^{THE} CANDIDATE

THE CANDIDATE

A Novel

SUSAN *WALES* AND *ROBIN SHOPE*

Revell
Grand Rapids, Michigan

Published by Fleming H. Revell
a division of Baker Publishing Group
P.O. Box 6287, Grand Rapids, MI 49516-6287
www.revellbooks.com

Printed in the United States of America

Library of Congress Cataloging-in-Publication Data
Wales, Susan.
   The candidate : a novel / Susan Wales and Robin Shope.
      p.   cm.
   Sequel to: The replacement.
   ISBN 10: 0-8007-3112-3 (pbk.)
   ISBN 978-0-8007-3112-0 (pbk.)
   1. Investigative reporting—Fiction. 2. Women journalists—Fiction. 3. Politicians—Fiction. I. Shope, Robin. II. Title.
PS3623.A3585C36 2007
813'.6—dc22   2007009504

With love to my parents, Mr. and Mrs. Arthur Joseph Huey, who have nurtured my faith, storytelling, and imagination since my childhood. And with gratitude to my cousin Tom Morgan, diver extraordinaire, who provided consultation for Jill's dive.

Susan Wales

To Gordon Yadon, friend and mentor to all who know him. Town's historian and keeper of Wisconsin's past. And the best storyteller in the Midwest. Also to my hometown of Delavan and all the people who live there.

Robin Shope

1

It's like just before the sun goes to bed down on the bay, those million sparkles on the water. . . . Like that mountain lake, it was so clear . . . it looked like two skies, one on top of the other. I couldn't tell where heaven started and the earth begun.

—Winston Groome, in *Forrest Gump*

Jill had spent a lifetime of summer evenings on the porch of her family home at the lake, but none seemed as quiet as this one. As she lit the candles, memories of those evenings began to roll through her head like a film clip—Scrabble games, thick slices of watermelon, and barbecues with friends.

Jill smiled as she recalled the lively suppertime debates with her dad. Her sister Kathy, prim and proper like their mother, would usually sit silently, but not Jill. She had always liked to voice her strong beliefs. Much to the chagrin of her mother and sister, Jill was still espousing her views. Only now, families around tables everywhere read them. But that was all about to change.

After Jill poured iced tea into the two glasses, she added a sprig of mint to each one, then settled into the porch glider to wait for her mother to bring their dinner. Back and forth, the swing's creaking chain chimed in the summer chorus of frogs and crickets.

Why hadn't she lingered at family suppers instead of wolfing down her food and dashing off to meet her friends at the local hangout, Eat'n Time? Today that diner was gone, her friends scattered across the country. And her father's chair was empty.

"Bon appétit," Pearl said as she appeared at the door, carrying their supper on a tray.

Pearl set the plates of roasted chicken and green salad atop the linen placemats. She stopped to watch the sunset, shielding her eyes with one hand as deep purple unfolded around the edges of the sky and a ginger sun slipped cloud by cloud toward the water, leaving behind a trail of pink ribbons scattered across the heavens.

"Going, going. . ." Jill said. Then, at the exact moment the fiery ball crashed into the azure lake, Jill exclaimed, "Gone! Wow!"

"Wow? Is that all the author can utter after a glorious sunset?" Pearl asked, raising an eyebrow. She pulled the linen back from the bread basket and offered Jill a roll.

"I'm a journalist, not a poet."

"And you're a publisher now," Pearl reminded her.

"Of a small-town newspaper," Jill added, carefully punctuating the word *small*. "A lot less impressive than investigative reporter at the *Washington Gazette*."

"Oh, but it sounds prestigious. I can just see Miss Cornelia's words in print on the society pages." Pearl fanned her hand across the air. "'The bride is the publisher of the award-winning newspaper, the *Lakes News*.'"

Jill rolled her eyes. "Let's not get too carried away, Mother."

"By the time you're married, you'll have won at least a couple of awards." Pearl patted Jill's hand in reassurance.

Jill pursed her lips, then chuckled. "So the truth's out. You don't expect me to marry for another decade or two?"

"Au contraire," Pearl retorted, her eyes twinkling. She speared a piece of grilled chicken as if it were a husband for her daughter and asked, "What girl wouldn't love to have your left hand, a hand with not one but two marriage proposals?"

"And a girl whose mother happens to own the only bridal shop in a ten-mile radius to boot." Jill raised her water glass high.

"Wedding shop aside, I know you're here to get away from it all so you can decide which of the charming young men you'll marry."

"No." Jill frowned. "I'm here to run the newspaper I bought, remember?"

"To whatever got you here, I'm grateful." Pearl clasped her hands and looked heavenward with a smile.

"After my last investigation, it didn't take much to bring me home." Jill shuddered at the memory. She leaned forward to confide in her mother. "And just tonight, I've made another decision."

Pearl leaped from her chair and hugged Jill. "Oh, darling, that's marvelous news. You must drop by my bridal shop tomorrow so we can choose your wedding gown. I bought several Vera Wang designs in New York with you in mind."

"Mother . . . shouldn't I choose my groom first?"

"Oh, I'm sorry. I almost forgot. Who's the winner? Uh, I mean, who's the lucky man? Is it Tommy or John? I'm dying to know."

"I'll bet you are." Jill clucked her tongue. "But this decision has nothing to do with a bridegroom."

Shoulders drooping, Pearl sat back down and took another bite of her salad. Between bites, she asked nonchalantly, "Okay, so what is this big decision?"

"I've decided I'm not going back to Washington. Tomorrow I'm calling Annabelle and Rubric to make it official."

"What?" Pearl gasped, dropping her fork. It tumbled and clanged against the china plate. "But Annabelle's given you a six-month leave of absence to find someone to run the paper. Why resign now? Especially since both your young men live in Washington. Unless you're telling me you've decided not to marry either one of them?"

"Relax, Mother. I haven't made any decisions about my love life."

"Then are you sure it's the best time to leave Washington for good?"

"I think so." Jill sighed. "I almost died in my last investigation, and since then, I've just wanted to live each day to the fullest. Home is where I need to be, with you." Jill felt tears coming to her eyes, and she blinked them back. "I want to watch the sunsets like we did tonight and to run the *Lakes* myself." Jill wrapped her arms around herself and hesitated. "I thought you'd be thrilled, Mother."

"If I believed it were true, I'd hop up on this table, shout amen, and do a tap dance to the 'Hallelujah Chorus.' But I know you too well, Jill Lewis." Pearl wagged her finger at her daughter. "Once you recover from your post-traumatic stress disorder or whatever you call it, you'll be back on the Hill involved in another life-threatening story while I'm finding your replacement at the *Lakes*."

Realizing her mother's words just might be true, Jill didn't protest.

Both women sank into a reflective mood as they silently watched the flicker of taillights and the last boats sputtered toward home. Loud, angry voices broke their mood.

Pearl frowned. "This lake's not what it used to be. Too many rowdy tourists."

"Probably a bunch of drunks. Should I call the lake patrol?"

Before Pearl could reply, the angry voices ceased. "Sounds like they've settled down now," she said, then excused herself. In a minute she returned with two slices of lemon pie and a pot of coffee.

As the women enjoyed the summer dessert, Pearl asked, "What are your plans for tomorrow?"

"Scuba diving," Jill announced, wiping meringue off her mouth with her napkin.

Pearl shook her head. "Good heavens! I think you'd be much safer in Washington. There's no telling what's rumbling around at the bottom of this lake."

2

I've never lost a game in my life. Once in a while, time ran out on me.

—Bobby Layne

Sunlight sliced across the lake's surface. Thirty feet below, Jill and her diving buddy, Donna, trailed a school of sunfish. Without warning, the iridescent sunfish scattered like shooting stars in every direction. Jill looked around for the source of their panic. There it was, gliding beneath her—a northern pike with yellow fins and rows of needle-sharp teeth. Typically, this species dined on the fish that lived in brushy pockets of coves and submerged caves, exactly the places where Jill, a novice diver, aspired to search for sunken relics.

Hoping to find a buried treasure to blog about tonight on the greenhorn diver's site, Jill pointed to the pike, signaling Donna to follow. Donna flashed thumbs-up and joined Jill in the chase. Swiftly, the women swam far away from the other divers, nearly colliding with a turtle in search of a breakfast of sunfish. Sufficiently bullied, the old turtle reluctantly paddled away into a limestone formation. Curious, Jill followed him. Looking inside, she gasped at what she saw snagged on a ledge of limestone—a treasure born of childhood dreams and untamed imagination.

The wooden dinghy was covered in barnacles and packed with mud and sand. It was impossible to tell the original color. Jill shined her flashlight on the side of the craft, reading a gold, cursive letter *T* hanging on by a single rusty screw. Jill searched, hoping to find more of the fallen letters near her feet. After looking through the mud and sand, she came up with only one more, a cursive *C*. Not much of anything to go on, *T* and *C*. Respectfully, Jill returned the letter to its resting spot. Once more, she rubbed her hand over the smooth surface and nearly caught a finger on a nail sticking out above an eroded area. From her diver's vest she pulled out a camera and snapped photos of the dinghy.

Pleased with her find, Jill turned around to show Donna, but there was no sign of her diving buddy anywhere. Since they weren't allowed to separate, Jill immediately kicked off to find her, but Donna was nowhere in sight. Had Donna surfaced and neglected to let Jill know? That was definitely a diver no-no.

Jill considered her options. Blowing her diver's whistle would needlessly alarm the other divers in the class. If she surfaced, she couldn't count the required time for today's dive toward her diver's certificate. Their instructor had repeatedly warned the buddies to stay together, so Jill decided she'd try to find Donna. But first, she had to check the gauges on her diving console.

With all systems go, Jill swam deep. The water grew murkier as she traveled; the distance blocked out the sun's rays. *Where are you?* Jill looked around for the northern pike. Maybe Donna had followed the fish, not realizing Jill had taken a detour after the turtle.

The warning alarm suddenly sounded on Jill's console. *It can't be . . .* But before she could check the alarm, her fins scraped the bottom of the lake. Quickly checking her depth gauge, she was alarmed to read it registered fifty feet below the lake's surface. Being alone, especially at this depth, was risky. It was time to resurface.

To increase her buoyancy, Jill deflated one of the weights on her diver's vest. With both feet she pushed off from the rocks on the bottom, but something tugged at her left ankle, holding her back. She leaned in closer to confront her captor and was relieved to see it was only a few long strands of milfoil weed tethering her to the bottomland.

Jill swung her foot back and forth to free herself, but this gnarly plant appeared to have a life of its own. The more she tugged at the weed, the tighter it gripped her ankle. She sloughed off her fin, but her foot still wouldn't budge. Jill imagined her final headline: "Jill Lewis Murdered by Lake Weed."

Giving one last jerk of her foot, she swiped her diver's boot against something sharp that sliced like a sushi knife slitting a shrimp. Pain seared her foot as a small red cloud colored the water. Knowing she had to get out of there, she grabbed the diver's knife and hacked away at the weed, eventually cutting herself free.

She wiggled her foot back inside of her fin and swam sideways to avoid the thicket of weeds. Trying hard not to snag her equipment, she carefully maneuvered between two five-foot pillars covered in plants. Stalagmites? Curious, Jill chopped a few weeds from a pillar to reveal a pale structure.

As she examined the pillar, Jill realized she was trapped inside a rib cage of gigantic proportions. The twenty-one ribs she counted extended along an enormous backbone with ringlike vertebrae forming an enormous barrel-shaped cage attached to a large pelvis. What a marvelous sight! The carcass dwarfed her by a few feet. After surveying the site of the skeletal remains, she discovered more of the mammoth-sized bones scattered haphazardly about the lake bottom.

No way these bones belonged to a native fish. The largest catch ever recorded on this lake was a sixty-pound pike. Whatever this monster was, it was too large to survive in a small lake for its hunting ground. Had it moved into this locale through an underground stream or river?

Anxious to research her discovery, Jill pulled the underwater camera from her vest again. She swam in and out of the rib cage, snapping photos and imagining the front-page story for her debut issue of the *Lakes News*. With her head filled with headlines, the slight hissing noise coming from her regulator was easy to ignore, but when a fine mist of bubbles tickled her face, Jill realized air was escaping from her tank. Horrified, she checked the pressure gauge on her console; her air supply still registered a little over half an hour, just enough to surface.

No more exploring. Before Jill kicked off, a loud noise blasted behind her like a revving motorcycle. Jill slapped her hands over her ears. A rush of bubbles gurgled about her head now, blinding her view. The bubbles were coming from her tank. She was losing air at an alarming rate. Panicking, Jill sucked hard on her mouthpiece, fearing the gauges had malfunctioned or, worse yet, all of her air had escaped.

There was still air in her tank, for now, but bubbles continued to encircle her head. The compressed-air-demand unit she wore on her back was designed to automatically shut down after each breath, but now the air was free flowing from her tank even when she wasn't inhaling.

She grabbed her underwater rescue whistle and blew. She knew she would black out within minutes after the tank was drained of air, and the surface was a long way away.

3

The fishermen know that the sea is dangerous and the storm terrible, but they have never found these dangers sufficient reason for remaining ashore.

—Vincent Van Gogh

As Jill floated upward, she caught sight of a ghostlike image moving toward her through the water. Donna? Or was she hallucinating? As the form grew closer, she saw it was Donna. Oh, what a beautiful sight!

Donna held out an alternate air supply regulator to Jill, who took gulping breaths just as a second murky form appeared above them. Their diving instructor, Chad Stokes, quickly hooked Jill up with an extra tank. Once he was satisfied that Jill was inhaling normally, he signaled for Donna to surface and then guided Jill toward the sunlight. Jill rejoiced as she saw sparkling beams of light bouncing around on top of the water.

Chad guided Jill to the dock and helped her onto the ladder. Donna waited for them on the dock. "Are you okay?" she asked anxiously.

Jill nodded as she pulled out her mouthpiece. After a few deep breaths, she felt euphoric.

"Just climb on up the ladder," Chad prodded. With a single push, he lifted himself out of the water and directly onto the pier.

Feeling weak kneed and jelly armed, Jill didn't have the strength to climb. To stop herself from falling back into the lake, she wound her arms around the steel rails and leaned her forehead against the top step.

Chad was about to head back up to shore when he saw Jill still waist deep in water. "Jill! What are you still doing down there?"

"Give me a few minutes. I . . . I don't have enough strength to get up there just yet. But I will," she promised with a feeble smile. "Just as soon as I get my land legs back."

Instead of letting her wait, Chad grabbed Jill's arms and pulled her up, scraping the whole length of her lower torso as she slid onto the pier. On her back, staring up at the blue of the sky, she could only imagine how black and blue her legs would look by tonight.

"Can you sit up?" Donna asked.

"Of course." Jill pulled herself into a sitting position.

Donna helped Jill remove her gear. As she pulled off one of her fins, a small puddle of blood ran out.

Jill winced. "It's no big deal."

Chad grabbed a towel off a stack from the diver's cart and tossed it her way. He made a second towel into a makeshift bandage around her foot. "There, that should stop the bleeding until I get back with the first-aid kit."

"Thanks," Jill murmured, hating the fuss. She made a face at the deep gash. Chad took her wrist to check her pulse while he timed it on his watch. The young man looked right at home in the Wisconsin resort area, with his deep tan and sun-bleached hair.

"Will I live?" Jill asked in an effort to be funny.

"If I don't get back with those bandages soon, you could bleed to death." Chad squinted. "You can smile now; I was only teasing." He glanced back to the shore, where the dive class still waited. "I better dismiss class; I'll be right back with that first-aid kit." He gathered his equipment and walked down the planks with Donna, making loud battering reverberations with his feet as he went. The other members of the class waited, wanting to know what happened. It took him several minutes to extricate himself from the group and escape into the dive shop.

Jill dangled her uninjured foot into the water. Trying to calm her nerves, she watched as sailboats gathered for a race. A gun blast signaled the start, and boats skirted the bright orange markers as the wind kicked up waves. Bits of spray cascaded over Jill. She had grown up by the lake without incident, but she now had a new, healthy fear of it. She'd wanted to learn to deep-sea dive for a possible honeymoon trip to the Bahamas. Right now, snow-laden slopes sounded best.

Minutes later, Chad ran back down the length of the wooden pier with the first-aid kit. He sat cross-legged beside her. "How's your foot feeling now?" he asked, lifting the towel to have a peek.

"It's feeling better. The bleeding hasn't stopped, but it's slowed down." Jill winced over the sting of the antiseptic.

"What did you cut it on, a rock?"

"I don't know, but whatever it was, it was sharp." Jill quickly realized it was going to take more than one measly Band-Aid to stop the blood from seeping out, so she put on five of them.

"With all the junk people toss into the lake, it could be anything. There's all kinds of stuff rolling around down there. You may need a tetanus shot."

Jill ignored his suggestion, trying not to think about her father's long-gone medical practice. But Chad's comment reminded her of the bones. "Have you ever heard stories about the lake monster?"

"Oh yeah, everyone has, but I don't believe a word of it. It's just the old-timers around here trying to stir up some excitement. After all, the stories aren't just about this lake; every lake community in the area claims to have their own version of the monster. You don't believe in all that bunkum, do you?" Chad looked at her as if she were a lunatic.

"Of course not," Jill answered, trying to brush off his suspicion. "But, I must admit, it's kind of fun to think about. When I was in high school, the town's historian told me about the lake monster overturning boats in the late 1800s, early 1900s. I fell in love with Delavan folklore."

"So now you think you might've cut your foot on the bones of the lake monster?" Chad burst out laughing.

"I'm not sure, but I've got some interesting photos in my camera." Jill reached for the camera from her vest but couldn't find it. "Hey, did you take my camera up with my equipment?"

Chad helped Jill to her feet. "I don't remember, but I'll look. Now, before you collect the prize for your archaeological find, drop by Doc Jenkins's office and get a tetanus shot."

"I'll do that on my way back into town. But I really need to find my camera first."

"We can look for it in the shop. By the way, what happened to you down there? Did you panic when you saw the bones?"

Jill stood a little straighter, anxious to defend herself. "I got separated from Donna. And then my tank went haywire, and I lost all my air."

"Why didn't you just surface?" Chad began flexing his fingers nervously.

"The way you ask it makes it sound so simple, but it wasn't. I got caught in the weeds and lost air too fast, and I guess I panicked."

"The worst thing a diver can do—panic. Are you sure you weren't getting air?"

"I'm positive."

"I checked all the tanks this morning myself." Chad started to sound defensive.

"I know you did, and I double-checked it, just the way you taught us," she told him. "But something happened down there, and it wasn't the lake monster's doing."

"Let's go to the shop and find out what happened. Dad's up there checking your equipment now."

Jill followed Chad to the beach and then across the small road and into the diver's shop. They found Mitch in the back room, where the tanks and scuba gear were stored. He was weighing the tank she wore during the dive. He smiled at Jill. "Hello, Jill. Sorry about the mishap. Chad told me there was a problem."

"Yes, but I'm fine now." Jill emphasized each word. Just thinking about how she felt nearly sent her into panic mode.

"This tank is empty." As Mitch read the gauge, his smile faded. "Let's see if I can figure out what happened here." Mitch started examining the tubing and the gauges.

"From what Jill described, I'm guessing her O-ring blew," Chad said.

Mitch frowned at his son. "But weren't the O-rings changed six months ago?"

"Yeah. I changed the O-rings on all of the equipment, just like you told me to. I always do what Daddy tells me. He's the one in charge."

"And you're sure you changed this one?" Mitch narrowed his eyes, obviously doing his best to ignore his son's blatant rudeness.

"Positive! Check the logs. It's all documented." Chad pointed toward the books, his face flushing.

"Just because it's logged in doesn't mean it was actually done," Mitch quietly stated.

"What's an O-ring?" Jill asked, partly to distract the family tension.

"It's a gasket used for sealing a connection. In this case, from the hose to the tank," Chad explained, visibly reining in his emotions.

With a pair of tweezers, Mitch meticulously pulled the ring from its seat between the tank valve and yoke. Holding it up for them to see, he announced, "Here's the culprit. Just as we thought: a blown O-ring." Mitch wiped it with a tissue and set it on a paper towel on the counter.

"That little piece of rubber caused all this?" Jill asked incredulously.

"So it seems," Mitch said. "It was an O-ring that caused the *Challenger* shuttle tragedy back in the 1980s too. A faulty ring caused the entire shuttle to explode."

"What would've caused it to blow?"

"Lots of things," Chad told her. "Sometimes it's the depth, or it can also blow in frigid temperatures." He rinsed his dive suit in a barrel and then hung it up on a peg.

"When I hit the bottom, it was forty-six degrees," Jill said.

"No. That's not cold enough to blow an O-ring." Mitch studied his son. It was apparent to Jill he didn't trust Chad's ability. "Something as small as a grain of sand can get in it and cause an O-ring to blow."

Chad's face turned redder. "We'll probably never know why it blew, but I'm guessing it was defective."

"You're guessing? One of your students could've died down there today, and you're just guessing? Well, I intend to pinpoint the cause. Do you check all the O-rings before every dive, like you're supposed to?"

"Of course I do! I already told you that. I do it all by the book!" Chad looked for something close to take his anger out on. Finding a mask handy, he slammed it across the room.

Mitch stared at his son long and hard. "Well, you missed something today." With a pair of tweezers, Mitch lifted the O-ring and held it under a magnifying glass for Jill and Chad to see. There on the right side of the ring was a tiny chink in the rubber ring.

"It could've been damaged during the dive," Chad was quick to point out. "This is your shop. You should check out the equipment too."

Jill spoke up. "If I had played by the rules, I could've easily surfaced in spite of this blown O-ring."

Mitch wouldn't let her ease the tension. "Chad should've emphasized the rules more to the class, so you would've known to surface immediately." He turned to his son. "So, you still think you're ready for your own dive shop, Mr. Know-it-all? Well, at least if you get one, I won't have to worry about any more catastrophes around here, will I?"

"Not if you're retired by then." Chad sharply nudged Mitch's shoulder on his way out of the shop. A moment later, Jill heard the roar of his truck and the screech of tires.

"Mitch, I feel just awful about this. It's my fault, not Chad's. He's a great instructor. He's warned us time and again about what to do and not to do. It was my own curiosity that got me into this mess. I'm afraid my high-risk career has lessened my judgment in dicey situations."

"That's very kind of you, Jill, but I accept full responsibility for my divers' mishaps. Ever since I told Chad I was selling the shop to someone else when I retire, he's been impossible to work with. Listen, I don't want you getting in on family arguments." Mitch opened the cash register, grabbed a hundred dollar bill, and tried to put it into Jill's hand. "Here's your money back for today's lesson."

"Please, keep your money. I learned a valuable lesson underwater today." Jill pushed the money back to him.

"Then the rest of your lessons are free," Mitch insisted.

"Actually, I think today's diving lesson will be my last."

"No way. A diving mishap is no different than falling off a bike. You've got to get back in the water as soon as possible." Mitch's eyes showed concern.

"I'll think about it," Jill demurred, but she had already decided she'd never go diving again. Feeling awash in claustrophobia, she grabbed her beach bag from her locker and headed into the dressing room to change into her street clothes.

On her way back to town, the emergency horns blared in spurts, signaling there was trouble somewhere in the area. Just as she put on her left turn signal to pull into Dr. Jenkins's office, a squad car and two fire trucks wheeled past in the opposite direction. Her eyes followed them in her rearview mirror until they disappeared over the hill.

After getting her shot and leaving the doctor's office, she drove to the bakery, anxious to get her next errand done so she could get back to the newspaper. John was due to arrive in Delavan this afternoon, and she was not at all ready. The clock above the counter told Jill that she had less than thirty minutes before John's estimated time of arrival.

Jill paid for the cake without stopping to chat with the cashier and limped back to her car. Just as she backed out of the parking space, her old office cell phone rang.

"Hello?" It was hard to hear the voice on the other end with such an old phone that had been dropped so often. Plugging one ear, Jill hollered into the cell. "Marge? Is that you? Marge?"

No answer.

"What's up, Marge?" Jill scrunched her face as if that would help her hear better.

"Jill? Didn't you hear me? Speak to me."

"Chill out, Marge. I heard you."

"Okay, then. Did you get the cake?"

"Yes, I've got Miss Cornelia's birthday cake in a box next to me as we speak."

"Good. I was worried you'd forget."

Jill rolled her eyes. "I'm glad you have such faith in me, Marge."

"Yeah, well, just hurry up and get here. John's already been here with a whole bunch of balloons for the party, but he's gone now."

"John was there?" Jill banged on the brakes. "But he wasn't supposed to arrive until this afternoon. He's early." Jill pressed on the car's accelerator. The purpose of John's quick trip from Washington was for the two of them to reconnect, and they only had twenty-four hours together. Why hadn't he told her he was arriving early?

"What did you expect? You knew he was coming; you should've been here. Daylight is burning."

"Just tell me where John went."

Silence.

"Marge, are you still there? I asked you where John went." Mad enough to toss the rickety phone from the car, Jill tried to calm her nerves as she hot-wheeled toward the office.

"All I know is that he's not here, boss woman. He got a call from the detective in Walworth County. You know Russ Jansen, the fine-looking, young detective."

"Why would Russ call John? And how did he know John was in Delavan?"

"Russ saw John cruise through town. One of the guests of Lake Lawn Resort drowned this morning. So it could be an assist."

"An assist on a drowning? Something isn't right. I need a name." She tapped nervously on the gas pedal with her foot.

"All Russ said was the divers were looking for a man's body."

"So that's why the emergency alert system sounded?" Jill glanced in her rearview mirror and swung her car in a U-turn. "Change in plans. I'm on my way to the Lake Lawn Resort to check it out now." Jill tossed the phone down on the seat. She could hear Marge screaming, "The cake! Don't forget you've got the cake!"

4

The hunger for love is much more difficult to remove than the hunger for bread.

—Mother Teresa

Jill forgot the possible lake monster and the cake needing re-frigeration as she stepped on the gas and aimed her car toward Highway 50. All 2,072 watery square acres of Lake Delavan spread out ahead of her on the other side of the family-friendly resort. Jill drove past stone gates and the golf course. Straight ahead was the one-story rustic hotel that had been built of river rock and limestone to blend in with the landscape.

Jill swung her Range Rover into the first available parking space. After she turned off the motor, she pulled down the vanity mirror and checked herself. Her windblown hair was unfixable, so she pulled it back into a ponytail. She hadn't bothered with makeup since her diving class, and the sun had already made a few freckles pop out over her nose and cheeks. Jill dug through her purse for powder and found none.

She hobbled between old Indian burial grounds on her way to the water and then finally reached the beach. Checking her foot, she was glad to see the fresh bandages still covered the nasty wound. Already there were the first signs of heavy bruising down both of her legs.

She saw John in the distance, standing tall and erect. Jill sighed. It had been a while since she'd seen him. And recently more than miles separated them. For weeks they had only talked on the phone, or rather, argued on the phone. Now he had come to straighten things out between them.

Jill swallowed her trepidation, took a deep breath, and gingerly moved past the knots of people gathered to watch the search and rescue team on the lake. Yellow police tape blocked the path closer to the edge of the lake. Officer Tom Connell guarded the area, but he waved Jill through after she flashed her newspaper badge. The pier's planks were still soft and wet with lake water.

John stood next to Detective Russ Jansen at the end of the pier. Now that she was seeing him in the flesh, she realized how much she had missed him. Never had John looked so good to her. It had been months since she had learned of John's faked death, which had pushed her toward Senator Tommy Harrison. But now all that seemed long ago. Was John the man she wanted, and not the flamboyant Tommy Harrison, who riddled her dreams with flattery and doubt? Was it possible she was falling in love with John all over again?

As if sensing her presence, John turned to Jill and gave her a tepid smile and a cordial hello. Jill felt taken aback by his cool, businesslike attitude. And just like that, the old comparisons resurfaced. Tommy was John's polar opposite. John stood waiting for Jill to come to him, whereas Tommy would have come rushing down the pier to meet her.

But maybe John appeared aloof because he was in his role as FBI Agent in Charge. After all, both their workplaces were not only inside an office but also at crime scenes. Jill resolutely continued down the length of the pier. When she reached him, his smile blossomed, only for her. Confusing thoughts about Tommy Harrison vanished.

John opened his mouth to say something, but he stopped when a police diver bobbed up from the water like a buoy. He hollered and gave a thumbs-up to the captain of the dive boat before putting his face back into the water and once again disappearing below the surface.

Jill turned her attention back to John. "Sorry I wasn't at the office when you arrived."

"No, I'm sorry. I was called out on this emergency before you got there," he told her. "I saw you limping. What happened?" He looked at her bandaged foot.

"Just a minor cut I got scuba diving. I'll tell you about it later." Jill pulled at her shorts again. Her injuries seemed insignificant when a man had just died in these waters.

Together, John and Jill moved to where Russ stood at the far end of the dock. With a tip of his dimpled chin, the detective acknowledged Jill's presence. An old walkie-talkie stuck out of his hip pocket, crackling with information from the dive boat.

Jill's cell phone rang before anyone spoke. When she answered it, she found it was impossible to hear anything on it due to its picking up the police calls instead. It crackled with noisy, white static. Deciding not to mess with it, Jill turned it off.

Russ took the talkie from his pocket and pressed it. "Find anything yet?"

"Nothing yet," a voice from the search boat reported back to shore.

Russ paced while responding on the walkie-talkie.

"What was happening at the time of the drowning? Were there any witnesses?" Jill asked Russ, pulling out her small tape recorder for the interview.

"A couple reported seeing a man in a rowboat spotting for some guy in the water, who turned out to be the victim . . . or rather, turned into the victim," Russ answered.

"Does his buddy have a name?" Jill slapped away at the mosquitoes trying to bite her.

"An important one—Congressman Fleming. Do you know him?"

"Yes, actually, I do know him." Jill was quiet for a moment, trying to process the fact that a cohort from Washington was here in her hometown and involved in a death. "What's the victim's name?"

"Joe Walker."

"I know Walker too. I met him when I interviewed Congressman Fleming when he was championing an environmental bill to protect Wisconsin native fish."

"I'm not much with politics, but that's a bill I do remember. It had to do with protecting native fish in the Midwestern states. Being a fisherman myself, I supported it and voted for Fleming again just because of it."

"That makes two of us," John agreed. "I had snakeheads crawling all around my yard at Egg Harbor, jumping from one body of water to the next. They were creepy."

Russ nodded. "Snakeheads were illegally smuggled into the United States from Asia. People wanted them for their fish tanks, and when the fish outgrew the tanks, the owners dumped the fish in nearby waterways. Since snakeheads weren't indigenous, they didn't have any natural predators, so they multiplied like crazy. Then they became predators of all our native fish. Snakeheads can actually walk for several yards on their bellies and move from one body of water to another. Fleming proposed a bill in Congress to allow state authorities to eliminate the snakeheads."

"Several fanatical animal rights groups protested the inhumane treatment of the snakeheads," John added. "Can you believe that?"

"Now I've heard it all," Jill said, shaking her head.

"When animal rights extremists made threats on Fleming's life, I recommended a security detail, and he used our off-duty cops when he vacationed in the area. I even worked for him myself a couple of nights. But nothing ever came of it, and the threats blew over fairly quickly." Russ talked without taking his eyes off the lake.

"Did you ever identify the groups?" John asked.

"It started as a combination of animal rights groups, but they organized and called themselves the SOS, for Save Our Snakeheads."

"Where was Fleming's bodyguard while all this happened?" John leaned against a wooden post and crossed his arms, blowing the mosquitoes away with short breaths.

More shouts between the divers and the boat were unintelligible.

Russ shrugged. "Fleming never used bodyguards after the snakehead mess died down."

"Any ideas about what caused Walker to drown?" Jill turned her own attention back to the lake.

"The witnesses I've been able to talk to said one minute Walker was there, and the next he was gone. Fleming wasn't alarmed at first, because he said it wasn't unusual for Joe to swim underwater. When he realized Joe wasn't coming up, he dove over the edge of the boat after him. A couple of witnesses saw what was going on and came over to help."

"Obviously too late," Jill mused.

"Too late for Walker, but they were able to save the congressman."

"Apparently, he nearly drowned himself while trying to rescue his friend," John explained to Jill.

"Where are the witnesses you talked to?" Jill looked around, hoping to get a statement for her article.

"Onshore." Russ pointed to a young couple standing with the congressman.

Jill recognized Chad, but she'd never seen the young woman who was at his side. *Chad's girlfriend?* Jill glanced over at Russ. "You don't mind if I ask them a few questions, do you?"

Russ turned to look. "Those kids and the congressman? Sure.

Be my guest. But promise me you'll leave the wife alone for a few days."

"Sure, I'll give her a few days." But *only* a few days. "Have you had a chance to talk to anyone else?"

"Not yet. This whole area, both lake and shore, is loaded with potential witnesses, and it'll take a while to interview them all. Right now, Officer Connell is interviewing everyone along the lakefront. He's taking contact information and trying to get to the vacationers before they leave. Still, there's no way to know who might have seen something. I'm sure we'll miss some, so I want to run a notice in your newspaper asking for any witnesses to contact us."

"Consider it done," Jill said, making a note. "But aren't you going to a lot of extra work for a drowning?"

"It pays to be thorough, especially when a congressional aide is involved."

"Good point. Thanks for your information. It was good to see you again." Jill offered her hand.

He shook it firmly. "Good to see you too, Jill. As I said, this looks like an accidental drowning to me, but if you find out anything suspicious, be sure to let me know."

Jill said she would and then set off for the witnesses. She pressed the small tape recorder in her purse to "on" as she approached Fleming. Premature gray hair hung like a wet towel over his tired face.

"Congressman, I'm so sorry to hear about Joe Walker. How are you doing?"

"Jill Lewis? I didn't expect to see you here." Fleming didn't smile, so it was a relief when he extended his hand in greeting, making conversation easier.

"I've moved back home to Delavan. I'm the new owner and manager of Delavan's *Lakes News*."

"Did the *Gazette* fire you again?" he asked without malice.

Jill smiled. Her relationship at the Washington flagship newspaper had been rocky at times. "Actually, it was a personal choice this time. Can you tell me what happened here?"

"I'm sorry, Jill. I can't . . . discuss it right now." He kicked at the sand. "Give me some time. This is more than losing an aide. Walker was my best friend for years. He is . . . was like a brother to me." His voice broke as he waved her away.

Jill murmured her condolences and walked away, leaving the congressman to compose himself. Now she directed her attention to Chad. The girl standing next to him had wild red hair that somehow worked with her hot pink swimsuit. Although her skin was freckled, it had tanned evenly.

"You've had a busy morning," Jill said to Chad. "I heard you saved the congressman's life. Two lives in one day."

"If only we could've saved his friend too." Chad appeared visibly shaken.

Jill offered her hand to the redhead. "I don't believe we've met."

"My sister, Lynn," Chad said.

"I didn't know you had a sister. Hi, I'm Jill Lewis."

Lynn smiled. "Chad told me you came back to run the newspaper. How are you, Jill?"

"Have we met before?" Jill searched her memory. She hated to forget people.

Lynn laughed. "No, we haven't met. But I remember when you were the homecoming queen at Delavan-Darien High School."

"I'm sorry, I don't remember—"

"Stop. There's no reason you should remember me. I was only in fourth grade when you were crowned, but I clearly remember that pretty blue dress you wore on the float during the parade through town. You looked just like Cinderella."

"Thanks. I always wanted to be a princess." Jill smiled. "What are you doing now, Lynn?"

"This is my last year at the university. I live on campus in Madison."

"Are you planning to join the family scuba business?"

"Oh no, I hate scuba diving. I'm going to law school after graduation."

"I know the feeling," Jill agreed. "Sorry to meet you under these circumstances, but if you're up to it, I'd like to ask you both a few questions about the drowning incident."

They both nodded in agreement, but Lynn spoke first.

"After Chad's diving classes, we watched the races. That's when we noticed the rowboat with the man swimming beside it over there." Lynn pointed in the direction of the dive boat.

"Fleming was rowing, and Walker was swimming?"

"Yes. They were working as a team. It looked to us like Fleming was timing his friend. One of the sailboats started to tip over, and that drew my attention away from the men. When I looked back again, I couldn't see the man who was swimming. I assumed he was on the other side of the boat, but when Mr. Fleming stood up and started yelling, I told Chad."

"I saw Mr. Fleming jump into the water," Chad picked up the story. "We drove the boat over to help."

Fleming, who was standing near them, must have overheard their conversation and decided to step forward. "I was trying to find Joe. One minute he was there, and the next, gone. If these two kids hadn't stopped me, they'd be fishing me out of the bottom right now too." Fleming looked devastated.

Jill was surprised that the congressman had offered additional information, especially in his present frame of mind, but she was glad he had. Something didn't seem right to her, but she wasn't ready to be hard-nosed about it just yet. "I'm sorry, Congressman Fleming." Jill touched his arm.

"I should've been able to save Joe. We've been partners since we were Navy Seals together. When I won my first election, I told him there wasn't anyone I wanted with me in Washington more than him. His advice was always solid. Joe was the one person I counted on, who I totally trusted." Fleming turned his head to the side to hide the tears.

"I'm sorry," Jill said quietly. "And you said Joe was swimming, not diving today?"

"Joe never went diving without a buddy." Forcefully, he shook his head. Chad shot her an odd look as Fleming continued. "Joe was getting his morning exercise, swimming across the lake. I was in the boat."

"It sounds to me that you did all you could. Tell me, did Joe complain of cramps or say he wasn't feeling well?"

The congressman shook his head.

"Swimming across the lake is no easy task." Jill squinted her eyes toward the south shore. "It has to be more than a mile across."

"It was nothing for Joe. He swam every morning."

"Do you know what he had for breakfast?" Jill didn't forget to concentrate on the smaller details, because you never knew what those details might reveal.

"We ate at the lodge together. He had a light breakfast—just fruit and juice, as I recall. I'm the one who gobbled pancakes."

"Pancakes, huh?" she asked with a lilt in her voice.

"Joe was the health nut, not me." Fleming patted his belly. "Obsessed. He had an Olympic-size pool in his backyard in Oak Creek and an indoor pool in his Virginia high-rise. Joe never missed a day of swimming that I know of."

"Sounds like your friend was highly disciplined."

"His father died of a massive heart attack at a fairly young age, and Joe was determined that it would never happen to him. With his rigid workout schedule and a healthy diet and lifestyle, Joe cheated fate. That is, until today. Maybe it was a heart attack that got Joe."

"That's a logical explanation, especially with his family history. Sometimes you just can't beat those genes." Jill held out her hand to Fleming, and he shook it. "Thanks for your time,

Congressman. If you think of anything else, will you let me know?" Jill handed him her new card imprinted with the *Lakes News* logo.

Leaving the three of them, Jill returned to the site of search and rescue. She felt odd knowing that a person lay somewhere at the bottom of the lake in the green silence, underneath all the boaters, sailboat racers, and jet-skiers laughing and enjoying life on the surface.

She walked back over to John. "Have they found Walker yet?"

"No. All we've found so far are old bottles, a few fragments of Styrofoam coolers, and a tackle box," Russ said.

Jill started to say something about people who dump their trash in the lake when she noticed wild gesticulations from the divers.

"We got him!" Russ hollered with a clap of his hands. "Look, they're bringing him back in the boat now."

The rescue boat sped back to shore with its nose high in the air. John and Jill followed the detective to the next pier, arriving just as the boat was landing. Inside it was a black body bag.

Turning toward the shore, Jill noticed that Chad and Lynn Stokes had taken off in their small outboard and were heading east down the lake. Only the congressman remained, puffing on a cigarette while running his fingers through his hair.

Jill turned to John. "Guess you didn't expect to walk into a new case when you got here."

"I'm always glad to help." His smile was pencil thin.

They watched the coroner's truck drive up. The attendants rolled the gurney down to the lake and loaded the body. The truck left to take the black bag to the morgue, and it wasn't long until the crowd dispersed. A few stragglers remained, along with a police officer left to guard the scene.

With nothing more to be done, Jill and John walked up the shoreline, between the Indian burial grounds and past the sprawling hotel, back to the parking lot. Walking close to John, she made the mistake of looking up into his eyes. As if having a mind of their own, her hands reached for his arms and pulled him toward her until he was in her arms. He smelled of lake spray and sunshine.

"Jill." John put his arms around her and kissed her. She loved the way his mouth felt against hers. Suddenly a car horn blared, and John pulled back to look around them.

"Isn't it a little late to check out if anyone saw you do that? The deed's done." Jill smiled and pulled him to her for another kiss. "Don't worry, nobody's around. Your reputation as a law-man is still safely intact."

"Yeah, but we can't act like a couple of love-starved teens if we want to be taken seriously," he reminded her with a frown. But then his expression softened. "It's great being back here with you, though. How are you, Jill? How are we?"

"I'm fine. I've missed you. And we have twenty-four hours to figure out the 'we' stuff. But I must warn you, I have to lean on your arm for the rest of today because of my injured foot." Jill squeezed him tightly. To her delight he stayed put.

"When I got the call from Russ Jansen, I figured this was the reason you hadn't shown up, and I'd find you here. Wherever there's breaking news, there's Jill," John said softly into her ear.

"I only came here to find you."

"I know my girl better than that. I figured this accidental drowning would be the highlight of your week, maybe month."

"It sounds so awful when you say it like that. I don't take pleasure in somebody's death." She frowned at him. "And I find Delavan just as exciting as Washington." She walked away from him and headed for her Range Rover.

"Where are you going?" John called out to her.

"Miss Cornelia's birthday party. Aren't you coming too?"

"Of course, I wouldn't miss it. That's the real reason I'm here, you know. After all, I was put in charge of the balloons."

"Well, Marge gave me the most important job of all. I'm in charge of the birthday . . . Oh no. The cake!" Jill groaned at the thought of the bakery box on the passenger seat. She panicked even more when she opened the door and was hit by a blast of steamy heat. Raising the lid on the box, she saw the frosting was melting. At least half of it had slid off the cake.

"I've gotta go soon or this cake will be pudding." She waved a quick good-bye to John and hopped in the car.

The first thing she did was turn the AC on high and aim it toward the box. Then she stepped on the accelerator and sped toward the office, anxious to rake some of the frosting back into place before Marge found out.

5

A true friend stabs you in the front.

—Oscar Wilde

An overhead bell jangled when Jill walked into the *Lakes News* carrying the birthday cake. Marge wagged her cell at Jill and shrieked, "Finally, you're back! I've been trying to reach you for over an hour. Where's the cake? Why didn't you answer your cell phone?"

"Sorry. I shut mine off at the lake, and I guess I forgot to turn it back on."

Marge followed Jill into the break room. "You're supposed to leave your cell phone on. How can this system work if you won't cooperate?"

"I'm cooperating, but there's bad reception out at the lake. My cell kept interfering with the calls on the police and dive systems, so I had no choice but to turn it off." Jill tore the lid off the cake box and found a butter knife in the drawer. She got to work fixing the frosting on the cake, hoping Marge wouldn't notice.

John walked into the break room with the bunch of balloons. "Where do you want these, boss?" he asked Marge.

Marge perked up over the way he addressed her. "I'm going to tie some of them to the lamppost outside, some in the foyer, and a few in here." Happy now, she took the balloons from John and disappeared out the door to decorate.

John watched Jill as she finished working on the cake.

"Miss Cornelia will be so excited that you made it to her party," Jill said.

"Just don't let her know that her birthday isn't the real reason I came." He took the butter knife from her fingers and set it down on the edge of the plate. Then he slid his arms around her waist and tugged her to him. "It's been a long time. I've really missed you."

"I'm glad you're here." Wanting to say more, Jill pulled away from him to shut the door. "It's hard to survive a long-distance relationship. Phones and email just aren't the same as having you here in the flesh."

"Yeah, I haven't figured out a way to kiss through email yet. That's why I'm here."

"To kiss me?" Jill smiled.

John didn't return her smile. "No, so we can work things out. We've been through a lot these past couple of months." He leaned against the counter and slid his hands into his pockets. "I wasn't going to ask this so soon, but we don't seem to have a lot of time. I need to be direct; it's the only way I know to be." He drew in a deep breath. "Are you ready to put what happened between us into perspective, so we can talk about marriage?"

Jill was taken off guard by his words, and she didn't respond immediately. "I'm sorry, John," she finally said. "I still need time."

John crossed his arms over his chest. "It's been months. How much time do you need?"

"I don't know. I'm just trying to heal from your last case and get this behind me."

John let out a frustrated sigh. "I know. And I'm trying to be as understanding as I can. But I can't wait forever, Jill."

Jill sat at a table in the break room. She looked down at her hands as she said, "Believe me, there's nothing I want more than to trust you the way I used to. But I'm afraid of being hurt again."

"You're acting like I hurt you out of mean-spiritedness or spite. You know I didn't have a choice when the agency staged my death. Sometimes I'm afraid that . . ." He sighed. "No, never mind."

"What? What were you going to say?"

He sat down next to her at the table. "Sometimes I'm afraid that this isn't just about trust. Sometimes I'm afraid this is more about Tommy Harrison."

Jill still couldn't look him in the eye as she gathered the right words to say. "You're right. I did grow close to Tommy during the investigation. He was there to comfort me when I thought you had died. I didn't plan for those feelings to happen. If I had known you were alive, I never would've allowed myself—"

Just then the door to the break room flung open. Jill looked up, expecting to see Marge. But instead she saw Olivia, an old friend from high school.

"Hello, hello!" Olivia said brightly.

Jill looked quickly at John. His demeanor totally changed. His ear-to-ear smile seemed to be working again.

"What are you doing here, Olivia?" Jill managed to say. "Last I heard, you were on special assignment in the Middle East."

"My assignment in Israel and Jordan is over, and I was recently transferred to the Washington office. I was disappointed, though, Jill, because just when I got there, you left for Delavan." She winked at Jill. "I won't take it personally, though."

Jill went over to give her a hug. "You look great, Olivia." And she wasn't lying. Olivia did look beautiful, with her long auburn hair and naturally rosy cheeks.

"And so do you," Olivia replied. "By the way, I'm on special assignment now, and you'll never guess where."

"I have no idea."

"I'll be right here in Delavan for a year!"

"Really? Delavan? I can't imagine what for." Jill suddenly remembered that she hadn't introduced John yet. She turned around and asked, "Have you met John?"

"Yes, I have, as a matter of fact." Olivia smiled warmly at him. "John must've told you we worked together for a couple of months when I came home for Dad's heart surgery. He was Craig Martin then, but he didn't fool me for a minute. I knew a Renaissance man like John wouldn't be behind a dusty old desk in Delavan." She pulled her long auburn hair into a knot at the nape of her neck and then trotted over to John and gave him a big hug.

"That's right. Olivia figured out pretty quickly I wasn't who I pretended to be." John sounded as though he were pleased.

"Is that so? Well, I must be really dumb, because it took me a lot longer than that to discover his true identity," Jill admitted, half joking.

John pulled the keys for his rental car out of his pocket. "If you ladies will excuse me, I'd better go pick up the birthday girl or there won't be any party." John gave Jill a quick peck on her cheek on his way out.

"What a great guy," Olivia commented after he'd gone.

Jill ignored that comment. "Olivia, you still haven't said what assignment brought you here to town."

"You! Dad told me you bought this paper, so I presented an idea for a photojournalist article about how a successful Washington reporter returns home to save a small-town newspaper from a hungry conglomerate. The story intrigued my boss too. So, can you believe it? For the next year, you and the *Lakes News* are my very own project! Normally, I would have asked ahead of time if it was all right, but since you and I were friends in high school, and this is my dad's old paper, I knew there'd be no problem. Am I right?"

Jill didn't appreciate the way Olivia had sprung this on her without asking first. And how on earth would she find enough space for Olivia in this office? "Okay, but it'll be a challenge to find a place to put you."

Olivia shrugged her shoulders. "Anywhere is fine by me. Even though my dad is the former owner, I don't expect to be catered to."

Somehow Jill doubted that.

"By the way, how are the finances?"

Boy, she doesn't waste any time, does she? Of course, that's Olivia for you. She always did charge full speed ahead, trampling over everyone and everything that got in her way.

"Fine." Jill looked out the window and noticed the flourishing weeds and the absence of flowers in the raised beds out front. "I think I should hire someone to do the upkeep on the outside, though."

"Sounds like that'll be expensive. Are you sure the finances are okay?"

It was obvious that Olivia wasn't letting this go. "All right, if you must know, the paper's not making any money yet. But I'm about to make some changes."

"Like what?"

"Take a look around; don't you think it's time to modernize? I want to replace our old technological equipment with state of the art, starting with the outdated desktop computers. I want wireless laptops. Also those old printers need to be replaced with laser printers." Holding up her office cell phone, Jill added, "I plan to get everyone a much better cell phone, one that is top of the line and has the talkie component built right in. These are way too old and don't hold the battery charge anymore. I also want to install a state-of-the-art telecommunications system—plasma TVs, with news from all over the world, broadcast right into our little office."

Olivia looked skeptical. "I hope you're not planning to do all this at once."

Jill returned to the forgotten cake and began fixing the frosting again. "Why not?"

"Well, for one, I came here to write a provocative story about a newspaper that learns to stand on its own two feet, not one that's resuscitated through your bottomless pit of trust funds."

Hmmm, maybe seeing my old friend won't be so wonderful after all. Olivia hadn't changed much; she was just as opinionated as ever, and just as eager to share those opinions with anyone who would listen. Jill folded her arms and tried to keep her voice from sounding defensive. "The newspaper will stay afloat just as it did for your dad, and all the owners before it."

"But you could really build this paper into something by bringing new advertisers into the *Lakes News*. Let the newspaper pay for itself. Dad never got out there and sold like he should have. What came in the door was sufficient for him, but Jill, you can sell! It's all about relationships."

Unfortunately, Olivia was right about that. "You have a point," Jill said begrudgingly. "It's not a bad idea to rely on my business sense and not my trust fund."

"With no help from your mom, either."

That was another situation that would prove difficult to handle. Pearl was always offering Jill money to do whatever she wanted with the newspaper. But Olivia was right: easy money wasn't the answer; hard work was the answer. And Jill told her as much.

"Good," Olivia said, "because I want to write a heartfelt article about a seasoned reporter who left one of the most prestigious newspapers in the country in order to do things her way." Olivia's voice was brimming again with encouragement. "There is one thing I'm curious about, though."

"What's that?" Jill braced herself.

"Now tell me, why did you really come back to Delavan?"

Jill did her best to hide at least some of her secrets from Olivia. Maybe if she moved toward the kitchen counter and wiped it again, she wouldn't be such a stable target. "Isn't it obvious? This is my home, and this is where my favorite newspaper was for sale."

"Did you come to save the newspaper from a conglomerate takeover, or are you really running away from a certain senator in Washington?"

Olivia's question startled Jill as she brushed invisible crumbs from the counter into the sink. "What? How did you hear about that?"

"Where gossip is concerned, Washington is a small town."

When Jill didn't answer, Olivia continued, "Tommy's the bad boy, and John's the golden boy. But I don't know you the way I once did . . . is it the bad boy you really want?"

"Don't believe what you read in the tabloids, Olivia." Jill opened the refrigerator door and took out the pitcher of lemonade.

Jill watched Olivia and sensed a fresh level of strain between them. But both of them pretended it didn't exist as they finished setting up for the party. It was a relief to hear John's loud voice as he walked in through the front door. It served as an alert that Miss Cornelia had arrived. It gave the few employees time to rush into the break room and turn off the lights as Jill hurriedly lit the candles. But the minute Jill saw Miss Cornelia she knew someone had leaked information about the party, because the birthday girl sashayed into the room, all dolled up in a hot pink chiffon dress with a matching hat covered in sequins and feathers.

"Ta-da!" Miss Cornelia, the society columnist, announced her grand entrance. "Yoo-hoo. Here I am, children! Now, who died? What's the emergency obituary that needs to be written today? And why is it so dark in here?"

Jill flicked the light switch back on as everyone yelled, "Surprise! Surprise!" Miss Cornelia played along, throwing her arms up in the air. It did Jill's heart good to see the older woman's joy light up her face as everyone broke into a rousing rendition of "Happy Birthday."

Marge handed Cornelia a package wrapped in a paper printed with every shade of pink. The older woman was delighted to see what was inside her box. "A gift certificate for the Firkin

Restaurant! Maybe we can make a night of it and see a show too." Miss Cornelia squealed again when she saw the beautiful pink nightgown trimmed in a matching pink boa in the next package. And she loved the rhinestone-studded bag and hat. Pink. Pink. And more pink. "I bet Jill picked out all these. We have the same tastes." Miss Cornelia elbowed Jill.

"Yes, we both love our pinks," Jill admitted to everyone.

Olivia was quick to elbow Jill too. "I can see the future," she whispered as she waved her hand. "There you are thirty years from now."

Jill gave her a look.

Miss Cornelia began hugging everyone in the room. "You're all so dear to me. I love you to pieces. God has been good and blessed me. Thank you."

"How old are you, Miss C.?" Marge wanted to know as Jill grimaced over the personal question.

"How old do you think I am?" Cornelia asked everyone around the room. By the look on her face it was evident she wanted a low number.

Unfortunately, Marge was the first to answer. "Seventy?"

"Seventy? Do I really look seventy to you?" Cornelia answered in a huff as everyone shook their heads no. "I'll have you know I'm not a day over fifty-nine."

"You'll end up you-know-where if you keep lying about your age," Marge warned Miss Cornelia.

"Shall I show you my driver's license?" Miss Cornelia reached for her purse.

"Don't worry, Miss Cornelia," Olivia said sweetly. "God forgives women who lie about their age. If he didn't, there wouldn't be any women in heaven."

Miss Cornelia glared at Olivia. "I'm not lying about my age. Whatever gave you that idea?"

Jill moved in to start a birthday game to distract Miss Cornelia. Otherwise, the fur and the feathers would fly.

After the birthday celebration was over, Miss Cornelia went right to work on the society column, devoting half a page to her birthday party. Marge sat at the front counter in front of her Elvis poster, answering the phone. Only Jill stayed behind in the break room to clean up.

Something caught her eye out the window. It was Olivia taking pictures of the building, the empty flower beds, and the sign with paint chipping from the edges. John was on his way out with a trash bag when Olivia spotted him. She stepped from behind the oak tree and snapped his picture. They laughed and stood talking for a few minutes.

"Jill?" Miss Cornelia knocked on the door frame to get her attention. "Is there anyone here who can drive me home?"

"Sure, I'll get John to drive you home," Jill said with a frown.

6

There is nothing certain in a man's life but that he must lose it.

—Owen Meredith

Back in her office, Jill rummaged through the closet for her purse. Earlier she had carelessly tossed it on the top shelf. Now, she had to stand on her toes to reach it. "Got it," she said as it almost tumbled down on top of her. She dug through the inside of the purse until she found the cassette of the interviews from this morning and popped it into the duplicator to make copies. Once everyone went home for the day, she'd listen to it in the quiet of the deserted office with the rattle of the window fan as background music. Relaxed and with nothing else on her mind, she'd sit with pen and paper taking notes the old-fashioned way, paying careful attention to voice inflections, stammering, and pauses. They revealed more than printed words.

Jill swung her chair around to her computer and decided to spend the next half hour googling the lake monster. Delighted when dozens of sites popped up on her screen, she scrolled down the list and clicked on several sites before settling on one with details of frequent monster sightings in the northern Wisconsin lakes.

At the turn of the century, it was common for the *Lakes News* to report frequent sightings of a lake monster overturning small boats and damaging piers. A few residents even claimed the monster had dared come onshore, supposedly devouring dogs, hogs, and other small animals.

Opinions of the sightings were varied. Some skeptics speculated there was no monster at all and accused the witnesses of nipping from the bottle. Others claimed the tales were gross exaggerations by old-timers who loved to spin yarns to frighten the lake's summer folk. Ultimately, when most of these sightings were checked out, the lake monster turned out to be nothing more than a humongous fish or colossal turtle.

The explanation that made the most sense to Jill was that the monster was a large and exotic snake that escaped from the Barnum and Bailey Circus. Lake Delavan was the headquarters of the circus during the off season in the nineteenth century. But when she compared the remains of the monster she had discovered on the lake bottom with those of a serpent, she debunked her own theory. Her monster's enormous rib cage was attached to a gigantic pelvis. No way did it resemble the body of a snake, even a gigantic one.

Next, Jill searched the *Lakes News* archives on microfiche. By the midtwenties, articles about the lake monster had virtually disappeared from the pages of the newspaper.

Intrigued by the photos of the bones, Jill decided to reread an article that appeared in the *Lakes News* in 1900, a vivid description of the monster by Rev. H. M. Clark, a man who was considered a reliable source. Jill guessed he was the great-grandfather of the local druggist Henry Clark.

> August 13, 1900. Saturday afternoon Rev. H. M. Clark, who for twenty-five years has faithfully led the Delavan Methodist Church, was fishing off the pier of the parsonage on Walworth Avenue when he heard a loud splash in the water. Expecting to see a

largemouth bass midair, Rev. Clark, whose vision was later documented at 20/20 by local optometrist Dr. Charlie Ford, reported that he saw the lake monster. In Rev. Clark's own words, "The dark green reptile reared up out of the water to height well over twenty feet. The serpent had eighteen-inch horns protruding out of his head, and stared at me with flashing red eyes. He flicked his forked tongue like a snake. Fearing it was preparing to strike, I felt relieved when it dove back underwater with a loud splash."

Mercifully, the reverend confirmed that his wife, Rosabella, known for her faintness of heart, was presiding at a bake sale for the Women's Missionary Society. Rev. Clark's son Andrew heard him hollering and came to his rescue along with several neighbors. Jim Hansen, a local fisherman, and two other men searched the lake for over an hour but found no sign of the monster.

For the past twenty years, many residents have reported sightings of the monster, but no witnesses possess the sterling character and fine reputation of Rev. Clark. Never could he be accused of partaking in strong drink or gross exaggeration. For this reason, the *Lakes News* hereby confirms the existence of the lake monster. We are hereby issuing an official warning to all residents of Lake Delavan to exert extreme caution when near or on the lake and to keep a watchful eye on your children and pets. Rev. Clark has announced that next Sunday his sermon will be based on his terrifying experience with the lake monster. A cordial invitation is extended to all the citizens of Lake Delavan, including the summer residents, to attend the Sunday service and hear Rev. Clark's chilling account of the horrific lake monster. The Osterland Family Quartette will provide the music, and the Women's Missionary Society will spread lunch on a table under the oak trees afterwards. Bring a covered dish if you plan to attend.

Jill chuckled as she read the article in the next week's *News* that described the Sunday sermon. The church was overflowing with standing room only. The line to enter the church was reputed to have extended around the city block. Over the next few weeks a hundred souls made a decision for Christ. The lake monster was a big boon to Christianity and business in these parts.

Back at the computer, Jill logged on to the University of Wisconsin at Madison website, where she found contact information for Dr. Holden, the head of the zooarchaeology department. He would know what to do with the pictures she'd taken of the possible monster.

Pictures! She'd forgotten all about her pictures. After the heated argument between Chad and his father had erupted, Jill had forgotten to ask Mitch about her camera. She picked up the phone and called the dive shop. Mitch answered.

"Sorry, Jill, I don't see the camera here, and no one has turned it in. But I'll keep looking around, and I'll call you if I find it. In the meantime, I'll tack up a note on the bulletin board in the dive shop that one is missing."

Jill thanked Mitch and hung up.

It was kind of embarrassing to email Dr. Holden without the photos of the rib cage, but her eyewitness account would have to do for now. She gave him a brief history of herself so she wouldn't be considered a nutcase, and then proceeded to describe the bones as best she could remember. Just before signing off, she told him about where the ribs were located at the lake bottom. Just as she hit the send button, the bells at the front door jangled. An hour had passed since John had left with Miss Cornelia, and Jill was sure that was him now. With a deep breath, she put the fun project aside and looked up. Instead of John, Detective Russ Jansen stood looking around the cramped newspaper office.

"Come in and have a seat, Russ," Jill said, pleased he had come. "Make yourself comfortable."

Russ settled his lanky frame onto one of the old chairs and then kicked up his legs on the corner of the desk. "Where's John?" he asked.

"It's been an hour since he left to take Miss Cornelia home. I'm expecting him back any minute," Jill said, realizing it was John he had come to see, not her.

"Don't count on John coming back anytime soon." Russ rubbed perspiration from his face with the back of his hand.

"Oh?" Jill looked up in surprise.

"Miss Cornelia is probably showing off her prize-winning tomatoes and the blue ribbons she won at the Walworth County Fair last year. It may be hours more before John shows up," Russ figured with a laugh.

"And John's much too polite to tell her he isn't interested in seeing her garden," Jill agreed with a laugh of her own. "Hey, we have cake and punch left over from her party. How about some?"

"No, thanks. I've got to get going. I'll catch up with John tomorrow." His size-twelve feet hit the floor, but he remained seated. He rapped his knuckles on top of her desk a couple of times.

Knowing there was something important on his mind, Jill said, "John has an early morning flight back to Washington."

"But he just got here."

"He did, but he's been promoted from an SA to an SAC, the Senior Agent in Charge, at the Bureau. Now, he can't be away for more than a couple of days at a time."

"Well, then I won't take up any more time." Russ heaved an exasperated groan. It was obvious he needed to talk to John.

"Before you leave, can we discuss the drowning, Russ? I need a little more background information for my article." While the best detective Walworth County had ever hired was still in her office, she'd take advantage of getting more information from him.

"Sure."

"How long has Fleming been coming to the lake?" Jill reached for paper and pencil to take notes.

"Mrs. Fleming told me both couples have been coming here for years. She said they preferred Delavan over the other lakes because of its beauty and privacy," Russ said.

"Well, I wouldn't refer to Delavan as private. Not in the past forty years anyway. Any word on how Mrs. Walker is doing since her husband's death?"

"The last time I checked on her, she was resting." Russ noted the time. "I'm sorry, Jill, but I've got an appointment at the morgue. I should probably get going." As he stood to leave, the leather cushion of the chair puffed up then quickly deflated like a balloon.

Embarrassed, Jill looked around the room at the cracked plaster, peeling paint, and old bits of furniture. Her predecessors hadn't been into decorating or maintenance.

"Call me if you have any more questions," Russ said. "Be sure to have John give me a ring when he gets back."

"Will do." Jill remembered the tape. She reached around and pulled a copy from the player. "Oh, before I forget, here's a copy of my interview with the witnesses. Sorry, it's not typed out; I didn't have a chance to transcribe it yet." Jill handed the tape to him.

"No apologies necessary." He smiled. "I'm one of the few investigators who still prefer it the old-fashioned way. Things can be lost in a neat, written translation. Thanks."

"That's what I always say. Hey, before you go, can I ask what's going on at the morgue? Has the coroner already written the prelim report on Walker?"

"That's why I was hoping to catch John. He's got such a brilliant investigative mind, I was hoping he'd come with me."

"I could join you," Jill offered, already grabbing her purse.

"First time a newspaper editor's accompanied me to the morgue. Are you sure you can stomach it?" Russ looked her up and down.

"We'll find out soon enough, won't we?" Jill noticed that her comment seemed to make him nervous, so she added, "I've never been to a morgue, but I've seen a few dead bodies in my investigations."

"Come on then." Russ headed for the front of the office, and Jill followed right behind him. As they walked out the door, John was just pulling into a parking space. "Perfect timing," Russ called to John as he got out of his car. "Glad you're back."

"Oh? Then there's news on the body?" John asked.

"Hope so. I'm on my way to the coroner's now. Jill's already agreed to tag along. Want to come?"

"Sure. I appreciate the invite." Even an FBI SAC needed an invitation to step into a case outside the jurisdiction of the Bureau. And Russ wasn't one of those egotistical cops who was easily threatened.

Jill and John drove in John's car behind Russ to the coroner's lab across town. John steered with one hand while he channel surfed the radio. Newscasters were interviewing political insiders to find out the answer to the radio announcer's question: "Why has Congressman Fleming dropped out of the race?"

"He's dropped out?" Jill asked in surprise.

"The news just broke on the radio when I was driving back from Miss Cornelia's house."

"That's why we need TVs installed at the *Lakes News*," Jill complained. "I never know what's going on in the world. Radios just don't cut it anymore. So Fleming dropped out because of Walker's death?"

"It's probably an overreaction to grief. I'm sure he'll change his mind."

"But he can't. It's too bold a move to be flip-flopping around on." Jill didn't think someone would go back on such a big political decision, but then again, strange things always happened in politics.

At the morgue, John, Russ, and Jill donned surgical gowns, snapped on plastic gloves, and covered their hair with cloth caps and their faces with plastic shields. Jill imagined herself in a science-fiction movie, entering a biowarfare room instead of the autopsy room.

As a national political reporter, she'd never had a reason to venture into the morgue until today. When she did, she noticed a special ventilation system whirling over her head, sucking out harmful odors and bacteria. The room had a walk-in cooler and double stainless steel sinks. The floor and walls were painted with an easy-to-clean, no-slip green acrylic. A strong bleach odor permeated the air.

The autopsy table stood under bright lights as the center attraction of the room, and it tipped slightly toward the sink to drain body fluids from the corpse. It was eerie to be in a room with a dead person. Just this morning Joe Walker had been breathing, but hours later he was dead at the bottom of the lake. Jill shuddered at the thought that she easily could have been Walker's morgue-mate.

Coroner Lopez, a short man with a slight mustache, pulled back the sheet and revealed the unclothed corpse. Jill tried to act nonchalant, as if seeing a dead body was no big deal. But it was. Walker's skin, dark blue from lack of oxygen, was bloated from spending time in the water. The Y incision began at the clavicle and met at the sternum. From there it traveled down to the pubis.

Lopez picked up the file folder from the countertop and read his initial report aloud. "The corpse is 5'9" and weighs 175 pounds. At time of death, he was 42. Brown eyes. The brain, heart, liver, and lungs are all within normal limits of a healthy male of his age. Now let me explain some points directly on the body." Lopez began at the toes with the recently clipped toenails, working his way up the trunk, noting bruising on the legs and groin. "Notice the cutis anserina, gooseflesh. It's common in an immersed body due to postmortem rigidity of short muscle fibers in the skin. But overall Joe Walker was in excellent health."

Jill felt woozy. John put his hand on the small of her back and whispered, "Steady."

"Any idea as to the cause of death?" Jill asked, willing herself to snap out of it and become proactive.

"The blood and alcohol tests will take at least a week to come back from the lab, but the victim was definitely strangled." Dr. Lopez spoke rhythmically in a clinical, dispassionate manner.

"Strangled?" the three of them blurted out.

"That's impossible," Jill added. "He was swimming at the time of death."

"I can't help you with that. I rely on science, and according to the petechiae of the eyes"—he opened the vacant brown eyes—"which is the hemorrhaging of the tiny blood vessels, he was strangled. See the pinpoint eye and lid hemorrhages?"

"Couldn't a heart attack cause that too?" Russ speculated.

"Nope, just strangulation. Lack of oxygen administered with pressure, here and here." He pointed at two places on the neck. "His throat is crushed, neck broken. The trachea and esophagus are smashed. He sucked quite a bit of water into his lungs, most likely when he was fighting off his attacker. I've got it over there in a two-liter bottle if you want to see it."

Russ said he did, and went over to have a look. Out of the corner of her eye, Jill could see him pick up the bottle and then hold it up to the lights. He turned it in order to view it from many different angles.

"How does one get strangled while swimming?" Jill asked no one in particular as she turned her back to Russ.

"It's a first for me," John sighed as he slid his hands into his pockets.

"Lynn and Chad Stokes saw the victim swimming beside the boat moments before he disappeared," Jill said. "They never mentioned seeing a struggle. Walker must have gone down and had something horrible happen to him underwater. Someone needs to go back and have a good look at the lake bottom."

"Water is a nightmare to have for a crime scene. It's unstable because of the current, and evidence gets lost easily," Russ explained now that he was done with his look-see. "But the forensic dive team has already been notified. They'll be coming."

"Now we know why the congressman just pulled out of the race," Jill speculated. "Reporters asking questions can be a whole lot more dicey than a DA's suspicions."

"Bad timing for a murder," Lopez said.

Jill took one last look at the body, then looked at Russ and John. "Yeah, instead of witnesses seeing Fleming saving Walker, they were actually watching his murder."

7

It is better to know some of the questions than all of the answers.

—James Thurber

"You're quiet," John mentioned as they drove along the lake road to Max and Char's for dinner.

"I'm just trying to recover from a day of murder and morgues."

Jill didn't want to talk about Walker anymore today. What she wanted to do was reconnect with John, and that could only happen if they spent real time together. After months apart, she felt they owed it to themselves to have alone time and talk things out face to face. What a luxury it would be just to have a normal date like most couples. But once again, something reared up at the last minute, and they had to set aside their personal issues to meet social obligations.

Jill gave him a half smile. Romance was on her mind, but she didn't want to encourage John too much. So instead, she noted, "Murder's not appetizing dinner conversation, is it?"

"You're right, but you've given me so many off-limit topics like marriage, morgues, engagement rings, honeymoons, scuba diving..."

"Okay, okay, I get your point. I'm sorry. I just want to have a normal date like other couples."

"I'd planned to take you on a normal date . . . to dinner at the Firkin, at least until Max called."

"Well, then I demand a rain check." Jill smiled and squeezed his hand. With the other hand she pushed back her blond hair that floated in the breeze of the open car window.

"There's a full moon over the lake. Why don't we call Max and Char and cancel our dinner plans? Let's rent a pontoon boat and go out on the lake tonight."

"Did you forget that it's you who insisted we go over there?" Jill answered with a smile.

"Okay, I'll admit I'm the bad guy, but Max said it was urgent he see both of us tonight. And you know he's not one to insist without good reason. But I'd much rather spend our one evening together alone."

"I like hearing you say that. But you're right about it being important to have dinner at the Clarks' tonight. Since I bought the town's newspaper from Max, I feel obligated. I wonder if Olivia has something to do with this."

A smile lit John's face. "Do I detect a note of jealousy?"

"Don't tell me you didn't notice the way she looked at you at the office this afternoon." Jill felt annoyed just thinking about it.

"Really?" he asked. John nearly ran off the road after taking a hard look at Jill to read her expression. When a splash of gravel hit the undercarriage of the car, his eyes went back to the road.

"At least try to hide your excitement," Jill said.

John again smiled as he swung the car into a church parking lot. "When I asked you to be ready an hour early, I thought we'd go somewhere and talk for a while." John shut off the car. "Our conversation was interrupted this morning, and we need to finish it."

Jill moved closer to John. "All right, let me start by again saying I'm glad you're here."

John drew in a deep breath. "And I'm glad to hear you say that. But I have to admit, when you asked me to come to Wisconsin, I got my hopes up, thinking you were ready to set a wedding date." John's frustration was evident in his voice. "But now I know Tommy is still affecting our relationship. I'm sorry, but I have to ask: are you still in touch with him?"

"It's all right. Your questions deserve answers, John, and I'm going to give them to you. The truth is, I've talked to Tommy Harrison three, maybe four times on the phone."

John bit down on his lip. "I suspected as much."

"Actually, his calls were no big deal. They were more like, 'How are you?' or 'Just checking on you.' There were no professions of love from him, certainly none from me."

"How did you feel to hear his voice again?" John let out a puff of air.

"The first call was upsetting. I hated hurting him."

"Well, he's not the only one who's hurt." John slammed his hand on the steering wheel in frustration.

Jill drew back. "I'm sorry, John, but I wish you would try putting yourself in my place. The Bureau told me you were dead. Tommy thought you were dead."

"So you immediately ran out and found a replacement?"

"That's not true." Now she felt annoyed. "Since I've been back in Delavan, I no longer feel anything but friendship for Tommy."

"Then what's keeping you from taking back my ring?"

At first Jill didn't answer. She silently struggled with her indecision. She wasn't really sure what was holding her back, but she had a lot of choices to pick from. "When you arrived at the crime scene in Alabama, and I discovered that you were alive, I was only seconds away from telling Tommy that I loved him."

"I see," John said quietly.

Jill hated seeing John so sad; she just hoped she could explain everything to him in a way that he could understand. "During my investigation . . . losing you, and having my own life threatened almost daily was more than I could bear. At the time, I was so traumatized, I was reaching out for someone . . . anyone who I thought could keep me safe. Tommy Harrison just happened to be there and offered me that safety. Tommy and I survived the investigation together. We faced death together, only to be rescued at the last possible moment. People bond when they go through stuff like that."

"I know. I see it happen at the Bureau all the time."

"So you know what I'm talking about? You understand?"

"I guess that's what's really bothering me. I do understand. Have you forgotten the same thing happened to us, Jill? That's why I let so much time pass before I told you how I felt. To make sure it was love and not just the male instinct to look after you and take care of you."

"So why can't you understand why I need time?" Jill pleaded.

"Time to find out if you're in love with Tommy Harrison?" John's face reddened, and his voice sounded shaky. "That's what this is all about, isn't it?"

Jill had never witnessed John this distraught before. She reached over for his hand. "Please, John, this is hard for me. Let me finish." She paused and began again. "After surviving the ordeal, my emotions were bouncing off the walls. That's why I came home to Delavan. Not to decide if I loved Tommy or not, but to get away and sort out my feelings about everything."

"I'm trying to understand and be patient." He sighed. "Right now I can't help but wonder if we'll ever make it to an island for our honeymoon."

"Maybe we should go somewhere in the mountains and ski instead," Jill suggested as she remembered this morning's lake accident.

"I thought you told me you dreamed of a warm climate where we could scuba dive together."

"I won't have time for scuba lessons anymore now that I have this murder to investigate," Jill said, afraid to tell him about the water phobia she'd just developed in hopes that it would disappear. "And I'm an excellent skier."

"Well, investigating crime is your greatest passion," he admitted.

"A passion we share," Jill reminded him.

John smiled and then kissed her cheek. "There's just one more thing I need to know."

"Go on." Jill felt nervous over what that might be.

"Why didn't you discuss buying the newspaper with me?"

Jill knew it was time to tell the whole truth. She took in a deep breath before saying, "I was left out of the loop concerning your phony death, and you were left out of my decision to buy the newspaper. I know it sounds childish, but I just wanted to do to you what you'd done to me."

Jill looked up to the steeple of the church. Loving John was the easy part. Working out a life that fit them both was much harder. She sighed. "It was a spur-of-the-moment decision based on needing to gain control in some area of my life, along with the need to leave Washington. There was Annabelle hounding me day and night for fresh stories, and then there was Tommy pressuring me to commit to him. And there you were pressuring me to take your ring. I needed distance from everything. Buying the newspaper and coming home to where I felt safe seemed to solve a lot of my problems at once."

"Now you live here, and I still live in Washington. I love you, Jill, but it seems like we have two separate interpretations of what our life together should be. Do you think we'll be able to reach a compromise?"

"Yes, with time I believe we will. First, we need to sort out our conflicts. In the period in between, I don't want to lose you."

"You'll never lose me. I have a lot to make up for, and I'm willing to prove my love." John reached around to the backseat of the car and pulled a rectangular box out of a bag. It was hard to see in the dashboard light, but Jill could still make out that wonderful shade of blue. *Tiffany's?*

He placed it in her hand. "This is the best gift I can ever give to you."

Jill wondered what it could be: maybe a pearl necklace or a diamond bracelet. She smiled and opened the lid. It wasn't jewels from Tiffany's. She lifted the gift from the box and looked through the first few pages. John stopped her when she reached the marriage records page along with the family tree.

"It's my family Bible. Someday, we'll be writing our names inside of this." The gentleness of his words was followed by the touch of his lips. And for a few minutes, Jill felt like they were the only people in the world.

8

A politician should have three hats. One for throwing into the ring, one for talking through, and one for pulling rabbits out of if elected.

—Carl Sandburg

Thirty minutes later, Char greeted Jill and John at the door and then led them into the great room. "Come on in. Jill, I haven't seen you since you got back to Delavan. How are you readjusting to small-town life?" Before she allowed Jill to answer, Char focused on John. "Max can't wait to talk to you tonight." She smiled and gestured to the couch. "Make yourselves at home while I let Max and Olivia know you're here."

After Char disappeared down the hallway, Jill said, "This was the scene of a lot of parties during high school. There's something about it that reminds me of your cabin up at Egg Harbor."

"Thanks, but my cabin never looked this good." John laughed quietly.

Before Jill could respond, Olivia walked in and greeted them. She lit up at the sight of John. Jill thought he looked pretty happy to see her too. And what man wouldn't be? Olivia was dazzling in a pair of gaucho pants with a silk shell underneath a sheer chiffon tunic laced with gold threads and beads. Her auburn hair was piled on top of her head and held in place with antique ivory combs. Large gold hoops accented with peridots dangled from her ears. With her olive skin and dark lashes, Olivia needed no makeup, only a touch of gloss on her lips with a dab of blush to accentuate her high cheekbones. A myriad of adjectives described her, but Jill chose one. "Stunning. You look stunning, Olivia." Olivia had a bohemian vibe that men loved. Judging from the look on his face, John was no exception.

"Thank you, Jill. John, my father's quite anxious to see you. He's got some pretty important business to discuss with you tonight. Do you have any idea what this is all about, Jill?" Olivia asked, pouring them lemonade.

"Not a clue." Jill took a sip from the glass Olivia offered her. "But I'm sure you do."

"You're right, I do have an idea. But, I say, let's make tonight frivolous and fun instead. I'm sure you're not in the mood for business with John here. Maybe you could come back tomorrow night to discuss business alone with Daddy, John?" Olivia winked, making sure her fingers brushed his when she handed him his glass.

"I can't. Tomorrow I head back to Washington." He raised his glass and then drank half of it in a single swallow.

"Why so soon?" Olivia asked, not sounding pleased.

"This was just a quick trip to see Jill."

Olivia turned to Jill. "Aren't you the lucky girl? Your man flies almost a thousand miles just to spend mere hours with you."

"That's love for you." Jill walked over to John and put her hand on his arm. "I'm flying to Washington next weekend to see him."

"Are you serious?" John asked, surprised but clearly pleased.

"Of course. It's important that we see one another on a regular basis."

Olivia changed the subject. "We're eating on the back deck

overlooking the lake. Mom and Dad should be out there now waiting for us. Dad's just about done grilling steaks." Olivia led the way and opened the sliding glass door for them.

When they arrived at the deck, Max grabbed hold of John's hand and shook it hard. He offered Jill a friendly hello. Then the five of them ate while watching the lake as the wood ducks took flight to their nests in a clatter of good-night calls. The sun set in a collection of warm colors. But when the mammoth-sized mosquitoes began to swarm despite the candles, everyone grabbed their plates and ran for cover inside and sat down at the mahogany table in the dining room. Char had just poured them all another glass of lemonade when Max began to make his pitch to John.

"John, there's something I want to discuss with you."

"I just hate mixing business with pleasure," Char scolded, wiping her lips with a linen napkin.

Me too, Olivia silently mouthed.

"You know this can't wait, sweetheart," Max said to his wife. Turning back to John, he said, "You've probably already heard the news that Congressman Fleming has resigned from the race."

John nodded. "But you seem to think his decision is final. I told Jill earlier I think he's just reacting to his grief."

"According to the lead man in our party for this state, Fleming's serious, all right. He offered his resignation, and we took it. And here we are in early August, nearing the eleventh hour of elections with no candidate and a crater in the campaign where our popular candidate used to be. Of course, the other side is elated. This election alone could decide who has the majority in the House."

"That's unfortunate," John agreed.

"Spoken like someone who cares about politics. Unfortunate is right, and we're not going to let that happen, now are we?" Max leaned in as if he and John would single-handedly take care of this.

"I'm sure the party will quickly draft a viable candidate." John shifted uncomfortably in his seat and kept switching his fork from one hand to the other. He looked at Jill for an answer she didn't have.

"Yes, we plan to do that right away."

"Daddy is the chairman of the party in this district," Olivia informed everyone, looking smug.

"So Max, who's your candidate going to be?" John asked.

"Who do you suppose?" Max directed the question to all of them.

"Oh, Daddy, please don't be so dramatic," Olivia begged as she set down her napkin. "Just come right out with it, will you?"

"Well, to be honest, there aren't many possible candidates," Max said. "I've been on the phone with the state chairman all afternoon. We tossed out names back and forth for hours." He whirled his glass of ice cubes.

"I'm sure you'll come up with a solid candidate." John held up his glass as if toasting, then took a sip.

"It just so happens that we did come up with a solid candidate. John, I, along with the other members of your party, want *you* to take Fleming's spot and run for Congress."

John choked on his lemonade. "What are you talking about, Max?"

"Frankly, we're relieved Fleming decided to drop out of the November race. Everyone would have been focusing on the murder and not the issues we care about."

"You already heard Walker's drowning wasn't an accident?" Jill asked, surprised. "That sure got out fast."

"Just because I'm retired from the newspaper business doesn't mean I don't know everything that's going on in this town, this county, and this great state."

"Wonderful! Then it's you I'll be calling on a daily basis." Jill smiled.

Max winked at Jill and continued. "Who can take Fleming's

place, you ask? John Lovell!" He raised his glass high. "The best man for the job!"

"Here, here!" Jill agreed, enormously pleased at the idea. Olivia led a standing ovation, cheering for John, who remained seated with his mouth wide open.

Max waved his arms around to quiet them all down. "Listen, John, there are people who'll be more than happy to volunteer and support you, and plenty of others with the money to finance your campaign. What do you say?"

"Whoa! Slow down, everybody." John shook his head. "There are a lot of folks out there who believe Fleming will change his mind after he gets over the shock of his friend's death."

"John, think about it," Jill said. "It's quite probable people will say Fleming murdered his friend. There were just the two of them together out on that boat."

"There are a lot of other folks who are more qualified for the job than I am." John sounded annoyed.

"But we don't want Fleming to run," Max announced. "And we don't want the others either. We want you."

"Even though there's controversy surrounding Fleming, he still has strong supporters," John said. "Besides, there has to be a thorough investigation before we can say Fleming murdered someone. That's how the law works."

Max looked serious. "There's something else that factors into why Fleming withdrew from the race. I think it's important for you to know the congressman's ledgers were audited at the end of last week. It seems he's been co-mingling his campaign funds."

"You're joking." This news took even Jill by surprise.

"Luxury trips for his wife and children to the Caribbean and France. He also bought some expensive toys for himself like boats and cars with the money from his reelection account."

"Wow, Max. You're the best interview a girl could get for her newspaper!" Jill dove for a pen and pad. "When did this happen?"

"Let me say again, it's not on the news yet. Breaking story is within a week, so you have time to beat the big papers for this one, Jill. I'm glad I can swing this your way. The indictments are being drawn up by close of the day after tomorrow. I have a friend with the DA's office. Only a few in the inner circle know, besides Fleming. He's lawyering up for the storm, but he'll never sit in Congress again."

Olivia leaned toward John and grabbed his hand. "So what this campaign needs is a young, vital man with impeccable honesty. That's you, John! I couldn't agree more with Daddy."

John leaned back, away from the chorus of enthusiasm. "Let's slow down. You're very kind, Max, and I'm honored, but I just got a major promotion." John squirmed in his chair. "I'm not even sure my residency is established in this state. I worked here on an investigation, but my legal residence remains in Chicago."

"Of course you're a resident. You own a cottage up in Door County, and you pay taxes. According to the Wisconsin state constitution, that's all it takes. Don't forget you also worked out of the Milwaukee office on one of your cases, and paid tax into this congressional district. Rest assured, I considered all the angles before offering this one up to you, John my boy."

"John, this is really exciting news. I think you should seriously consider it," Jill pressed.

Char smiled at Jill. "I take it you wouldn't mind being married to a congressman?"

Before Jill had time to answer, Olivia added, "Maybe my next exposé will be on how an independent woman learns to be a sidekick to her famous and popular husband."

Jill shot her a look.

"Next, John can run for the Senate," Olivia said. "And then president!"

"Now wouldn't that be exciting, Jill ... you could be First Lady," Char said.

"I want to marry John whether he's a newspaper editor, a director of the FBI, or a congressman," Jill blurted out.

"You do?" John looked surprised.

Jill laughed then leaned toward him to kiss his cheek. "In fact, John and I were discussing our honeymoon on the drive over here this evening. Weren't we, John?"

John looked carefully at Jill and then slid his hand out of hers and back to his lap. He gave her an annoyed look, and when Jill glanced at Olivia, she could see a small smile on her face.

"This whole day has been full of surprises. I just don't know what to make of this situation, Max . . . or any situation." John avoided looking at Jill.

"What's John's platform?" Char said brightly, obviously trying to defuse the tension in the room.

John laughed for the first time since the conversation had turned to politics. "I haven't had time to think this over, and now I'm being asked to lay out my political agenda."

"What's in your heart, John?" Olivia sweetly asked, threading her fingers through one another and leaning her chin on her hands. Jill tried to ignore Olivia's coy portrait-pose.

"Education, immunization for all children rich or poor, grants for college tuition, bringing more industry to the state while safeguarding our environment . . . for a start. I would also love to court the car industry to open a factory here featuring hybrid cars."

"Bravo!" Max applauded as Char smiled with approval. "You're a natural-born candidate and leader. And with Jill at the helm of my old newspaper, she can throw that weight behind you."

"All ten thousand subscribers," Olivia said sarcastically.

Max ignored that remark and beamed at John. "Folks will be thrilled with your background in Homeland Security and the FBI. Just what our country needs now . . . a man like you to govern the country."

"So now I go from running for Congress to president in a

matter of moments. I'm flattered by your confidence in me, but I still think it's a matter I need to discuss with my family and Jill. How soon do I need to get back to you on this?"

"The sooner the better, Johnny boy. We need to act swiftly. We've got to make up valuable ground, and being without a candidate makes the party appear weak."

"Will next week be soon enough?"

"Yes, but no later than that," Max warned.

"My initial gut reaction is to tell you no, so if someone else comes to mind, please defer to him or her."

"That won't happen," Max said with complete confidence.

The clock in the entry hall struck eleven, and John stood to his feet. "It's been a lovely evening and a delicious meal, but if you'll excuse us, I think Jill and I should get going."

"Of course, you two young folks want to be alone." Char smiled while Olivia looked down at her lap.

"Thank you for that delicious meal and exciting dinner conversation," Jill said to Char. "Olivia, I guess I'll be seeing you tomorrow at the office."

Olivia didn't respond but simply nodded her head.

The family stood on the outside steps waving good-bye as John and Jill pulled out of the drive. In the car, Jill snuggled up to John and asked, "How about a moonlight drive around the lake?"

"Sounds perfect. And we can talk about what you think about Max's proposition." The glare of oncoming traffic washed the car in constant streams of light until they reached the less-traveled Lake Road. "Do you think I'm the best man for the job?" For someone usually so confident, John sounded unsure of himself.

"They could look the world over and never find a better man than you." Jill spoke with conviction. She believed her words with all of her heart. "Besides, anything that brings you back to Wisconsin sounds good to me."

"I doubt that I'd be spending much time with you, though.

Not only would that job keep me in Washington for much of the year, but I'd be spending a lot of time on the road when I campaign."

"That's true. But I know you could make such a difference in the world, John."

John sighed. "If I do run, it could mean pushing any personal plans off for a year. But that shouldn't bother you, since you said you need more time anyway."

Jill tried to ignore that little dig. "I'll help as much as possible with the campaign. But right now I need to get the newspaper updated and on its feet too. Olivia challenged me today not to use my family money to modernize the office, so I need to think about how best to do that. Speaking of Olivia ... you need to understand my past relationship with her. Olivia has always been competitive with me. We competed in sports, for the lead in the school play. And now she's competing for you."

"She is?" John scrunched his eyebrows.

"Don't tell me you didn't notice. It was so obvious the way she acted around you tonight."

John laughed. "It's cute that you're jealous, but I think it's all in your head."

Jill shook her head. "I don't think so. I've known Olivia for a long time, and I think she's waiting for me to take a misstep so she can rush in and take my place."

"No one could ever take your place." John reached for her hand and gave it a squeeze.

For the first time since she'd come home, Jill felt like it was easy to be with John. *Funny what a little jealousy can do*, she thought to herself as John drove them slowly around the lake.

"It's getting late." The clock on the dash read just about midnight.

"Oh, dear, and poor Mother is waiting up to see you. Be prepared: the first question out of her mouth will be if we're engaged yet," Jill warned him. "John, this has been such a good evening.

It reminds me of how good we are together, what a great team we make." She took in a deep breath. "Now that you understand my point of view, I've changed my mind and would like to be engaged to you again."

John was quiet for a moment. "You're changing your mind pretty suddenly," he finally said. "Seems a tad suspect to me."

"I know that's just the suspicious FBI agent in you talking. You have nothing to be suspicious of. What do you think of a summer wedding?"

"Whoa, I don't know about this. A lot has happened tonight with too much to think about. Besides, I don't have the ring with me. It's in Washington."

"Since when do you need a ring to set a date?" Jill poked him in the side.

"Hours ago you weren't ready to make a commitment. Don't think I didn't notice the transformation in you when we were at Max's. What changed between then and now?"

Jill raised her eyebrows. "Nothing's changed."

He shook his head. "Sometimes you make me crazy, Jill."

"Good crazy or bad crazy?" She smiled at him hopefully.

"Maybe a little of both. It's just that I think this isn't about you wanting to commit to me. This is all about another competition between you and Olivia. And now walking into the house without a ring to show your mother is just too much."

"John!"

"Admit it. You're jealous of Olivia and scared of your mother," John teased as he drove into the driveway of Jill's lake house.

"I am not jealous or scared! Oh, just forget it."

"Speaking of your mother . . ." John smiled as he pointed toward the kitchen window, where Pearl was peeking out at them. "Do you mind if I don't come in tonight? I adore your mother, but I'm really tired, and Pearl will want to have a long talk. After this conversation with you, I'm just not up to another round."

"Mother will be disappointed, but . . ." Jill pulled at the door handle and got out.

"Okay, then, I'll quick pop in to say hello. I don't want to offend two Lewis women in one night." John got out of the car too.

He walked behind Jill as Pearl swung the door open. "Come in, come in. There are too many mosquitoes out there for you to be lingering. How was your meal at Max's? What did Char serve?" Just as John suspected, Pearl was up for conversation.

"Max cooked steaks on the grill," Jill answered. "The corn was good too."

John smiled apologetically at Pearl. "Pearl, it's good seeing you, but I really can't stay." He gave both women a quick peck on the cheek and then backed out the door. Jill couldn't believe the kiss he left her with was as benign as the one he'd given her mother, but John was apparently unhappy with her.

Mother and daughter watched John's taillights disappear into the darkness. After his car was no longer in sight, Pearl broke the silence by asking her daughter if they had gotten re-engaged.

"Actually, I don't really know," Jill said, folding one arm over the other.

9

Jealousy is all the fun you think they had.

—Erica Jong

Dreading the start of another early day, Jill set her alarm clock for 5:00 a.m. It was already midnight, and too late to call Marge to remind her of their 6:00 a.m. reenactment of the drowning incident.

As she lay in bed, her mind darted from Olivia to the lake monster. Through tired eyes she watched the clock hands as they crawled past 3:00 a.m. before she gave up on sleep and got out of bed. She changed the bandage on her foot to a waterproof bandage and was pleased to see how well her skin was healing under the sutures in just a day. But her legs were still a mess with the bruising; blacks and blues shifting into greens and yellows. For a moment, she thought about Chad and wondered if he'd meant to be helpful when he pulled her up on the pier, or if he pulled her up against the edge because he was angry with her for not moving as quickly as he wanted her to. She decided to give him the benefit of the doubt.

By 4:00, she was showered and dressed and on her way to the office. It was pitch black and dead silent when Jill unlocked the door of the *Lakes News*. Not even a solitary car rolled over the cobblestones at this hour on a Friday morning. The only sound Jill heard was the occasional bark of a dog in a distant yard, or a bird awakening from its snug nighttime perch.

She flung her beach bag into her office and went to the break room to start coffee. When the coffee was ready, she poured it into her favorite sunflower mug and doctored it with loads of flavored cream and sugar. Mug in hand, she retreated back to her office.

Jill sat down at her desk and sipped the coffee. Yuck, she never could make a decent pot . . . a good reason not to be the first to arrive at the office. She needed to get to work but didn't want to be in the middle of something when Marge showed up. What to do until then? Jill logged onto her computer and clicked on her email box. A dozen little envelopes dropped down, but not a one from Dr. Holden. Deciding to put off answering her mail until later, Jill reached for the file at the top of the stack in her in-box. Ah, the lake monster.

Jill went to the greenhorn diver's blog and anonymously blogged about yesterday's giant submerged rib cage. It was nice to have something interesting to share with others. Then she read through other blogs of relics discovered in protected lake reservoirs.

For the first time since yesterday, Jill remembered the dinghy she found hung up in the limestone cave. She picked a well-sharpened pencil out of her drawer, and on a pad of paper she played around with the letters *CT*. Was that part of someone's name, or initials? Could it be the name of an old company? Jill typed the letters into her search word browser but came up with nothing she could use. She considered making the dinghy into a cute lost-and-found story for the paper, but then rethought it. With the murder of Fleming's aide and John's possible run for Congress, she didn't want to get off topic in her paper right now. She needed to write strong stories so she could prove herself and be taken seriously. Writing something cutesy wouldn't do that. For the present, she'd just sit on her find.

Jill went to Fleming's website. There he was, smiling broadly as he stood next to his empty leather chair. She leaned into the monitor to closely study his features. The camera had somehow caught a wild-eyed look at the time this picture was taken. *Did you murder your best friend?* Jill began to bookmark sites to refer to when she began her article on Walker's death.

A bang at the window sent Jill straight up out of the chair. An uneasy feeling swept over her as she used the end of a ruler to part the blinds and peek outside. There was nothing but darkness all around. The yard lights at the neighbor's had gone out. Jill moved to the next window and again used her ruler to part the blinds. She leaped back when she saw the silhouette of a man. Anyone prowling around at this hour was up to no good, that was certain. With one hand, Jill grabbed the phone, and with the other she picked up Max's forgotten bust of Dwight D. Eisenhower. Before she had the time to dial the last 1 of 911, she heard a familiar voice outside her window.

"Jill! Jill, it's just me. It's Chad."

Laughing with relief, Jill put down the phone and carefully returned Dwight to his rightful spot on top of the file cabinet. She pulled up the blinds by the string. Sure enough, it was Chad Stokes standing in the shadows. She waved him around to the front of the office. "What are you doing up so early?" Jill asked, seeing that the wall clock said it was barely 6:00 a.m.

"Sorry, I didn't mean to scare you," Chad said as he scooted into the office.

"I'm okay." When Chad stepped into the light, Jill noticed his disheveled appearance. "Is something wrong?"

"I've been up all night."

"Mmm. There must be a diver's rule about getting a good night's sleep before diving. I guess I'm not the only one to break the rules, huh?" Jill teased. "Doesn't your dive class start in an hour?"

"My diving classes were canceled, or more accurately, I was canceled."

"Oh, I'm sorry. I hope it wasn't because of my accident."

"You had nothing to do with it. It's my dad. He fired me and then kicked me out of the apartment behind the diver's shop. I'm jobless *and* homeless."

"That's terrible. How about some coffee? It's pretty awful, but it's all I have to offer."

"Anything warm will taste good to me. Hey, why don't I make a pot of coffee for you? My brew is dynamite. It's just the kind that puts hair on your chest."

"Just what I need . . . not the chest hair, but a dynamite pot of java." Jill ushered him into the break room. Noticing his attire, she said, "Shorts? No wonder you're cold. Wisconsin summer nights can get pretty cool." She saw Marge's sweater hanging off the back of a chair, and she offered it to Chad.

"Thanks," he said, slipping it on. "All I have are these clothes." He poured the pot of weak coffee down the sink. "I was freezing sleeping out in my truck, so I can't tell you how glad I was to see the light on at the *Lakes News*. What about you? Why are you here so early?"

"I couldn't sleep. I had to be here at my office by six anyway, so I just decided to come early and do some research. Hey, Chad, I just had an idea."

"I'm listening," he said as he measured the coffee.

"Why don't you work here?"

He shook his head. "Uh, I don't know a thing about the newspaper business."

"You don't need to know about journalism for this job. What I need is someone to help carry heavy files up into the attic, wash windows, paint, mow, and do general work. You can be my go-to guy. Whenever I need an errand, I go to you! It's no big career move, but it'll help you survive until you can sort things out with your dad."

"It's the best offer I've had all day. I'll take it."

"Well, we haven't discussed salary yet, but I must warn you, the pay is lousy."

"Even minimum wage is fine with me."

A few minutes later Chad reached for two mugs on the shelf and poured a cup of the freshly brewed coffee for each of them.

While Jill fixed her coffee with cream and sugar, Chad gulped his drink down. Finished, he set his mug in the sink. "I'm going over to the dive shop and see if I can crawl through a window to get my things. What time should I report for work?"

"Marge usually comes in around 8:30."

"Then so will I. I'd better get going. I can't show up at my new job the first day dressed like this, now can I?"

"Oh, while you're at the dive shop, would you look around for my underwater camera again? I must have left it there yesterday. I really need it back."

"You want those photos of the lake monster, don't you? You really believe it's him?"

"Yeah, just like I believe in Santa Claus." Jill did her best to make light of the situation. "But pictures or not, I'd really like my camera back."

"I'll try to get back here soon."

"That sounds great, but if you need time to sort things out with your dad first, then you can start on Monday."

"I'm not ready to talk to my dad yet, but I am ready to start work. What do you need me to do first?"

"I need you to start categorizing the old newspapers in the storage closet. They date back to the first issue in the mid-1800s."

"Why would you want to save all of that?"

"It's our town's history. We need to hold on to every issue. Maybe someday we'll have a place to display some of those old newspapers. Anyway, on Monday, I want you to go to Wal-Mart and buy some medium-sized plastic bins."

"I can do that for you today. How many boxes do you need?"

"As many as they have in that particular size. Charge it to me here at the paper. If they give you a hard time about that, then let me know, and I'll go down and pay them up front. I want the newspapers categorized by week, month, and year, and mark the dates on the outside of the box."

Chad whistled. "That's a huge undertaking. But I'm up to it."

"It is, and I'm counting on you to do a good job for me. Please don't spend any more nights in your car either. Set up a cot in the break room until you find a place to live. I wish we had a shower to offer you, but we don't have one here."

"Thanks for coming to my rescue, Jill, but if I ask him just right, I'm pretty sure I can bunk over at my cousin's for a while. He's a sign painter."

"Really? Come outside with me; I think I may be able to use his talents on making a new sign for the place too." She walked Chad outside, where a fresh pink sky was pushing the darkness away. "See this old wooden sign? I want it replaced." Jill tapped the sign, and it swung askew and fell off the hardware. "Yes, I definitely want it replaced."

"I'll get him right on it." Chad picked up the sign and dumped it into the back of his truck. Then he climbed into the driver's seat of his Chevy pickup and drove off.

Jill looked at her watch; it was after six, and Marge was now quite late. Jill called her on both her land phone and her office cell but got no answer. Guessing Marge was a no-show, Jill got to work on her article. She also wrote an open plea to the community for copies of all pictures taken of the sailboat race the day of the drowning, as well as any video.

The sooner she got her hands on some video, the faster this investigation would snap along. What worried her was the lack of capability the paper had in clearing the pixels in any video people might provide. There was no way she could afford the equipment. But the FBI had just the right technical gear at both their Chicago and Milwaukee offices. Maybe John could get permission for her to use them . . . She glanced at the clock on her desk and was shocked to see it was already eight o'clock. *Where's Marge?*

The front door jangled. "Marge?" Jill got up from her chair and went for her beach bag that had her swimsuit and a towel inside. But John walked into her office. She didn't try to hide her smile. "I'm so glad you stopped by to see me. You did come by to see me, right?"

"I sure did, and after the way we left things last night, I like the sound of those words. By the way, I didn't see Marge at the front desk." He pointed out the door in the direction of her desk.

"I'd dearly love to know where my assistant is." Jill shook her head. "She was supposed to meet me here at six this morning, but I haven't heard from her."

"Maybe she overslept?"

"Maybe, but she seemed excited about us reenacting the drowning at the lake this morning. Want some coffee?"

"Uh, no thank you. I've tasted your coffee before." He made a face. Jill laughed.

"Well, the coffee elf appeared this morning. I think you'll find his magic brew to your liking." She excused herself and returned with a steaming mug of coffee for John. Grinning, he sat down in a chair and took a sip. His eyes lit up. "Mmm, this is good. Don't tell me you learned how to brew this coffee in your cooking class?" He took another sip, a much larger one this time.

"Chad Stokes made the coffee right after I hired him to be my guy Friday," Jill announced.

"No kidding? Chad Stokes, the witness in the drowning incident? Keeping those witnesses close, huh?"

Jill laughed. "No, my motives are purer than that. Chad's dad fired him and kicked him out of his apartment at the dive shop.

Since he was my instructor when I had a diving mishap, I think he suffered the brunt of the blame. It's the least I could do."

"That's right; you were supposed to tell me about that." John's voice filled with concern. "I'm listening."

"My air supply malfunctioned. Later found out it was an O-ring. But what could have turned out to be a tricky underwater situation, Chad had no problem taking care of. So now this is my way of helping him."

"So, Jill feels guilty and has decided to take care of him?" John said as if speaking to another person in the room.

"No, Jill needs help around here," Jill sassed right back. "Anyway, I'm sorry we had a bit of a rough time when you first got here. What a waste of time when we have so little of it lately. You fly all this way to be with me, and I act . . . unreceptive. Sorry. I just get in the groove of being with you when it's time for you to disappear again." Jill came around from behind the desk and plopped down on his lap. She put her arms around his neck and hugged him, nearly making him spill his coffee. John set his mug on the desk and then wrapped both his arms all the way around her. Jill felt him sigh as he kissed her.

"By the way," she finally said, "have you given any thought to the idea of running for Congress?"

"Actually, I did, and to tell you the truth, when I woke up this morning, I felt pretty excited about the idea. Tell me, what do you think about it?"

She gave him another kiss and then said, "This is what I think. You're the perfect man for me and the perfect candidate for our state, and I'm committed to doing whatever I can to get you elected."

"Whoa, slow down. I didn't say I was definitely running. I'm just warming up to the idea."

"I know we hit a big bump last night when we discussed this, but if you do run, should we put our engagement on hold? Just for a little while at least."

"Absolutely. Being engaged to you might really hurt my chances for election," he teased. Then he raised an eyebrow and shrugged his shoulders as if he didn't know what to do.

"What?"

"Seriously, have *you* ever thought about running for office, Jill? The whole time Max was trying to talk me into running I thought about you. You've got a lot more experience in politics than I do, and you're much better known in these parts. I didn't bring it up at the time because I wasn't sure how you'd feel."

"Only in my nightmares. It's much more fun to write about politics than actually be in politics."

"That's too bad. You would be elected by a landslide, Jill." He squeezed her closer and laid his head on her shoulder. "The happiest days of my life were spent in Wisconsin."

"I agree. Wisconsin summers are some of my best childhood memories," Jill murmured, missing those carefree days.

"I was talking about the time I've spent here with you." He hugged her tightly and then looked at his watch. "If I'm going to make it to O'Hare in time for my flight, I'd better get going. You can never tell how bad the traffic is going to be until you're actually on the road. Walk me to my car?"

"I'll do ya one better. Since Marge stood me up, I've suddenly got a free morning. Let me ride to Chicago with you so we can spend some more time together, and then I can take the afternoon train from Union Station back to Walworth." Jill stood up and pulled him to his feet.

"That sounds like a lot of trouble to me. Are you sure you want to do that?"

"Positive."

Just as the two of them were leaving, a car came screeching down the road, did a wheelie at the corner, and barreled up next to them in the parking lot.

Marge nearly fell out of the door. "I'm so sorry, Jill! Is it too late to go to the lake?"

"It is now. I'm on my way to Chicago with John, but I'll be on the train back early afternoon. You can pick me up, and we'll go out to the lake then."

"Well, I need to talk to you before you go. It's urgent."

"John, would you excuse us for a second?" Jill asked, pulling Marge to the side.

"No problem. I'll wait for you in the car." He climbed into his rental and powered up the AC.

"What's wrong, Marge?" Jill asked in a whisper. "Are you all right?"

"I was here early this morning so we could go to the lake, like we'd planned. That's when I saw Chad Stokes walking around the outside of the building, looking in the windows. I parked up at the back of the property under the pine tree where he wouldn't see me. I know he got into the office because he left wearing the sweater that Miss Cornelia gave me last year. I waited until he drove off in his truck, and then I followed him back to his dive shop. I parked across the road, turned off my headlights, and watched as he went in through a window. I wasn't sure how to handle that, since his dad owns the place and Chad works there. I didn't call the police, but I stayed put until Mitch showed up. Then there was all this screaming and hollering. It was awful. Chad left with a duffel bag."

Jill sighed. "I'm sorry to hear that those two are still at it. As far as Chad breaking into the *Lakes News*, don't worry about that, Marge. Chad saw my car in the parking lot and wanted to talk to me. And what you saw at the dive shop this morning was only a continuation of yesterday's argument that Chad had with his dad. Chad was only going back to get his clothes, since Mitch kicked him out. For now, I've hired him to do odds and ends for us until he works things out with his dad."

Marge put her hands on her hips. "What about my sweater?"

"Relax about the sweater; it's just a loan. He was cold from sleeping out in his truck."

"I don't understand you, Jill." Marge folded her arms in a huff. "Here the paper is so tight on money, and you hire someone else."

"It'll be fine. Stay connected to your cell. I'll call you later." Jill turned her back on Marge's frown and walked toward the car, where John waited for her.

John drove toward the interstate that took them into Chicago. The day was already humid, so they rode with the windows up and the air conditioner on full blast.

"Did you tell your dad the news about your possible candidacy?" Jill knew how close John was with his dad and was interested in knowing his take on it. His dad's opinion could sink or sail John's aspirations.

"I called him, but he wasn't at home, and that's not the sort of thing you can leave a message about. Dad's always had an interest in politics. I think he'll be very supportive."

"I think so too. It gives him one more reason to be proud of you, and I can't wait to headline you in my paper!" Jill bubbled.

"Let's not get carried away here," John said; he sounded like he was running short on patience. "There are a lot of things for me to consider. For one, I really love the job I have now. I'm not looking for a new career at this point in my life. The only way I'll accept this nomination is if I feel it's a calling."

They didn't say much to each other for the rest of the ride to the airport. Once at O'Hare, John and Jill sat side by side in two of the hard chairs lining the huge windows. The summer sun beat through the glass onto their backs. Jill looked at her watch. Only a few more minutes before John would need to hustle through security in time to board the plane.

"Will you be back soon?" Jill asked softly, wishing they could start their time together over again.

"I thought you were coming to Washington next weekend. Don't tell me you already forgot?"

"Of course not. I'm coming. I just like it when you're in Wisconsin."

"Me too." John looked at his watch. "I think I'd better go through security. Thanks for riding along with me." He gave her a kiss on the cheek, but what she really needed was a lingering kiss followed by a declaration of love. She grabbed his hand before he could leave. "We're okay now, right?"

John nodded. "Of course. We just hit some rough water is all. But we're solid."

Suddenly a familiar voice rang out. "What a coincidence, meeting you two here!"

Jill blinked. "Olivia? What are you doing here?"

"I woke up this morning and decided to go back to DC today to take care of some business. Don't worry, Jill. I'll be back in a week, maybe two."

"What about your story?"

"I've got plenty of time for that. My deadline's almost a year away. What flight are you on, John?" Olivia asked with a flirtatious smile.

He held up his boarding pass for her to see.

She grabbed the ticket and read it. "Oh, I don't believe it, but we're on the same flight . . . what a coincidence! Maybe we can sit together?"

"Well, that's cozy," Jill mumbled.

"What did you say, Jill?" Olivia asked, narrowing her eyes.

Jill glanced at John. He acted clueless, but she could tell he was uncomfortable by the way he tugged at his collar.

"Hey! Here comes Max with your bag now." The men greeted one another with a handshake, and then Max handed Olivia's bag to her. Like a gentleman, John took the bag for her. "Max, could Jill catch a ride with you so she won't have to go to Union Station downtown?"

"Of course. I'd love the company." Max looked pleased. "I should've called you to find out what time you were coming to the airport so you could've saved me a trip into the city. Have you made a decision about my little proposition yet, John?"

"Not yet. But you have my word, Max. By the end of next week I'll have an answer for you."

"Good," Max said, slapping John on the back.

Olivia put her hand on John's arm. "Come on, John. We need to go through security. There's not a lot of time left."

"Just a minute. I need to say my good-bye to Jill." John walked Jill back a few yards in order to be out of earshot. As if he could read her mind, he said, "Hey, you don't have to worry about Olivia and me."

"I'm not worried about you. It's Olivia and her little games that bother me."

John took Jill into his arms and delivered a full-lipped kiss right on her lips. Then he turned back to address Olivia. With mischief in his eyes, he said, "You can fill me in on all of your and Jill's escapades when the two of you were in high school."

"Oh, believe me, I've got some great Jill stories."

"And I want to hear every one of them."

10

The best protection any woman can have . . . is courage.

—Elizabeth Cady Stanton

Jill and Max talked about John's candidacy as they walked back to the car. The heat in the city was sweltering, and the humidity in the air made it even worse. Jill counted her blessings that she was at her mother's lake house for the summer. The cool breezes dropped the thermometer by twenty degrees.

On their ride back to Wisconsin, Jill worried about Max, noticing he looked tired. There was so much she wanted to ask him about Fleming's misappropriation of funds, but she decided against it for now. Last year he had suffered a heart attack, and now, with all this campaign business, she didn't want to add another stressor by asking questions. She called Marge to tell her Max was driving her back to Delavan and instructed Marge to meet her at Lake Lawn Resort.

"Be sure to bring my beach bag," Jill said. "It's under my desk."

"And where will you change?" Marge asked.

"Get one of their cabanas for me, okay? Make sure it still has a good lock on it."

"Isn't this a job for Chad to do?"

"Chad has other things to do today. Please, Marge. Besides, it's you and I who'll be doing the reenactment." She paused. "Unless you want Chad to take your place?"

Marge sighed heavily. "Oh, all right, you don't have to ask Chad to step in for me. I'll just do my job as well as Chad's."

An hour later they pulled into the resort. Max stopped in the circular drive of the hotel and handed Jill a folder he took from the backseat.

"What's this?" she asked as she opened the folder.

"Copies of Robert Fleming's campaign contributions along with the receipts of the money spent. The audit's there too."

"Wow, how did you get the audit?" Jill was thrilled, but she had to be sure it was authentic.

"From someone inside the political arena. It'll be a matter of public record soon, but I wanted you to see it first."

"I appreciate this, Max. Do you mind taking this back to my office for me? You can lock it in the safe; I haven't changed the combination." Jill handed the folder back to Max.

"Sure, no problem. I'll make sure this is secured. You know, Jill, I have great confidence in your ability to run this newspaper. I know I made the right choice in selecting you as the next owner."

"I didn't know you had other bids."

"Just before I sold it to you, Olivia had shown some interest and quickly changed her mind. Now she told me she's interested in the paper again. But she's too late, obviously."

"Olivia wanted to buy the paper? Why did you sell it to me then? It's been in your family for three generations."

"I know. We've been begging that girl of ours to take over the newspaper for the past four years, and then when it's too late, right after you bought it, she tells us she wants it. But that said, you're the one who can take it from a small-town paper to a popular state paper, not Olivia. She loses interest too fast and likes to move around."

"Thanks for the vote of confidence. And for the ride," Jill said. Suddenly she understood Olivia's attitude toward her. Jill got her paper, so Olivia was determined to take John.

"I enjoyed the company. And Jill, if you ever do decide to sell, would you talk to us first? Just in case Olivia changes her mind again." Max lifted an eyebrow.

"I will, but right now my plans are to pass it from generation to generation in my family."

"Well, then it's in good hands."

Jill gave Max a hug and got out of the car. Next she hurried to the pier and found Marge pacing back and forth, waiting for her. She had rented an exact duplicate of the boat Walker and Fleming had used.

"Wow, I'm impressed. You keep up this good work, and I'll make you my right-hand woman, Marge."

"I'm already your right-hand woman."

Jill smiled, feeling thankful for such a faithful employee as Marge. Not only was she sincere, but also she was totally unpretentious and had an uncanny way of stating the obvious.

"But I smell a pay raise with a private office, and my own assistant! Maybe surfer dude would like to be my assistant. Here's your beach bag." Marge tossed it to Jill. "And you can change in that blue and white cabana right over there."

In moments Jill had her swimsuit on with her cover-up over it, which hid her leg bruises. Her waterproof bandage seemed snug enough. She reported back to Marge on the deck. "Okay, which one of us is rowing and which one is swimming?" she asked, praying she wouldn't have to actually go into the water. Her heart rate increased just standing there thinking about it.

Marge pulled off her sundress, revealing a bathing suit. "The swimmer would be me! I'll be Walker, the dead guy. You can be Fleming, the congressman." Playfully, Marge began to sing the well-known oldie from the sixties before plunging into the water. "She wore an itsy bitsy teenie weenie yellow polka dot bikini . . ." She surfaced then spouted out a stream of water from her mouth.

Next, Jill timidly climbed into the boat. Her pulse began to race when the boat started rocking. She sat directly in the center of the forward seat and placed her purse by her feet. Picking up the oars, she locked them in and began to row. At first she could only manage rowing around in an off-kilter circle as Marge impatiently treaded water. Jill was used to driving flashy motorboats, so long, heavy oars were foreign to her. She finally got the hang of it and straightened out the bow of the boat before heading in the direction of the opposite shore, just as Walker and Fleming had done. Only today there was no sailboat race. In fact, there wasn't much traffic on the lake at all.

Panic rose up in her again. But when she caught sight of the bright orange life preservers at her feet, she felt better. Lake safety 101 said she needed to have one of them on, but the reenactment had to be pure, so she resisted buckling one on to her body.

Jill thought for a moment and then asked, "Exactly where do you suppose Walker was swimming in relationship to the boat?"

"Far enough back from behind the boat so he wouldn't get bonked by an oar."

"That means the boat was ahead of Walker by a few yards so Fleming could keep an eye on the swimmer as well. Okay, let's try that and see how it works." Jill bit her lip with determination.

"Gotcha!" Marge was off and swimming hard. It was surprising to see Marge transform into such a graceful, strong swimmer. Impressive. Carefully, Jill maneuvered the boat around her and remained in front, but not without weaving precariously in an unintended zigzag route. Clearing the point of land that stuck out in the water like an elbow, they stopped about fifty feet from land. Jill pulled in and locked the oars.

"Why are you stopping?" Marge hollered.

"I think it happened about here." Jill looked around. "I wonder how close Walker was to the boat when he went down."

"Like this?" Marge asked, and with that she took a deep breath and dove beneath the water. Jill sat looking at her watch, waiting for the seconds to tick by. The boat shifted with the motion of the water, and she inhaled the scent of the lake. She loved it, and it reminded her of how good it was to be home.

Willing herself back to the task at hand, Jill said out loud to herself, "Okay, the witnesses said Fleming sat and waited a bit for the swimmer to resurface."

Suddenly, Marge popped up out of the water. "Aren't you going to rescue me? I ran out of breath waiting for you!" Close to the boat, she waggled her arms above the water.

"Rescue you?" The thought never occurred to her. Jill assumed she would play the part of Fleming, and Marge would be Walker. She didn't want to leave the boat for any reason. She just wanted a sense of what things looked like from the boat that day. "You know, Marge, I don't really think I need to go in . . . I can't, not after the other day . . ."

"Running scared?"

Where does Marge come up with all these clichés? "It's not safe for us both to be in the water without a spotter is all."

"We agreed to a reenactment. So let's reenact!"

Jill still didn't budge. Marge sighed. "Isn't this supposed to be an authentic investigation?"

"It's not how things are always done . . ."

Marge's eyes widened and her body stiffened. "Jill, there's something really strange right here under the water near my feet. Oh my goodness! There it is again!" In an instant, Marge disappeared under the water. Bubbles floated up and burst at the top.

"Not funny, Marge!" Jill leaned over the side of the boat, trying to see down into the late summer's algae-ridden waters.

Then Marge shot up from the water, screamed for help, and again disappeared.

With her heart pumping wildly in her chest, Jill knew she had no other choice but to save Marge's life. Jill stood to her feet, making the boat rock a little. Shaking, she gazed down into the water again. How easy it would be to slip beneath it and never be seen again. She picked up a life preserver and tossed it into the water. No hand reached up from the depths to grab a hold. Now Jill leaped over the side, sending the boat rocking from side to side as it moved slowly off by a small current. Jill bobbed to the surface, then took another breath and went back down again. Marge grabbed Jill and wrestled with her underwater. She grabbed hold of her shoulders and shoved her further down. Panicked, Jill quickly responded by shoving her back and shooting back to the surface with Marge right behind her.

"What are you doing? Are you crazy?" Jill gasped for air while choking and swallowing water. Fear settled in, but she covered it with anger.

"Don't you want to struggle underwater for a bit?" Marge asked innocently.

"No, I don't!" Jill screamed, reaching to hang on to the side of the dinghy.

"But isn't it necessary to see how the strangulation took place?" Marge's eyes were glassy with lake water. "This is a murder."

"Only if you want to murder someone else!"

"This has to be real." Marge yanked at Jill's arm and shoved her back under the water again. Jill responded by swimming away from her.

Both women bobbed to the surface again, this time yards apart.

"You're a lunatic!" Jill hollered.

"You got away from me, didn't you? Get my drift?" Marge winked with a smile. "I know you are a little-miss-play-by-the-rules sort of gal, which I find to be quite disappointing. But think . . . the struggle made us move to a different location from where Walker's body was found."

As anger over Marge's trickery subsided, Jill was able to focus on what Marge was saying. "You're right. Walker's body was found directly in front of the largest pier at the Yacht Club but two hundred yards out. We've drifted perpendicular to the pier. Fleming and Walker couldn't have fought with one another. Fleming stayed by the boat that was found near the body. Maybe a third person waited below."

"The real murderer."

Marge gave her a thumbs-up and went back down. Jill followed her, and they engaged in a light shoving match. Bubbles rushed out of their mouths, and two pairs of arms and legs swung around as their hair floated about their faces. Jill lightly placed her hands on Marge's neck, but Marge was able to easily lift her feet to her chest and use them as a battering ram against her attacker's body. Aware they were done for now, the two women gave one another the thumbs-up and swam to the surface, gasping for fresh air. When enough air filled their lungs so that they could comfortably speak, Jill said, "When we were fighting below, we kept coming back up to the top. If Walker and Fleming had been fighting, then they should have been spotted coming to the surface for air. Something, or someone, dragged Walker out much further so no one witnessed the struggle."

"And we just proved that." Marge breathed heavily.

"We sure did, but who? And why?"

They looked up to see the small boat had moved off again several yards and was approaching the center of the lake, which put them in danger of possibly not being seen by a passing motorboat. They swam in haste to reach the rowboat. Jill grabbed onto the side and tried to hoist herself up and over, but in doing so, the boat began rocking as if it was about to flip. Marge swam to the opposite side to hold it steady. However, she discovered that nothing is ever really steady when you're in the water. The small craft pulled away from them again.

"Maybe we should just hold on to the dinghy and try to swim it back to shore," Jill suggested.

"Sounds way too difficult to me. Let's just leave the boat. Chad can come out for it later. We can put on the life preservers. I think I can reach them." Marge swam to the boat. She lunged for a preserver but nearly swamped the boat.

"Stop, Marge! Swimming to the shore with just preservers is too dangerous. It's better to stick with the boat and wait for help."

"Who's going to help?"

"Another boater or the lake police will come along eventually."

"Ha, the lake police boat only cruises for a few hours each day. We'll be shriveled prunes if we wait for them." A buzz reverberated in their ears. "Look! I think someone's coming to our rescue already!" Marge hollered, waving her arm.

Jill looked up to see a blue outboard fiberglass boat approaching, an Eliminator Fundeck. A fountain of water whizzed from its tail.

The women each held up one hand to wave while holding on to the rowboat with the other. As the Eliminator cruised closer, Jill realized that it wasn't slowing down. In fact, it was headed right toward them.

"Marge!" Jill screamed. "Get away from our boat! It's going to be hit!"

Each let go of the sides and swam in opposite directions as fast and as hard as they could to get away. In a moment, a terrible crash reverberated over the water as shreds from the rowboat rained down on them. The waves that the boat left in its wake moved the women farther away from one another. Dog-paddling for her life, Jill was mortified to see the stern of the glistening motorboat as it kept right on going down the lake without so much as a backward look.

The waves kept erupting, beating Jill with force as foam blew from the tops of wave crests. Jill looked around and called for Marge. Finally, she saw her form floating just inches below the surface, face down. Jill's long arms knocked through the debris to reach her friend. When she turned Marge over in her arms she cried, "Marge, Marge!"

One eye opened and then the other. "What are you doing?"

"Saving your life!"

"I'm fine."

"No, you weren't. You were unconscious." Jill let go of her.

"I was playing dead. If the boat intentionally hit us, I wanted them to think we're dead, but once again, you really blew it."

"We need to stick closer together. We'll have a better chance of being seen." Jill grabbed one of the life preservers.

In a few minutes the sound of an approaching boat rumbled in their ears. Was the boat coming back for them? And if so, what were the intentions . . . rescue or harm? As the boat got closer, Jill was relieved to see the words "Delavan Lake Police" written on the side.

The captain turned off the motor and allowed the craft to drift next to them. A ladder came over the side, and a hand reached down. Looking up, Jill saw the hand belonged to Russ.

"I was with the lake police when we spotted you girls out here. Don't you know it's dangerous to be out in the middle of the lake without a marker?" He fished Jill out and then extended his hand to Marge.

"Marge and I were reenacting what happened over the weekend . . . when someone smashed our boat into kindling . . . look, there's one of the oars." Jill pointed to it floating nearby. The captain of the lake patrol, Steve Carter, pulled it in with a pole.

"What kind of boat hit you?"

"A fast one," Marge replied.

Jill shot Marge a look. "A blue outboard fiberglass, an Eliminator Fundeck. It came right through the center of our boat and just kept going."

"I don't suppose either of you saw which direction the boat went?" Carter asked.

"No, we were too busy getting out of its way," Marge answered.

"Actually, it headed west," Jill informed him.

"With the sun's reflection off the lake, they probably didn't even know you were there," Russ surmised.

"Well, they surely knew we were there when they hit us. Can't you get them on not stopping to render aid?" Jill asked.

Carter nodded his head. "I can, but you'll need to fill out an accident report. Right now, if you ladies are all right, I need to drop you at the lodge's pier, and then we'll try to locate the craft in question." Carter pushed the boat to full throttle, heading for shore. "It'd be a good idea to check out the public boat docks first. If it was an out-of-towner, they'd be pulling their boat out of the water about now. We want to catch them before the boat is hitched to a truck. Keeping this incident contained is the only way to handle it."

"Let's not waste time with dropping us on dock. I want to check it out with you," Jill insisted as Marge vigorously nodded her head in agreement. "We're wasting time."

"Okay, let's get to work," Russ told Carter.

Carter turned the boat in a large *U*, aiming first toward Township Park at Community Beach. A wide stream of water gushed behind the boat as he slowed to cruise closely along the shoreline, looking for boat lifts and trailers. There weren't any, not even under the leafy shadows of the cluster of great old oaks. Carter turned the steering wheel of the boat toward the center of the lake and pushed the hand throttle to full speed as Russ sat on the back of the seat, holding binoculars to his eyes. It was hard talking above the loud hum of the motor, so they all sat silently searching for the Eliminator. Only a few boaters were on the lake, but the Eliminator was not among them. They slowly cruised past other public boat docks, the Delavan Lake Marina and

Reeds Marina. Each time, Russ stepped off the boat and spoke with the owners and employees. No luck. No one knew anyone who owned a boat like that.

Next, they concentrated on the inlet to see if the boat was hidden there. Carter opened the boat at full throttle, and they seemed to fly across the lake. The bottom of the craft bumped across the surface of the water, making the occupants hang on to the inside boat railings to keep from being torpedoed up and out of it. This was the rush of the hunt that Jill loved.

Up ahead, Jill noticed the angle of the lake curve and the point of land. In the middle of that union, covered by a thicket of trees, was her mother's house, which had been designed and built by Frank Lloyd Wright. It was the mark she used in high school to help her keep her bearings when boating or swimming. It always guided her back home.

The boat moved slowly through the winding webs of inlet streams, carefully navigating around the maze of dilapidated wooden piers and boats. Nothing. Another few hours took them around the entire shoreline of the lake. A few times they thought they may have found the culprit, but when they disembarked at the piers to have a closer look, they saw no damaged vessels. Many boats were pulled up on lifts, some were even covered with tarps, but Russ and Carter couldn't touch them without a search warrant. Russ made notes of the addresses in order to contact the owners later.

"Could that boat ramming you have been a deliberate assault?" Russ asked.

"I'm beginning to wonder. Like you said, between the bow up so high in the air, and the glare from the water, he probably didn't see us. But it makes you wonder why he didn't stop once he hit the boat."

With no piers or inlets left to search, Carter pulled the police boat up to the lodge's dock and helped the women out.

Marge and Jill walked up the steep shore of the beach. By now dusk was darkening the sky. Jill went into the cabana and quickly dressed. Then she checked her bandage. It hadn't budged, and it had done a good job keeping the wound dry. Jill waited while Marge took her turn in the cabana, and together they walked back up to the *Lakes News* truck. Looking through the windows, they saw that both their office cells were on the front seat. The women looked down at them and then up at each other.

"This reminds me of a matter I need to take up with you, Jill," Marge said. "You left your office cell back on your desk last night, so I brought it to you today. You need to have it on you at all times."

"Well, Marge, it looks to me as though it was a good thing that happened, or it'd be at the bottom of the lake . . . Oh no! My purse! It's at the bottom of the lake! Where's your purse?"

"I locked mine in the trunk." Marge crossed her arms over her chest. "You know, Jill, it amazes me that you've survived all these years without my help."

11

I am done with great things and big plans, great institutions and big success.

—William James

On Saturday, Jill spread before her the contents of the confidential folder Max had given her the day before. Copies made from the original receipts and documents spilled across her work space. She painstakingly noted every record and then placed it into its own category. And how fast those categories multiplied: large ticket items like motorcycles, small expensive items like jewelry, vacations in the Caribbean and France, nice dinners, designer clothes. Jill handled each piece of potential evidence with great respect and care. Within days she'd be the one to break open this story. It was pretty heady stuff for a small-town paper. But it was the norm for Jill.

Jill smiled gratefully at Chad when he set the unrequested mug of coffee in front of her. She took a quick sip, watching his back as he tiptoed out of the room, not wanting to disturb her. The coffee tasted great and was even the perfect temperature for drinking. Jill set the mug at the side of her desk and went back to her piles of documents.

A menacing current of air swept in through an open window next to her desk, doing damage to her neat piles. Jill set the mug down with a thump and sprang to her feet. She went from window to window all the way around the room, slamming each down in a hurry as gusts of wind rode sheets of rain into the room. Chad assisted Jill's cleanup with a handful of paper towels. When the water on the floor and windowsills was sufficiently mopped, Chad carried out the sopping towels. Jill gathered up the receipts and began her categories of piles all over again, shuffling through copies of Fleming's documents. Just as meticulously as the first time, Jill read through each individual document. If there was anything Jill hated, it was losing time and having to do a well-done job all over again.

When she was done recategorizing her piles, Jill decided to focus on the last two years' worth of receipts for anything that remotely appeared to be the embezzlement of funds. Everything Jill looked at she regarded as suspect.

She spent the afternoon on the phone, making inquiries to businesses in the United States, where the big-ticket items were purchased. Next she verified vacations he'd taken with his family in the Caribbean and France. *Had someone died, leaving him a bundle?* Jill wondered. She did a thorough background check, but nothing turned up to explain this sudden burst of wealth. No, the money Fleming spent belonged to the taxpayers. There was no other explanation for it.

An unnoticed receipt on the floor got Jill's attention. She reached down to retrieve it, and her mouth went dry when she read the purchase order. It was for a boat, an Eliminator Fundeck. Of course, there were hundreds, maybe thousands, sold in this area. It didn't necessarily mean Fleming's boat was the one that plowed into them. But this single piece was too significant to ignore. It could turn out to be the most incriminating.

When Jill felt composed enough, she pressed the button on her phone that buzzed for Marge at the front desk.

"What?" Marge asked while snapping her gum.

"I need your help in this investigation . . . Marge? Marge?" Thunder pounded right overhead, making the room shake and the windowpanes rattle in their frames. Even the lights flickered.

The door to Jill's office flew open as a flash of lightning lit the room and Marge careened in with pen and paper in hand. "You have no idea how long I've waited for this day. I'm now an investigator. I'll put an ad in tomorrow's paper for a new receptionist. Don't worry, I know you're busy, I'll do all the interviewing." Marge dropped into a chair and swung one leg over the other.

"Well, let's not hire anyone for your position just yet." Jill took a deep breath before she spoke. "What I need for you to do is locate all boat companies in a hundred-mile radius to see if they winter any blue Eliminator Fundecks. Get the make and model along with the owners' names and addresses. Next I want you to talk to the owner of . . ." Jill picked up the receipt for Fleming's boat and read, "Boats Galore in Whitewater to see if you can get a photograph of the boat Fleming purchased from them three months ago. Talk to the boat dock managers to find out if Fleming keeps his boat docked on the lake in Delavan. If not, find out where he keeps it. I want to know if he pulls it onto the lake each time he uses it. Maybe a friend houses it for him."

"You don't think that it was Fleming who tried to kill us, do you?" Marge's mouth gaped open.

Jill placed her palms up in the air and shrugged her shoulders. "We just have to get all the facts."

"I don't know; this is a lot of responsibility you're giving me," Marge said, suddenly sounding reluctant.

Jill narrowed her eyes at Marge. "Okay, what's going on?"

"This assignment you've given me requires lots of extra work. I'm out of breath just thinking about it." Marge sat up straight and began to breathe heavily.

"Are you trying to say you want more money?" Jill rocked back in her chair and crossed her arms.

Marge leaned over the desk. "Plus an assistant."

"Even I don't have an assistant, Marge."

"You don't need one. You've got me." Marge pointed toward herself.

"And you need an assistant?"

"Yup, but call it backup for the front desk."

"Oh, now that's something I can do. I'll put Chad on the front desk when you're gone." Jill felt pleased with herself for checkmating Marge's request.

"Are you sure about that? Shouldn't we have Miss Cornelia take care of the front desk for me?"

"No, she'll feel it's a demotion. What I mean is, she has her hands full with her column and the obits as it is. It's just answering the phone and taking messages. Chad can handle it."

"Just answering the phone?" Marge reared back. "I'll have you know it's a very complicated job. A lot of psychological savvy is needed to handle the phone calls. Not just anyone can do it. But hey, you're the boss, just don't blame me if things go haywire." Marge spit out her gum into the trash.

"I'm willing to take my chances." Jill chuckled.

"You got it, boss lady. And don't forget about my raise."

"Marge, I gave you a raise when I took over."

"Meager. It was a meager raise that doesn't even keep up with the cost of living."

"Look, I've told you you're going to have to wait until I can recoup some of my expenses. We'll talk more about it later. Much later."

"Fine, but you'd better say your prayers that the *New York Times* or the *Washington Gazette* don't come calling with more pay and benefits."

"I'll take my chances." Jill winked.

"Don't say I didn't warn you." Marge walked toward the door

and headed for her desk as a soft rumble of thunder skirted the sky.

Jill turned her focus back on writing her article for the paper. For her readers' sake, she laid it all out precisely and simply, so the facts were easy to understand. Line by line, she wrote the sequence of events and backed each one up with cold, hard facts. Then she printed the article and took it to the press personally to be sure it was front-page news. She also brought along two more articles, the call for video and pictures of the race, and the request from the police department for any possible witnesses to please step forward.

Before the *Gazette* went to press, Jill went back to her office to fax her story to Rubric, smiling over the fact that a small-town newspaper and a Washington powerhouse would have the exact same story appearing on the same day. This would mean more trouble for Congressman Fleming, both at home and in Washington.

———

On Sunday night, Jill sat in bed with her knees drawn up beneath her chin as she talked to John on the phone. She went into great detail about the fun she'd had with Marge up to the moment the boat crashed into them, and how fearful they had been of drowning. "And worst of all, my expensive purse is at the bottom of the lake," Jill said. "But at least I didn't lose my ring!"

"You still have the plastic ring?" John asked.

"I sure do. I'll keep this one forever." Jill kissed the plastic emerald, the funny little ring he'd given her the night he proposed. He'd replaced it with the "real" ring, the family heirloom, but when she thought John had died, she'd given it back to his father.

"Why haven't you been wearing it?" he teased her.

"It's broken."

"Well, then maybe it's time for a new one."

Jill was delighted to hear John talking rings again. *A very good sign*, she thought to herself.

"Didn't I tell you five more rings came in that package of party favors in case you needed to replace it?"

Jill's heart scuttled to the bottom . . . no mention of her emerald engagement ring. "Sure I remember."

"I don't have any more emeralds, but there's still a ruby, a diamond, a sapphire, a topaz, and a pink one in the package. Take your pick."

Trying to hide her disappointment, Jill replied, "Why don't you pick out one for me?"

"I noticed you haven't asked if I've decided about Congress yet."

"It's hard, but I'm trying to behave."

"That's my girl. I'm still undecided, but I feel a definite excitement about it. I just have to be sure this feeling is from God. Keep praying for me."

"I will." She slid her long legs under the sheets and settled back into her pillows.

"Are you sure you and Marge are okay?"

"A couple of tough old broads like us? We're fine." Jill didn't want to worry him.

"Promise me you'll stay away from the water until I get back to Delavan."

"Does that include bubble baths?" Jill asked playfully.

"As long as the bathtub isn't too deep, no," John teased, and then his voice turned somber. "I can't bear to think of losing you, Jill."

His words made her feel more secure. "I miss you, John. I wish you were here."

"Well, we'll be seeing each other next weekend."

"Oh, that's right." Her thoughts were more on the story than seeing John. She went to her laptop and quickly jumped online to book a flight to Washington.

"Don't tell me you changed your mind again?" John sounded out of patience with her.

"Of course not," she said. "I've been cruising to meet this deadline since the *Lakes* only comes out biweekly. Had I missed the deadline, I'd have to wait until next week to break the story."

"And you and I both know it'll be old news by then," John said.

"Exactly. Thanks for understanding the pressure I'm under here. Hey, by the way, I printed that request for videos and pictures of the sailboat race. Can we use the equipment at the Bureau to scan it for clues for Walker's drowning?"

"Bring your responses to Washington this weekend, and we'll use the equipment at the Bureau to go over them."

"I was hoping you'd offer!"

"What time are you getting in on Friday?"

Jill quickly scanned the flights. "Around six o'clock Friday evening. I'll have to email you my details."

"How about I make dinner for us at my place, and then we can spend a quiet evening in front of the TV eating popcorn? I think I even have a Scrabble game somewhere."

"Trying to win back the championship from me? I'm not so easily beat. I grew up on that game."

"It'll be a spirited game for sure. Do you have other plans for our weekend?"

It was obvious to Jill that John's question shouldn't be taken at face value. He was gauging the value of this weekend on Jill's response. If she said she had no other appointments, that meant her only Washington business was him. If she said she had appointments, he could misinterpret her visit as just another reason to come to the capital. Jill opted for the truth. "After I decided to come see you, I also made a few business appointments for Saturday. I'll call you as soon as I get to my apartment on Friday. I want to catch an earlier flight so we can spend more time together."

"That sounds wonderful. I can't wait to see you."

"Me too."

"Okay, so catch me up on the investigation now."

That was just what Jill wanted to hear. "Max provided a full disclosure on the misappropriation of the Fleming funds. I have detailed documents proving the congressman spent over a hundred thousand campaign dollars on personal pleasures. Never have I been handed a point-by-point synopsis. I mean, the article practically wrote itself. It will appear in Wednesday's edition."

"Congratulations! The *Lakes News* is looking like the *Gazette*."

Jill laughed. "Maybe so; Rubric's agreed to print my article simultaneously in the *Gazette*, so by Friday our *Lakes News* story will appear on the front page of every newspaper in the country."

"This calls for a celebration! Now get some sleep, and I'll see you Friday." John sounded as excited as Jill felt.

When Jill got to the office Tuesday morning, she had a message from Glenn Carlin, Fleming's campaign manager. She decided to call him back right away.

"Jill Lewis returning Mr. Carlin's call," she told the receptionist.

"Oh, he's been waiting for you. I'll put you right through, Ms. Lewis."

In a moment, Glenn picked up. "Jill, thanks for getting back to me so quickly."

"What can I do for you?" Jill spun about in her chair, feeling on top of the world.

Glenn didn't beat around the bush. "When can we meet?"

"I'm not sure." Jill put him off, knowing full well he was just as eager to meet with her as she was with him. But it was a game she always played, and she played it quite well. "What's this about, Mr. Carlin?" Jill wanted to act a bit aloof when she was actually delighted that he'd called.

"What do you think? The charges you've made against Fleming, of course. I hear you're about to disclose some financial documents."

"They're not just some kind of document; they're official and verified."

"Ah, so you do have them?" Glenn laughed, obviously pleased Jill dropped her information like an amateur.

She chastised herself for falling for his trick like a rookie. She regrouped. "What does it matter? We can meet or not. It'll be public record soon anyway, but if you still want to meet with me, I'll be flying to Washington this weekend."

"What a relief I don't have to fly up to Wisconsin."

"Have you forgotten the good people here pay your salary, Mr. Carlin?"

"Can we meet at my office at two o'clock Saturday afternoon?"

"I'll be there." Jill noted the appointment in her BlackBerry. "By the way, I'm sorry for your loss."

"My loss?"

"Weren't you and Walker buddies?"

"We tolerated one another, but I . . ."

"Didn't care for him?"

"It wasn't that. He was a nice enough guy, but he and Fleming didn't always see eye to eye," Glenn told her.

"Really?" This was contrary to what Jill had heard. "Can you tell me anything more specific?"

"It was always about money. Fleming always backed big-budget programs, and he couldn't spend his own money fast enough, whereas Walker was legendary for his penny pinching. They argued over where money should go and how it should be divided and spent. It was an ongoing problem," Glenn explained. "Walker didn't act so much as an aide but took on more of an advisory role. It wasn't a good working climate for either of them, and I had the feeling after this next election, Fleming wanted to shake Walker loose."

"Really?" This news stunned Jill. "And whose side were you on in all this?" Jill prodded to keep him talking. She plucked a pencil from her desk and began taking notes furiously.

"Neither. I don't take sides. I've found that Washington careers last longer when you keep your opinions to yourself."

"Fair enough." Jill didn't believe him for one minute. Glenn Carlin was known for his backroom backstabbing. But she let it go. "Were you aware that Walker was training for a triathlon?"

"Wasn't everybody aware of that? The man was obsessed."

"Did you help Walker train too?" Jill twisted the phone cord around her finger.

"Not really. But the three of us dove together until the congressman put on an extra twenty pounds; he's had blood pressure problems, so Walker and I went down together while Fleming acted as our boatman."

"Did you ever go to Lake Lawn Resort with them?"

"No, I'm usually pretty well stuck here in Washington. Listen, I have another call coming in. See you Saturday."

12

*When you finally go back to your old hometown, you find it wasn't
the old home you missed but your childhood.*

—Sam Ewing

On Thursday morning, Jill bought a large purse with a small price
tag. On her way to the office, Jill decided to drop by a String
of Pearls to see how her mother and sister Kathy's new bridal
shop was coming along. It had been a week since the last time
she'd been at the store. When she opened the door, Jill heard a
chime rendition of "Here Comes the Bride" playing above her
head. *Cute*, she thought.

Pearl stopped examining paint chips for the walls and looked
up at Jill. "Oh, darling! I'm so glad you're here. Kathy and I were
just discussing what color we should have the painters do the
walls—don't you think green is a more appealing color?"

"Mother!" Kathy protested.

Jill looked around the shop. "I'm thinking something in the
pink family, and you could use the other colors sparingly as ac-
cents . . . and bring in lots of wedding cake white."

"You know, Kathy, Jill may be right," Pearl said.

Kathy smiled at her sister. "I didn't think you had the Lewis design gene in you, but maybe I was wrong."

"Please don't think your personal designers have forgotten all about your office," Pearl said as she gestured toward herself and Kathy. "As soon as the shop opens, the *Lakes News* is at the top of our list of design disasters to remedy. That place hasn't been tended to in years."

"Actually, Mother, this time around, I've decided to do it myself."

"Oh no. Kathy and I won't hear of it!"

"Kathy just said I inherited the famous Lewis design gene. Don't you think I can handle my own office?"

"I'm sure the remark about the design gene was merely a compliment, not a license to decorate!"

"Now that you've sufficiently destroyed my design confidence, I think I'll get back to the newspaper, where I know exactly what I'm doing." Jill delivered a smile and then moved toward the door. On her way there, she stumbled over a mannequin's head. She scooped it up and looked into the painted face topped with a glob of black hair. "Did someone lose something?" Jill held it up.

"The groom," Kathy said, relieving Jill of the head. "Go get your own Prince Charming. This one belongs to the bride over there." Kathy pointed to a naked bride-to-be stretched out on the counter.

"Kathy, show her the dress for this bride," Pearl instructed her younger daughter. "I think I've found your wedding dress, Jill. Hang on one minute."

"Great. Now that you've found my dress, maybe you can find a groom for me."

"You've got two. How many more do you want?" Pearl pooh-poohed her eldest daughter as Kathy hurried into the back room. In a minute she returned with an ivory gown trimmed in gold brocade. "Ta-da! What do you think? Exquisite for Christmas, isn't it?"

"Mmm, it's way too fluffy."

"What?" Kathy asked. "It's perfect. I would've loved to have worn this dress."

"Probably because it looks just like the one you did wear, Kathy. I want something simple, understated. Elegant. No lace and fluff. Maybe a simple silk peau de soie or a satin."

"That sounds like mine," Pearl said with a smile. "I wore Muv's dress to my wedding."

"That's the dress I want to wear." Jill pointed at her mother's wedding picture hanging on the wall. "I love it because it's very forties with sleek, simple lines."

"Jill's just given me a marvelous idea, Mother," Kathy said. "We should carry a few vintage gowns at String of Pearls."

Pearl patted Kathy's cheek. "You're brilliant, darling. Jill can still be our first bride. We'll sell her Muv's dress as a part of our vintage collection."

"What? Pay to wear my own mother and grandmother's wedding dress?"

"Just a token cost of a dollar or so, so we can truthfully advertise Jill Lewis as our first bride," Pearl explained.

"If that's the case, we'll go bankrupt waiting on Jill to become our first customer," Kathy said.

Pearl clucked her tongue. "Apologize to your sister. Just because Jill's made a mess of her life doesn't mean we shouldn't be supportive and remain positive."

Jill smiled to herself at the realization that her mother hadn't noticed that her own comments were offensive. "It's okay, Mother. Kathy's right. Best not to wait around on me."

"Girls, girls. I thought you'd outgrown your bickering by now." Taking Jill by the hand, Pearl coaxed, "Come with me, darling. I want to show you the new shipment of wedding gowns."

"Another time. I've got to get to work." Jill pulled away and escaped out the front door.

Jill shuddered to herself as she headed to the office. Trapped in a bridal shop with a perpetual bridesmaid and a mother-of-the-bride wannabe was a deadly situation for a runaway bride.

The moment Jill breezed into the office, Marge pounced on her. "Where have you been? Just tell me, how can you run a story about Congressman Fleming and not be here to answer all the phone calls? I tried reaching you on the office cell but . . . where is it? I don't see it anywhere on you." Marge circled Jill, pulling at her clothes trying to find it. "Is it in your pocket?"

"I believe it's still in your car."

"It's probably turned off too, am I right? I should dock your pay for this one."

"May I remind you that you have no control or say whatso-ever over my pay? Hand me the message slips, and I'll return all the calls."

Marge grabbed a handful from her desk and handed them to Jill. "The rest are piled up on your desk."

Jill took the message slips. After returning a few calls, she spun about in her chair.

"Here are more messages," Marge said as she dumped another bunch on Jill's desk. "I couldn't ring them through with you on your office line."

"With this news hitting the papers all over the country, the office needs some fast sprucing up," Jill told Marge. "Get a hold of Chad for me right away and tell him to go by the nursery. In the new window boxes that Chad needs to install, I want deep purple petunias, pink and white moss rose, and trailing vinca. Along the walkway we need a riot of color with black-eyed Susans, pink daylilies, larkspur, silver mound, and cosmos. The new *Lakes News* sign should be delivered this afternoon."

"What new sign?" Marge asked while making a list of Jill's instructions.

"Didn't I tell you? Chad had his cousin, who's a sign painter, make a new one, and they're hanging it this afternoon."

"How can I reach Chad? Does he have one of our office cell phones?"

"Isn't that your job? To keep up with the staff?" Jill asked.

"A receptionist has to rely on her employees to keep her informed of their whereabouts," Marge said haughtily. "But I think I do have his cell phone number someplace."

"Have you even made Chad aware of the rules around here? If you have, and he doesn't comply, let me know and I'll have a little chat with him, okay? Now sit down and let's make a list."

Marge carefully took down Jill's instructions and went back to her desk to try and locate Chad.

As Jill watched Marge exit her office, she noticed the peeling paint around the doorway. She recalled the uncomfortable conversation about decorating that she'd endured at the bridal shop and decided to draw up a list of improvements she wanted to make in her office. New paint, definitely. Probably new window treatments, and maybe some new office furniture. But Jill decided to hang on to the antique wooden desk, a handmade treasure of oak with large drawers and decorative copper pulls. The desk was over a hundred years old and had become an icon. To her, it stated that she, Jill Lewis, was the editor, the first woman in a long line of men who'd sat behind it.

"Marge!" Jill called, wanting to see if she had reached Chad yet.

Jill gasped when suddenly Chad was standing in the doorway. "Oh my goodness, you scared me!" she yelped.

"Sorry; I just wanted to let you know that I'm standing in for Marge at the front desk."

Jill's heartbeat started slowing down to normal. "Okay, where is Marge?"

"She went to buy a new investigating business suit at Bradley's Department Store. Said she'd be back right after lunch."

The last thing Jill needed was someone who put fashion before job. But she put Marge from her mind and focused on Chad. "I'm hoping for a deluge of tapes from the sailboat races. As they arrive, will you make copies of each one of them?"

"You got it. Anything special you're looking for on them?"

"Not really sure. It just has to do with the case I'm working on, is all. By the way, did Marge mention to you about the landscaping I need done?"

"I have the list right here in my pocket."

"Great. Were you able to get those boxes?" Jill checked things off on her personal list as they discussed them.

"Yes, I have about fifty of them in the back of my truck. I'll unload them and put them together. Then I'll start through those newspapers."

"Be sure to catalog them," Jill reminded him.

"I'll be right on it, as soon as the outside of the building is taken care of."

"By the way, were you able to find my camera?"

"Not yet. Sorry. Since I can't get back into the dive shop to look for it, you may have to replace it with a new one."

After Chad had gone, Jill booted up her laptop and began flipping through the thick pile of pink messages. Annabelle, Jill's former boss from the *Gazette*, was among the first callers, followed by three dozen other messages. As expected, there were also several calls from Congressman Fleming's headquarters in both Wisconsin and in Washington. Jill smiled at the growing stack of messages from reporters and producers from most of the prominent newspapers, magazines, and networks in America.

"Watch out, big guys, Jill Lewis is back on the front page," she said, still thumbing through all the messages.

Her next phone call was to Annabelle.

"Well, I'm glad you found the time in your busy schedule to

return my calls," Annabelle sniped. "But what can you possibly find to do in that town that would keep you so busy?"

"I sent you a story. Didn't you notice?"

"Oh, I noticed, all right. It's a winner. That's why I'm calling. I'll double your salary and pay your moving expenses if you'll come back to the *Gazette*."

"But I've got a newspaper in Delavan to run."

"You get someone else to run that little Podunk paper and get your rear end back here where you belong."

"You won't call it Podunk when I win another Pulitzer," Jill said, imagining Annabelle flipping her hair nervously around her shoulders.

"If you don't win it for me, I'll wring your neck. Besides, aren't you over that post-traumatic stress disorder you claimed to have?"

"Yes, I'm fine. In fact, I feel great. With this murder to solve and now with the Wisconsin congressman dropping from the race, I'm in my element."

"It shouldn't take too long to find the murderer, and the motive, in that little town."

"There are more places to hide around here than at the grocery store, you know," Jill chided. "There's also the laundromat, and behind the bleachers at the high school gym. By the way, this weekend I'm coming to Washington. On Saturday I have an appointment with Fleming's top aide, Carlin, but what I really want is an interview with Fleming himself."

"If you find anything interesting, I want the *Gazette* in on it," Annabelle ordered, as if Jill still worked for her.

"I'll think it over."

"Why don't we talk this weekend? Can you squeeze Rubric and me in your plans?" Annabelle was obviously turning on the charm.

"I have late Saturday afternoon free. How about then?"

"Perfect. But be sure to call me and let me know the exact time, okay?"

"Let me check with John about the time, and I'll get back to you."

"John? You're back with John?" Annabelle sighed heavily. "My money was on Tommy."

13

The duty of a newspaper is to comfort the afflicted and afflict the comfortable.

—Adage

Jill made a left turn onto a narrow side street of midsized houses. For the most part they all sported large lawns. The numbers on the mailboxes made it easy to find the Walker home nestled among shade trees in the middle of the block. Jill parked her car at the curb and turned off the engine. The house was painted white with black shutters and had a wide front porch. Jill lifted the lion's head brass knocker and released it, allowing the force of gravity to hit it against the frame. It was a few minutes until the door opened.

"Come in," Mrs. Walker said, pushing the entry open wider so her guest could walk into her house.

"Your home is lovely." Jill followed the pretty widow into her kitchen. Her red hair was bobbed close to her head, and her stylish glasses only emphasized her large green eyes. Although Mrs. Walker's manner was cordial, there was the unmistakable mark of grief in her red-rimmed and puffy eyes. She invited Jill to sit down at the kitchen table and offered coffee, an icy glass of orange juice, and a plate of banana bread straight from the oven. "I'm so glad you gave me a heads-up about your visit. I hate it when folks feel they can just barge right in on you. Thanks for your consideration."

As she sat across from the new widow, Jill worried it might be difficult to glean information from her since the grieving woman's feelings were still at the surface. Yet, if she waited for the healing to begin, too much time would have passed to solve this murder. At times, Jill had to remind herself that the cases she investigated were sensitive matters to others. She jockeyed the conversation around so she could find a way to get the widow to open up to her.

"Please accept my condolences. I'm sorry about your husband's death."

"I wish God had taken me before Joe. He could've handled this so much better than I'm handling it. There are so many details, so much to do, and I haven't the foggiest how to get it all done." The widow's tears fell into a handkerchief she grabbed from the waistband of her slacks.

"I'm sorry." Jill touched the woman's hand.

"Everyone's been so kind. I've been inundated with food, but I woke up this morning and had to keep busy so I made this banana bread myself. Please, have some, it's still warm." She lifted the crisp linen cloth off the bread and pushed a silver butter dish in front of Jill.

Ordinarily, Jill refused food or drink during the course of an interview, but this time she felt she needed to set aside those rules to be genial. Before reaching for the banana bread, Jill said, "I have a mild peanut allergy. Does this bread have any nuts?"

"You're in luck. I never bake with peanuts. Normally, this bread would be full of walnuts, but I'm out of them. Truthfully, I haven't felt up to going to the grocery store. Please go ahead and try some." Mrs. Walker tipped the side of the plate toward her guest.

Jill helped herself and took a bite. "This is amazing! It's so delicious."

"I'm glad you like it. I'd give you the recipe, but Joe's mother would disown me if I ever let it out of the family." Mrs. Walker sighed and stared at the bread, her thoughts obviously elsewhere.

"I'm not much of a cook anyway, so it doesn't matter," Jill admitted before taking another bite. Across the room were a variety of framed photographs of Joe Walker's athletic pursuits—swimming, running, and scuba diving—on a wall. Jill stood to her feet and walked over to have a look at them. "Joe was a Navy Seal?" Jill asked, feeling a bit warm. *Don't they have air-conditioning?*

"Yes, he loved being a Navy Seal. Even after his stint ended, he continued to dive. He belonged to the DCA, the Divers' Club of America. Are you a diver, Ms. Lewis?"

"I've tried it, but it's not my thing," Jill said, now facing the woman. Lightheadedness washed over her. She braced herself to recapture her balance and strained to focus on Mrs. Walker's next words.

"When we were first married, Joe pressured me to go down with him. I'm not a great swimmer, so it terrified me. But Joe thought the underwater world was a secret kingdom. After my first and last dive, I told him it would remain his secret place."

"The things we do for men. I feel seasick just thinking about it." Jill shook her head in agreement so she could connect with this woman. "When did Mr. Walker first become interested in diving?"

"Are you sure you want to hear about that?" She seemed like she wanted to talk, and Jill was more than ready to listen. Discreetly, Jill reached inside her purse and pushed on the tape recorder. Mrs. Walker watched her and didn't object.

"I'd love to," Jill prompted, turning the volume control up.

"When Joe was a teenager, he and his grandfather used to

dig at dump sites to find lost objects to sell for extra money. A century ago, there wasn't a sanitation system, so in those days people dug holes in their backyards to get rid of their garbage and trash. All kinds of interesting things were disposed of that way. Today, hobbyists like Joe dig up these materials. You wouldn't believe the things land hunters find."

Mrs. Walker jumped up and led Jill out to the screened-in porch in back of the house. "Everything you see out here is from Joe's digs."

Lining the porch were shelves overflowing with pieces of glass, old medicine bottles with stuff still corked inside, and buckets. There were things Jill couldn't identify. "What's this?" Jill pointed to an unusual object in the corner.

"An old corn husker. And that stove in my kitchen is one of my most prized possessions, an old Chamber stove. He got it from a dig in a deep valley in northern Wisconsin, near Hillsboro, and restored it. In college, Joe's interest in buried treasure spread underwater. Then he joined the Navy ROTC, and in the service he became a Navy Seal."

"What other interests did your husband have?" Jill asked.

Mrs. Walker's shoulders slumped, and there was a pause before she spoke again. "His biggest interest was his job, but he was quite the history buff too." She dabbed her tears with a handkerchief as Jill dabbed at her nose. Mrs. Walker misunderstood that gesture for empathy, and that was quite all right with Jill. Mrs. Walker continued, "In recent years, he's become a physical fitness fanatic. But his first allegiance was always to his job, to Robert and his needs."

"You said that in a way that makes me think the relationship bothered you." Jill tilted her head.

"At times, I felt their friendship came before our marriage." Mrs. Walker shook her head, remembering an unhappy thought. "When my husband first met Robert in the navy, he announced, 'I've met a man who's going to be president one day, and I'm going to help make that happen.' I knew exactly what that meant."

"What?" Jill moved closer to listen.

"It meant that he would dedicate his life in order to make it happen. Joe was a man of action. And since that day, he's devoted his life to Robert and his ambitions. In his mind, it was as serious a commitment as his marriage to me. But you know, Ms. Lewis . . ."

"Please, call me Jill." Now her tongue felt tingly.

"And you can call me Anna." She began again. "Joe was the brain behind Robert's success, but that's my side of the story. Once I encouraged Joe to run for office, but he insisted that he lacked Robert's charisma. Joe called himself the brains and Robert his mouthpiece. Oh, the political arguments they'd get into." Anna shook her head.

"What kind of issues did they debate?"

"Oh goodness, let me think a minute now. Well, I know Joe was very conservative when it came to the government doing things for the people. He felt strongly about working for what you earned, but Robert felt that there were those who needed a helping hand and they should get financial help at those times. At least Robert appreciated my Joe and respected him when he offered his ideas. I'm thankful for that."

"With so many other lakes closer to Oak Creek, I'm curious why your two families vacationed on Lake Delavan." Jill changed the subject as they returned to the kitchen and sat down.

"I can't tell you for sure, because Joe and Robert chose the vacation spot. And Crystal and I enjoyed the antique shops there while the men were diving or swimming. Sometimes the four of us went boating on the lake, but most of all, we loved the solitude."

"Was it customary for Joe to swim across the lake on these visits?"

"Yes. Early every morning, Joe went for a swim in the lake.

And since Joe decided to train for a triathlon, we've gone there even more lately. He was trying to expand his lungs so he could hold his breath longer. It worked too. I think at last count he got up to over five minutes."

"Wow, it seems unlikely that anyone would be able to do that."

"Oh no, let me show you." Anna got to her feet and searched for a magazine. When she found it, she paged through it until she found the right article. She laid it on the table and pointed to the paragraph. "This man can hold his breath for nine minutes. Joe did those same exercises all the time."

"Amazing." The next question was trickier, and Jill had asked it dozens of times inside of her head on the drive up here. "Did Joe help Robert pick out his Fundeck boat?"

"Fundeck boat? What kind of a boat is that?" The woman looked perplexed. Just this morning, Jill had purchased a boating magazine just to have the picture of this particular boat. From her purse, Jill took the picture of the Fundeck and placed it in front of Anna.

Anna shook her head. "You say Robert and Crystal own a boat like this one? If they do, I've never ridden in it, nor have I seen it."

Jill took a moment to refocus. "Since you spent so much time in Delavan, did you ever consider just buying a cabin there?"

"Oh no. We love staying at Lake Lawn Resort, and recently they were offering condominiums for sale. We had just put a deposit on one. But I can't afford it anymore." Anna pursed her lips hard.

Unexpectedly, someone banged on the back door, causing the women to jump. Jill was mildly surprised to see Congressman Fleming with a teenage boy, who walked on the bottom edges of his tattered jeans. The congressman stepped in the kitchen while the boy stayed behind on the porch. Jill narrowed her eyes, not pleased at all to see him.

Jill hid her feelings and then politely rose to shake his hand. "Hello, Congressman."

Fleming seemed surprised to see Jill as well. "Hello, Jill. This is the last place I expected to see you today. I seem to keep running into you. This is my son James. James, this is a reporter from Delavan, Jill Lewis."

"Hi, James." Jill held out her hand.

With his hands remaining in his pockets, James didn't bother to look at her as he mumbled, "Hi."

Typical teen, Jill thought.

"I came by to see how you're doing, Anna," Robert said, now focusing his whole attention on the widow. With a brotherly gesture, he placed his hand on her shoulder.

"As well as can be expected." She swiped a tear from the corner of her eye.

Jill sniffed and wiped her nose again.

"I'm enjoying Jill's company this morning."

"I've brought James to cut your lawn." Fleming looked at his son, who slowly skulked out the back door and headed for the shed to get the mower.

"Would you like to join Jill and me for some juice and banana bread, Robert? I have a pot of coffee going," Anna offered.

"Nothing for me, but sure, I'd be glad to stick around for a few minutes. I have no place to go." He took a chair. His body language told her he was not happy to see her there. He stared at Jill while tapping his fingers on the tablecloth. "Hot enough for you?"

"Yes, it is." Jill looked around the room as a long moment of deafening silence followed.

"Oh, Jill, let me get you some fresh orange juice. What's in the pitcher isn't as cold as what's in the fridge." Anna nervously got up from the table.

"Let me get that for you, Anna," the congressman offered, going to the refrigerator himself as Anna sat back down. Jill could hear him rattling around behind her with a glass and ice cubes. Finally, he set the new glass of orange juice down in front of her with a thud. "Thanks," she said. The glass looked sloppy, and when Jill picked it up, her hands got sticky. She kept her eyes on him as she drank.

It was time to stop the congressman from intimidating her. She'd be the intimidator. "It's no secret you've dropped out of the race. There must be an interesting reason for that. Would you care to share the reason with my readers?" She took out a steno pad and pen from her purse.

Fleming coughed uncomfortably then rose to his feet. "You two go ahead with your visit while I supervise James. I noticed some bushes need trimming out there. I'll take care of that for you, Anna." He stared long and hard at Jill. She held his gaze. Fleming was the first to give and turned away. As the door opened, Jill heard the whine of the mower eating grass along with the sweet aroma of freshly cut lawn. When Fleming shut the door, the kitchen grew quiet again.

Jill jumped right back into questioning. "Did Joe spend most of his time in Washington?"

"Only when Congress was in session. When Joe and Robert were back in Wisconsin, a senior aide, Glenn Carlin, was left in charge of the Washington office. More bread?" She held up the plate.

Jill refused a third slice. Her stomach was suddenly churning so badly even the sight of the bread made her ill. She fought back the nausea by taking deep breaths. "The three of them were good friends?"

"Not at first. Joe recruited Glenn for the position after the senator he worked for lost his reelection bid. Joe thought Glenn would be a great addition to their team, especially since he was a diver too. But when Glenn first went to work there, Joe complained about his attitude."

"How so?"

"Apparently, Glenn acted as if working for a congressman instead of a senator was a demotion. He thought he was too good to work for Congressman Fleming."

Jill's eyes began to burn. Having torn her napkin to shreds from dabbing at her runny nose, she now reached into her purse for Kleenex to dab at her eyes. Her thinking felt altered, but she managed to ask, "Did Glenn ever dive with your husband and the congressman?"

The widow nodded. "That's when things at the office seemed to improve. It was really nice for Joe to have a diving buddy again." She smiled at the memory.

"But didn't the congressman dive with Joe?" Jill already knew the answer, but she wanted to hear what Anna Walker had to say.

"It wasn't for lack of desire, but Robert was forced to give up diving when he gained a lot of weight and subsequently developed high blood pressure. But he still went along on the diving excursions and drove the dive boat for Joe and Glenn. Joe commented a few times that he was becoming odd man out. When Robert suggested going to Delavan again this weekend, Joe jumped at being with his buddy without Glenn."

Feeling jittery, Jill moved her feet about and began to quietly rock back and forth in her chair. It took all her willpower not to spring for the door. Obviously she had to leave quickly, but she wanted to preserve some dignity as she went out the door. Anna didn't seem to notice Jill was feeling unwell.

"Did your husband have any enemies?" Jill looked her in the eyes.

She nodded. "Because Joe loyally stood behind Fleming, I'm afraid the congressman's enemies became Joe's enemies too. And it's no secret that Robert Fleming had a lot of enemies."

"Like who?"

"Do you have a week?" Anna laughed softly. "In politics you can't please everybody, no matter how hard you try. A person contributes to your campaign, and then expects a favor. Sometimes that favor is possible to grant, and at other times, impossible."

"Most people who give money do have a motive."

"Joe found that out the hard way. And then came the snakehead fish bill. And guess whose job it was to appease the snakehead fish lovers?"

"Joe? How did he accomplish it?"

"He couldn't make that odd fringe group understand that these horrible creatures were the fish equivalent of rats. Even when he explained that the snakeheads were in no danger of extinction and had to be eradicated not only for health reasons but also environmental purposes, they refused to listen." Anna shook her head.

"But there wasn't one specific enemy?"

"If there was, I never knew about them. Joe shielded me from a lot of things. He thought I was too delicate to handle the stress. But look what I'm handling now, and not very well, I might add. I guess Joe was right."

"Oh, Anna, under the circumstances, I think you're handling everything very well."

"Thank you, Jill. That means a lot to me to hear those words." Anna smiled gratefully.

"Anna, I appreciate your time in answering my questions. And the bread was delicious. Again, I'm so sorry about your husband," Jill said as she reached for her purse and stood up from the table, feeling the start of a horrid headache to add to the mix of ailments she had developed.

"Thank you. I know you'll write a wonderful obituary about my Joe."

Jill turned white as she held on to the chair. "Excuse me?" she asked, realizing that Anna thought this interview would lend itself to an obituary, not a murder investigation. "You must have misunderstood. I'm not writing his obituary."

"Is it more of a human interest story? How about some photos then, to run along with your article?" Anna asked. "I can get out some picture albums, and we can select the pictures together, but just remember, I want them all back in the same condition as you got them." She went to the bookshelf in the living room and pulled out some albums. The woman looked so happy Jill found it difficult to tell her the truth. Anna turned to Jill and smiled. "Look," she said pointing to a particular photograph. "This is how we looked the day we got married. Don't we look so young here? And this is from our latest trip to the Caribbean."

"Anna, just a minute. We need to talk."

Anna's eyes widened. "Something's wrong, isn't it? Tell me what it is."

"Anna, I'm an investigative reporter. I'm not writing your husband's obituary, but I am writing a story about his murder." Jill bit her lip. She'd let her information out. The only reason she was privy to this information was because Russ and John let her in the autopsy room.

"Murder! No one mentioned murder to me! How do you know about this?" Anna shouted the word so loud that it brought the congressman running from the backyard and through the door. "Thank goodness you're here, Robert!" Anna ran over to him and started sobbing uncontrollably on his shoulder. "Ms. Lewis just told me that she's not writing Joe's obituary. She's not writing a human interest story about him either. She's trying to make up some cockamamie story that Joe was murdered. Get . . . get her out of here, Robert, please."

"I'm afraid I'll have to ask you to leave, Jill," the congressman insisted.

At that moment, Jill felt too ill to defend herself properly, but she had to ask: "But Congressman, haven't you or Anna spoken to the coroner?"

"I asked you to leave in a nice way. Please go! Get out of here." The congressman's voice was getting louder, his tone more abusive. "Get out or I'll call the police and have you thrown out."

"But didn't the coroner notify either of you with the cause of death?" Jill was startled by the omission.

"No, he hasn't. Now please leave." The congressman turned and put his arm around the widow.

It was hard not to meet the congressman's icy gaze. Jill's vision blurred as the wallpaper pattern began to move like water bugs. She pushed the screen door, hurrying across the porch to the yard.

Dogging her steps, the widow pushed through the door and followed Jill. "We're waiting for the body to be released so we can make funeral arrangements. Are you the one holding things up, Ms. Lewis? Do you have any idea how hard this has been on me?"

Jill dodged Fleming's son James, who had turned off the motor and was standing there gawking at the two women. Jill turned around to face the widow. "I'm so sorry, Anna." She turned the corner of the house and ran to her car. Sliding into the driver's seat, she looked up to see that Fleming had come down off the porch and was now behind Anna. He caught up with Jill and pushed half his body into the car so she couldn't shut the door.

His eyes were bloodshot and angry. "Why did you come here today? Was it just to stir up trouble?"

"I'm writing a story. I had no idea that neither Anna Walker nor you were informed that Joe Walker was murdered." Jill jerked on her seat belt and then turned the key in the ignition, hoping he'd remove his body from her vehicle. She took her foot off the brake, and the car began to slowly roll. Despite his weight, Fleming kept up with it. Jill kept watching his feet, praying they wouldn't get run over by her tires.

Since he persisted, she decided to question him. Either she'd get answers or he'd move back. "You're going to face a lot more charges than misappropriation of funds. Why did you have Joe murdered? Was he going to turn you in for stealing from your campaign funds?"

Fleming looked shocked at her words and stepped back. Jill floored the accelerator. Her tires spun out from the curb. Driving south toward the interstate she struggled to focus her energy on getting back to Delavan safely.

14

Words are, of course, the most powerful drug used by mankind.

—Rudyard Kipling

Gripping the steering wheel, Jill sped toward the interstate. Tears mingled with perspiration and trickled down her neck into her shirt. *Concentrate*, she willed herself, but images of the wild-eyed Fleming kept popping back into her head.

Jill felt hot, even a bit claustrophobic. She was twisting the knob on the air-conditioning full blast when the brake lights ahead of her suddenly lit up. Stomping the brake pedal, she barely missed the car's bumper as she jerked to a stop.

She panicked, knowing she was too ill to drive. She pulled into a parking lot and called Marge to come and get her.

By the time Marge arrived, Jill felt more in control of herself. She left her car parked and got in with Marge.

"What's up with you?" Marge shook her head.

"Shh, let me think," Jill pleaded.

With a clearer head, she began to review the time she'd spent at the Walker residence. Anna Walker had seemed quite pleasant until the very end of the visit. But things went haywire about the time Fleming showed. Did one of them slip something into her food or drink that made her ill? Could she have been poisoned?

There was a way to find out. She gave Russ Jansen a call on her cell and discussed the situation with him. He didn't seem to be enthusiastic about her theory, but he must have believed there was some validity to the claim because he started asking questions about what each person ate and drank. Jill thought for a moment. "Anna didn't have any orange juice, but she had coffee."

"So that could rule out the coffee. You had coffee and orange juice? Is that all?"

"Uh, I had two slices of her banana bread, slathered in butter, but I don't think Anna had any herself."

"When Fleming and his son dropped by, did they have anything to eat or drink?"

"No, the son was only inside for a moment. Anna asked Fleming to join us. I distinctly remember how relieved I was when he refused. So, neither Fleming nor his son had anything to eat or drink, at least while I was there."

"Did you see Mrs. Walker pour both your coffee and hers from the same pot?"

"A silver coffeepot was on the table, and yes, she poured the coffee from it into both of our cups. But the glass of orange juice was already set at my place at the table when I arrived."

"Okay, so that means if there was any poison, it was either in the banana bread or the orange juice."

"Or the butter!" Marge hollered into the phone.

"Thanks, Marge," Russ said with a chuckle. "Jill, tell Marge I want her to take you by GE General in Milwaukee and get a tox screen. I'll call ahead and order one, so you should be in and out of the emergency room in no time."

"Yeah, right," Jill said with a chuckle.

～w～

They were in and out of the emergency room and back on the road to Delavan in four hours.

"I never thought the day would come when I'd be hoping to find drugs or poison in my system." Jill licked her lips. "But can you just imagine the headlines?"

"Just listen to you. You're half dead, and all you can think about is the newspaper. But you're right, it'll be the most exciting front-page local news we've had since Senator Burke's thugs tried to drown you. Oh, I almost forgot. Not since the FBI agent threw you into that pit with those vipers. I've gotta say, it's so much more exciting with you around. I'm glad you're back."

"Uh, thanks. Wait! How will I get my car from the parking lot? I can't just leave it there. I have to drive to O'Hare at the crack of dawn. I'm going to Washington, remember?"

"You can't get it today. I'll drive you to the airport in the morning, and when I get back, I'll drive Chad over here to pick up your car."

"What would I do without you, Marge?" Jill said with a laugh.

"Just remember that when it comes time for another raise."

"Back off." Jill turned businesslike. "Have we received any videos or photographs from our ad?"

"A few. Chad's already copied them for you."

"Good. Would you package them so I can carry them on the plane with me? Also, talk to as many of the Eliminator Fundeck dealers and the owners on the list as you can."

"Businesses are slammed with tourists and won't be able to give me the time of day. Weekdays are slower, more conducive to conversation. I should wait until Monday for that. Besides, I had an idea about where Fleming might be keeping his boat."

"Where?"

"At his own house."

"That thought never occurred to me. But Anna isn't aware of

Fleming owning a boat like that. If it's there, he has to be keeping it in his garage, or a storage unit."

When Marge dropped her off at home, Jill had the house to herself, since Pearl was still at the shop. After a quick bath, she slipped into her cotton nightgown and sat cross-legged on the bed with her laptop to do some research. First, she scanned her emails to see if Dr. Holden had responded to her message about the lake monster. He still hadn't. She had to find her camera! Next she looked for an email from John. Nothing was in her inbox, so she googled Glenn Carlin to get background information on him before their meeting on Saturday.

Scanning the research on Google, she read that he was regarded as a successful image-maker. His background appeared solid; he championed charitable causes like higher education programs for welfare recipients in order to get them out of the system. He had previously worked as the top aide for a well-respected senator from New York.

Her cell phone rang as she was scrolling through the info on Google. "Hello?"

"Hi, Jill. It's Russ. I just talked to the lab at the hospital. They'll do your workup in the morning when they're fully staffed."

"I expected we'd have to wait." Jill sighed, impatient to find out what had happened to her.

"How are you feeling?"

"Much better, thank you. Tomorrow I'm flying to Washington."

15

For all sad words of tongue or pen, the saddest are these, "It might have been."

—John Greenleaf Whittier

Her bumpy flight arrived in Washington smack-dab in the middle of a summer storm. Lightning streaked the sky with thunder rumbling all around as the plane touched down. Surprisingly, Jill felt fine. Perhaps yesterday's ordeal had been caused by something she'd eaten or a sudden flu bug that dissipated in twenty-four hours.

She headed straight to her apartment building. As she walked through the lobby, an unmistakable profile waited for her. Senator Tommy Harrison rose to his feet and walked quickly across the marble floor toward Jill.

"Tommy?"

"May we talk?" He picked up her luggage.

Jill glanced around and agreed. "Upstairs in my apartment."

Once inside her door, she noticed that though it was scorching outside, it was freezing in her apartment. Trying to gather her thoughts, she did little things like readjust the thermostat and look at her mail while Tommy deposited her belongings outside her bedroom door.

They took their seats in the living room, facing one another.

"I've been counting the days until you returned to Washington and to me," Tommy finally said.

"Don't try to schmooze me, Tommy Harrison. I've seen your smiling face splashed across the pages of *W* and *Town and Country*. Last week, even *People* magazine had a full-page spread of Washington's most eligible bachelor with his arm around that young starlet, what's-her-name."

"So, you're jealous." He grinned at her.

"No, I'm pleased to see you're enjoying yourself." Jill stood up and walked toward the windows, passing within inches of his chair. To her surprise, he reached out for her hand, but she sidestepped his touch and opened the Roman shades. Summer sunshine poured into the room. Here was her beloved Washington. The dark clouds had moved west, and right behind them was her bright forecast.

Tommy followed her over to the window. For a few seconds neither of them moved. Then he reached up and touched her face with his fingertips. "I adore those freckles," he said softly.

Jill swatted his hand away but felt her anger melting. "How did you know I'd be in Washington today?"

"Annabelle mentioned it to me when I ran into her at lunch. I took my chances on catching you in the lobby."

Jill sighed. "Okay, now tell me why you're here."

"There's buzz on the Hill that John's been offered a stab at Fleming's seat. If he takes it and wins, that levels the playing field a bit. You get to choose between a congressman and a senator. I stopped by to make sure I'm still in the running."

"Mmm, political multiple choice. I've never played this game before," Jill admitted, a bit irked by his nerve to bring up the subject of John.

"Let's hope you know how to play. It'd be a pity to settle for the runner-up when you could have the grand prize."

Jill raised an eyebrow, impressed at his nerve. "So, you're the grand prize?"

He laughed. "Judging from your ice-princess stance, maybe not. This game seems to be over before it started." He laced his fingers together and stretched his arms. "So, I guess the rumors are true. You've made your choice. You're going to marry the congressman, not the senator."

"Who told you that?"

"Your friend Olivia."

"You know Olivia?" Jill asked. "Why am I not surprised?"

"We met at a cocktail party earlier this week. She's an intriguing woman."

"And a troublemaker," Jill grumbled. "Olivia had no right to tell you anything about my private life."

"Look, I'm just here to hear it for myself . . . from you." There was anxiousness in his voice.

Jill touched his hand. "I'm sorry, Tommy. I was going to call you and tell you."

"But you were afraid because you knew once you connected with me again—"

Jill cut him off. "No." Now the room felt too warm. Somehow, she had to find the right words to turn him away without hurting him too much. "You'll get over it, Tommy."

"But will you?" he asked, raising his eyebrows.

Jill ignored his question. "With your charm and good looks, not to mention your money, the women will line up to the top of the Washington Monument and back for you. You can have your pick of anyone you want, and you know it."

"Except for the only woman I want . . . you."

Jill laughed nervously. Hoping to shift the focus, she quipped, "My mother once told me men always want what they can't have."

"What would your mother tell you to do now?" Tommy stared at her.

"Run!" Jill laughed, trying to make light of the tense moment.

But Tommy didn't laugh. He reached out and took her by the arms, pulling her closer to him. She dodged his first kiss but didn't move from his arms right away. Sensing her emotions, he pulled her closer, awakening her memories with his familiar scent, evoking the feelings she once had for him. Jill couldn't move.

"You're not backing away. Does this mean . . . ?" He stopped. Not waiting for her answer, he slightly brushed her lips with his.

Unable to resist, Jill kissed him back. All her pent-up feelings—her regrets, her affection, her fear—poured into that one kiss.

When Tommy pulled away, Jill's heart churned with a mixture of relief and sadness.

He was silent for a moment, and then he put his hands on her shoulders and stared at her. "You're giving me mixed signals. Do you want me in your life or not?" He paused, waiting for her to respond, but she refused to answer him. Her lip quivered, and then she ran into her bedroom and locked the door. She knew she was overreacting, but she had to lock the door to protect herself not from Tommy but from her own choices.

He apologized to her through the door. "I'm sorry, Jill. I didn't mean to push you. I'll wait out here until you're ready to talk. Unless you'd prefer that I leave?" he asked tentatively.

"No, I . . . I'm okay . . . Give me a minute." Her head was spinning. *What am I going to do?* Seeing Tommy so unexpectedly unnerved her. Surprised by a sudden rush of feelings that began to resurface, she wondered if Olivia was right. Was it the bad boy she really wanted?

Jill sat up on her bed. After drying her tears, she went into the bathroom to splash water on her face.

When Jill walked out of the bathroom, Tommy gave her a smile that practically knocked her off her feet. He stood up. Still not sure how this would turn out, she faced him and began, "To be perfectly honest, I've reached a decision." She brushed a tear from her cheek.

"If it's more time that you need, tell me. I'll wait. I love you, Jill."

She spoke resolutely. "Tommy . . . I don't need more time. I'm sorry, but my decision is made. It's John. It's always been John."

"Not what I expected to hear after that kiss," he said quietly as he stared intently at her.

Without looking at him, she said, "No, I'm sorry, Tommy. I should have never let that happen."

He reached out to her. "Maybe that kiss should tell you that maybe you aren't ready to make that commitment."

Jill pulled away. "Please, Tommy. For weeks, I've put a lot of thought and prayer in this. Don't make me second-guess myself."

"You can honestly look me in the eyes and tell me you don't love me?" Tommy asked.

She sighed. "Yes, I can. The truth is, it's over between you and me. This wasn't any kind of a contest. John is the man I loved first, and he's the one I will love last. I should have called you to say that it was over between us. I wasn't being fair to you, but for a while I just didn't know how I felt about either of you." Jill felt so guilty for leading him on for so long that she couldn't meet his eyes.

Tommy didn't say another word. He turned and walked slowly to the foyer. Jill followed at a safe distance and watched him as his hand twisted the doorknob.

"Tommy, I don't want you to walk away angry. Please . . ." She wanted to see a glint of understanding and forgiveness on his face, but if it was there she never knew. He didn't look at her as he walked into the elevator and out of her life.

Although she looked forward to her evening with John, Jill struggled to put the haunting scene with Tommy behind her. As she got ready for her date, she popped some music into her CD player and hummed along with it in an effort to forget about Tommy. And she *was* excited about seeing John's townhouse in Alexandria tonight, especially since the odds were greater that it would soon be her home too. Just as she was dressed and about to step into her high heels, her cell phone rang. It was John.

"Jill, I'm sorry. I can't make it for our date tonight." He said nothing more. He sounded apologetic, but no explanation followed the disappointing news.

Trying to hide her disappointment and frustration, Jill said, "Are we star-crossed lovers or what? Last weekend was way too brief, and it seems like this weekend is turning out to be the same way."

"Is that a pout I hear in your voice?" John asked.

"It is." Jill went for her nightgown at the back of her bathroom door.

Again, John didn't apologize or offer details. "Hopefully, this won't be an all-nighter, so it shouldn't ruin our weekend. Let's meet tomorrow at eleven at the Grille. We can go over the tapes from the sailboat race after that at the Washington Bureau."

Jill went to her BlackBerry and looked through her standing appointments. "The Grille I can do, but right after that I have a meeting with Glenn Carlin, followed immediately with one at the *Gazette*. But don't worry about it. Tomorrow's fine as long as I can get to my appointment with Carlin by two."

"Sounds great."

"Oh, wait, my other line's ringing. Can you hold on for a minute?"

"I've got to run, so take your call, and I'll see you tomorrow. Love you," he said, and he was gone.

All dressed up with nowhere to go. Jill felt sorry for herself as she clicked onto the other line. It was Russ Jansen.

"Good news! You can relax and enjoy your visit to Washington. All panels are clear. No poison."

"Not a trace, huh? That's a relief. I guess it was nothing more than a bad case of the stomach flu."

16

Love is the irresistible desire to be desired irresistibly.

—Louis Ginsberg

Saturday lunch with John was just what Jill hoped—casual and trouble-free. After ordering juicy cheeseburgers, John said, "Sorry I had to drop out of our plans last night. There's a lot going on at the agency, as usual."

"Anything with political overtones?"

"If you're asking if I have anything for you to investigate, no." He laughed as though he could hear her thoughts. "But, I do have some news today that should make you happy."

"Oh?" Jill spoke in a low voice. She had an inkling of what John was about to tell her but remained quiet. She didn't want to be accused of putting words in his mouth.

"I've made my decision, Jill . . . and you're the first to know. I'm accepting the offer to run for Congress."

Wanting to set off fireworks, Jill instead reached for his hand and squeezed it. "John, that is wonderful news. I'm so thrilled to hear that!"

"Top secret. I'm waiting to announce it back in Wisconsin

next week. No one can know about this outside a very small circle."

"Please say you'll make the announcement in my newspaper." Her feet danced under the table.

"That goes without saying. I was thinking I'd make the announcement at Millie's Diner. What do you think?"

Jill was taken aback that John was asking for her advice. It was something new, and she liked it. "George Bush made his announcement for the presidency at a little diner in Crawford, Texas, and it worked for him. Just be sure to make it at noon when the place is really hopping. Oh, but it can't be on Monday, because that's the day they're closed. What did Max say when you told him? He must be relieved."

"Max doesn't know yet. And neither does my dad. Didn't I tell you that you're the first to know?" John grinned at her.

"You don't know how much that means to me," Jill whispered, her eyes misting. This decision proved to be a definite step in the right direction—in her direction.

"Are you surprised?" John asked.

"Only that you made your mind up so soon. The last time we spoke about the possibility of your candidacy, you were still vacillating. Tell me what it was that removed those last remnants of doubt."

"I've thought about my decision for days now. Last night I prayed for some kind of sign. It's been weighing heavily on me, as you well know. Before I could say amen, the phone rang, and it was Max calling to tell me that several old party-line supporters remembered my dad from when he was active in the Illinois party years ago. They liked him a lot. Hoping son was like his dad, several calls were made across the Wisconsin state line, and party conservatives stepped right up to replenish the campaign funds. The real clincher was that a few big money men from the opposite aisle jumped party lines and put in contributions as well. The funds are there. I guess a clean record in law enforcement goes a long way in Washington."

"That's great, John. Fund-raising's always the hardest part of any campaign."

"Don't get me wrong," John was quick to say. "I'm not flattering myself so much to say that I'm God's only choice. I'm just taking this new step in the direction he wants me to go. Having the funds along with the backing of so many supporters gave me the confidence I need."

"What's the next step?" Jill asked, ready to jump in and help.

"The party leaders in Wisconsin have met with several top political strategists," he said excitedly. "They say I have an excellent shot of winning the seat, even a better than 50 percent chance."

"That's awesome." Jill gave him a sunny smile. "Especially since you haven't even declared your candidacy yet. Once you do, the percentages will climb even higher in your favor."

"But don't worry, I don't plan to rest on my laurels. I still plan to hit the campaign hard." He lightly banged the table with a closed fist.

"Here, here," Jill cheered softly. She lifted her water glass in a toast. "Here's to Wisconsin's next congressman."

John picked up his glass of water and clinked it on her glass. "And now for what I believe is my best direction of all, I'd like to propose another toast."

Intrigued, Jill raised her glass higher.

"To our engagement," John said, tipping his glass against hers.

Jill nearly dropped the glass when she heard the words. "Engagement?"

For his answer, he dug down into his pocket and took out the emerald ring that she'd worn before their lives had become so complicated. Eagerly, John took Jill's hand in his, and then he slipped the ring onto her finger. "I love you, Jill, and I want to spend my life with you. For the third time, and what I hope is the last time, will you marry me?"

Jill became so choked up she couldn't speak. She kept blinking at the ring while dozens of thoughts spun through her head.

"I hope you haven't changed your mind again. Please say yes before I have heart failure and they have to carry me out of here on a stretcher," John teased her as a worried look crossed his face.

"I . . . I'm just so surprised, I'm speechless." Jill looked down at the ring and then back at John. "What I mean is, won't this engagement be detrimental to your campaign? Think about it. It might be better for you to remain unattached during your run for office."

"Are you joking? Jill, you're my best asset. Without you by my side to encourage and counsel me, I can't do this—I won't do this. But win or lose, I'm asking you to be my wife. Will you please answer me before my heart stops beating?"

"Yes! I'll marry you, I'll be your wife," Jill declared.

This wasn't quite the extravaganza that their first proposal had been, but it was definitely the most meaningful to Jill. Having believed John was dead, and then almost losing him to her fickleness, Jill knew she would never risk losing him again.

John reached across the table and took her hand in his. "Let's make it soon, if you're willing."

"You'll have to clear it up with my wedding planner." Jill laughed. "Mother will be tickled about us finally getting married, but I'm afraid I don't have the courage to tell her it'll happen right away. She'll probably need a year to make all of her grandiose plans. There'll be wedding showers, dress fittings, choosing the invitations, getting the right caterer . . ."

"Let me handle Pearl," John said firmly. "We don't need all of that."

She smiled at him. "I agree."

John gave her hand a squeeze. "Are you as happy as I am at

this minute? I've never been happier in my entire life. Not even the first time or the second time I proposed."

"And I've never been happier either. It makes me ask myself why we've waited so long."

"*You've* waited so long . . . I wanted to marry you months ago, remember?"

Jill nodded. "I do remember, and this is an old topic, one I never want to discuss again. It's time to move along and keep the door closed on that past. We've forgiven one another, and now we have a future to plan. Right now, I've never felt so sure about anything in all my life." Last night she had experienced a sorrowful ending, but today was a joyous new beginning.

John didn't hold back his grin. "I agree. From now on it's from this day forward."

"Amen." Jill closed her eyes, savoring the moment. "This is the best day of my life, knowing you really do love me and want to marry me. And then there's the election." Jill was so excited she bounced around in the leather booth.

"You're actually looking forward to being a congressman's wife, aren't you?" John said with a laugh. "Now that I've made up my mind, I am excited about running for office. Truthfully, I'd never considered politics before, but it feels so right. And with you, the journey seems even more possible and twice as exciting." John tossed his napkin on the table and came around to Jill's side of the booth and scooted in beside her. He wrapped his arms around her and kissed her until the waiter announced his arrival with a slight cough.

Without a trace of embarrassment, Jill thrust her ring under the waiter's nose. "We just got engaged!"

The waiter offered his congratulations, and then Jill said, "I think we need some ice cream sundaes to celebrate!"

The waiter plopped down their cheeseburgers and moved John's place setting to Jill's side. Then he did a perfect about-face to retrieve the sundaes.

"Burgers and ice cream sundaes? Shouldn't we order caviar or something?" John asked her.

"No, it's perfect just the way it is. Our waiter unknowingly just started a lifelong tradition for the two of us—burgers and sundaes to celebrate. It's kinda quirky and suits us, don't you think?"

17

Some cause happiness wherever they go; others whenever they go.
—Oscar Wilde

An hour before her meeting with Glenn Carlin, Jill ducked into the Library of Congress for a quick review of Fleming's voting record, as well as the bills he had sponsored.

To prepare for her meeting with Glenn, she had done extensive research at the library's website over the past couple of days, but she hoped to find an obscure fact or figure to impress him with in the library's additional resources. Glenn had a reputation as a savvy congressional aide, but Jill was primed to outfox him this time, especially since she'd blown it in their initial conversation. Still angry with herself for revealing far more about the Walker murder investigation than she had intended, she planned to redeem herself.

She hoped to find a motive for Walker's death hidden somewhere in the fine print of the Snakehead Bill, so she searched for additional information on the bill. She loaded the microfiche in the machine and scrolled through it. After a while, she said, "Nothing new here." Not about to let it go, though, she decided to expand the area of her search. To do that, she had to read over any other bills Fleming had supported in the past. Like a student cramming at the last minute for an exam, Jill worked quickly.

At the computer terminal, she located the information and scrolled through it. There wasn't anything new there. The thought occurred to Jill that she might be centering her attention in too narrow an area. She expanded her search to all of the bills Fleming had sponsored. Moving along the timeline, she saw that the Snakehead Bill was the only one, but that was not so unusual for a junior congressman. Following the passage of that bill, he was appointed to the powerful Environmental Committee, but once a member, he had rarely contributed anything of significance that Jill could see.

She looked at his voting record and discovered that he only showed up about half of the time when a bill came to the floor for a vote. Checking his overall attendance, Jill found that Fleming had been gung ho his first term, rarely missing a meeting on any of the committees on which he served. During his last two terms, he had missed the majority. Closer inspection revealed the same voting pattern. His first-term attendance was near perfect, but over the last two terms, it was downright pathetic.

Jill recalled that Walker was always pushing Fleming into voting the way he wanted. But the records proved that Fleming hardly ever voted at all. Jill hoped Glenn would be forthright and explain his comment to her about why that one particular environmental bill meant so much to Fleming, when nothing else had. Jill left without needing to make a copy of a single page.

Promptly at two o'clock in the afternoon, she arrived at Fleming's offices. The outer office was empty, and the door to an inner office stood open a couple inches. "Mr. Carlin . . . Glenn? It's Jill Lewis. Are you there?"

No one returned her greeting. In fact, nothing in the office stirred, so she opened the door all the way. It was Saturday, after all, so it wasn't unusual for there to be no staff in the office. Deciding to wait, Jill sat on an exquisite antique sofa. A painting from the Washington Monument series by Wisconsin-born painter Georgia O'Keeffe hung over the sofa. *Were these compliments of the campaign funds?*

After ten minutes, Jill dug out her BlackBerry to find Glenn's cell number. If he didn't appear in another few minutes, she'd call him to remind him she was waiting. On the coffee table was a copy of the *Washingtonian*. Jill picked it up and began to flip through it.

"Ms. Lewis." A voice spoke to her from the doorway.

Jill looked up. It wasn't Glenn. It was Fleming himself. She couldn't disguise her shock at seeing him. Not sure she wanted to be alone with this man after the scene at the Walker residence, Jill slid further back in the couch. She hated feeling cornered.

"Stop burrowing like a pathetic little rabbit. I'm not going to hurt you." Fleming seemed almost lighthearted.

"I'm here to meet with Glenn Carlin. Do you know where he is?"

"Yes, I know, but I thought I'd better meet you first. I'm very picky about who I give interviews to."

"So I've heard." Jill picked up her briefcase.

"Since Anna and I overreacted at our last meeting, I thought perhaps I should explain. We both found your visit unsettling."

Jill raised an eyebrow and then asked, "Will Glenn arrive later? There are things I need to discuss with him."

"I'd prefer to meet with you myself. You and Glenn will just be talking about me anyway. Why meet with him when you can interview me? I'm the one with all the answers. Come on back to my office, Ms. Lewis. You can keep the door open if you like."

"That won't be necessary." Knowing she appeared vulnerable, Jill had to quickly switch her manner. She got to her feet and stood tall, giving off an air of self-assuredness. She slowly picked up her purse while she gave him a long stare.

"It's time for me to explain to the people of the great state of

Wisconsin. Since you're a hometown girl, I want you to break the story . . . in the *Washington Gazette*, of course. Can you do that?"

Intrigued, Jill willingly followed Fleming down the hallway to his office. "I see no problem, that is, as long as I can run it simultaneously in the *Lakes News*."

"Ah, that little paper? I don't have a problem with that." The congressman pointed to a chair, and Jill sat down, placing her tape recorder on the desk. He kept the door open by a few inches.

"Before we begin, I have a question about the Snakehead Bill you brought to the floor a few years back."

"Yes, that's right. It was four years to be exact. It was a popular bill, the best thing I ever did in my congressional career." Fleming was acting like a sports player who is constantly showing off his one trophy. He pulled out a Cuban cigar from his humidor and reached across the desk for a lighter but stopped midair before he lit it. "Mind if I smoke?"

"As a matter of fact, I do mind." Jill met his gaze. "And so does the federal government . . . no smoking is allowed in federal buildings or anywhere on Capitol Hill."

As if not expecting this response, he stared at her for a moment and then capitulated by returning the cigar to the humidor and setting the lighter upright next to it.

"The Snakehead Bill was not only a popular bill, but it was a worthy one," Jill agreed. "I just find it interesting that this was the only bill you championed. I'm curious—what made this your single passion?"

"I'm not a wave maker, Jill. I like things slow and calm, like fishing early morning on a glass-smooth lake." He threaded his fingers behind his head and leaned back in his chair.

Jill laughed. "You've certainly gotten into the wrong field for that then. But if you didn't want to make political waves, so to speak, then why did you make them this one time?"

"I hate to admit it, but I did it for Joe Walker. Don't get me wrong, I believed in the bill. I spent enough time talking about it to my committee that year, but everyone was more interested in the Alaskan oil drilling. However, Joe was an activist, and he pushed me, giving me the courage. Joe remained more interested in exploring waterways than I was, and since I grew this anchor around my waist"—Fleming patted his belly—"he spent more time under the lakes. This bill brought us closer for a while."

"Did it bother you not to be able to go along diving with Joe anymore?"

"Of course, but I really didn't feel motivated enough to really do anything about my weight." He patted his big belly again. "As you can see, I enjoy life too much, especially food. Joe heard about the snakeheads and how they integrated into our streams, lakes, and rivers. One time he found one in Delavan and killed it. That was one of the reasons the lake was emptied, cleaned, and restocked." He ran a hand through his hair.

"Was he always on the lookout for the snakeheads after that?"

"Yeah, it was like he was obsessed. He looked for them on every swim." Fleming shrugged. "But he never found any again. Even though the bill was initiated by Joe's prompting, I feel good about being able to contribute in a very significant way to the environment. I think it's part of the reason I kept being reelected. Wisconsin is filled with lakes, and the people who live there are strong environmentalists. I gave them back their native fish. Now, let's move on to the real reason you're here. It's about Joe's murder, isn't it?"

"Yes, it is."

"Well, I'd rather talk about something else. Like John Lovell." Fleming moistened his lips.

"I'm not sure I know what you mean." It suddenly occurred to Jill that Fleming was the one interviewing her.

"You know what I mean. I'm still friends with members of the party. Put this in your paper: I'm going to run after all." His voice thickened.

"Without your party's backing?" Jill was stunned. "You'll run as an independent then?"

"I suppose I could, but I won't have to, since the party's agreed unanimously that I should remain in the race. They've given me their blessing and their backing, and I trust you will too, especially after you hear my story." Fleming opened the humidor and snatched a cigar but didn't light it. Instead, he rolled it between his fingers, then held it to his nostrils and breathed in the aroma. He was calm again, confident.

"But Congressman, even if you're cleared of all wrongdoing where Joe Walker's death is concerned, how can you possibly run with the charges for fraud and misappropriation of funds?"

He glowered at her. "Promise me you won't ask any more questions until I've told you everything."

"All right, go ahead. I'm willing to listen."

Focusing on the tape recorder, Fleming quickly leaned over and removed the tape. "There are things you can print, and then there is the unprintable." Then he sat back in his leather chair and folded his large hands on the desk. "Ms. Lewis, I believed that Joe Walker was the best friend a man could have. He was like a brother to me. Had you asked me a few days ago, I would've sworn Joe would've willingly taken a bullet for me. I certainly would have for him. I trusted the man with my career, my family, and my life."

"Go on."

"I found out that Joe Walker wasn't my friend at all. He was stealing from me as well as from the great folks of Wisconsin. Joe set me up, Ms. Lewis. It wasn't me who took the funds from the campaign, it was Joe Walker."

Jill crossed her arms over her chest. "Excuse me if I'm skeptical. The Fundeck was bought under your name, not his, and so were all the vacations your family went on."

"What are you talking about?" He narrowed his gaze at her.

Jill leaned forward. "You recently purchased an Eliminator

Fundeck. I have stacks of receipts, and each one bears your signature."

"You've said quite enough." Fleming's temper flared. He broke his unlit cigar in two before tossing it into the trash.

"I find it convenient that you blame Walker now that he's dead," Jill replied as she got to her feet.

"The truth will be forthcoming in a matter of days." He obviously wasn't backing down from his lie.

"Let me help you with that. Give me the evidence right now. I have two papers to publish it in, and the readers are waiting to hear all about it." Jill pressed her hand on the desk in front of him and leaned on it. She wanted to intimidate.

"You can have it after you convince Lovell not to run for my seat."

His comment was so unexpected that it made Jill falter. She withdrew her hand and stepped back. "So you think I have bargaining power, is that it? You'll give me the information only if I talk John into not accepting the nomination. No deal." Jill walked to the far end of the room and took a seat farther away.

"Jill, it's better for our state to keep its incumbent congressman," he said in an attempt to reason with her. "I've got power in Congress that it would take years for John to achieve. Don't you see the merit in my running as opposed to a new candidate?"

"Why? You don't vote on any bills. You barely propose any, save a bill that was Joe's passion. There's no burning in your soul to make a difference for the people you serve."

Fleming looked down. "There are people who need me there."

Jill stood. "Is this all you have to say?"

Fleming looked up at her but didn't say anything.

"Then I take that as a no. You aren't going to offer me a rebuttal as to the charges against you and where Walker's murder is concerned?"

He glared at her.

"Mr. Fleming, you have wasted my time." Jill walked across the room and snatched up her empty recorder.

As she walked out of his office, he yelled to her, "Heads will roll."

Jill couldn't get away from Fleming fast enough. Riddled with anger, she hurried down the steps and practically ran into Glenn Carlin.

"Jill? What are you doing here?" Glenn was startled to see her. "Congressman Fleming told me you called to cancel our appointment."

"No, I showed up at two, just as we had planned, but Fleming was there to meet me instead of you."

"He lied to me?" Carlin heatedly asked.

"Don't worry about it. I think I have all the information I need. But, I do have one question for you."

"Okay, what's that?"

"On the phone, you told me that Walker always tried to get Fleming to vote his way on bills. But according to public record, Fleming only voted half the time."

"If it hadn't been for Walker, Fleming never would have voted," Glenn said.

Jill couldn't help but wonder why Carlin, Fleming's own campaign manager, would say such negative things about him to her, the press. Was this his way of distancing himself already? That had to be it. Carlin wanted a long life in Washington, and that meant aligning himself with winners and distancing himself from political ruin.

Jill glanced up and noticed Robert Fleming standing on the landing above them, watching them.

Glenn noticed him too. "I better get going. See you another time, Jill." Glenn continued up the steps as Jill descended them. There seemed to be no escaping Fleming's gaze.

18

Saddle your dreams afore you ride them.

—Mary Webb

On the elevator up to the *Gazette* offices, Jill felt her excitement to see everyone, beginning with Landry at the front desk. As the doors opened, Jill stepped onto the marble floor and was surprised to see a young man in Landry's place.

"Where's Landry?" Jill looked around, trying to find a familiar face.

"She's off on Saturdays," a twentysomething man with a skinny neck sticking out of his starched collar explained. "I'm Armando Muniz, the new weekend receptionist. May I help you?"

"Oh. Yes. I have an appointment with Annabelle and Rubric."

"Name?"

"Jill Lewis. I used to work here."

"Oh, that's right." Armando smiled. "Which one did you choose?"

"I beg your pardon?"

"I couldn't help but notice your engagement ring. Did you

choose the senator or the FBI agent? Lots of us here in the office have sizable bets hinging on your decision."

Jill dropped her briefcase to the floor and rubbed her temples with the tips of her fingers. "Who's in on this bet?"

"Nearly everyone."

Fuming that her former colleagues had the audacity to set up a betting pool based on her future, Jill didn't respond. She loudly tapped her shoe on the marble. Armando wisely shut his mouth and pressed the intercom. "Ms. Lewis is here, Ms. Stone."

"Send her down to the conference room," Annabelle instructed.

Armando walked from behind the reception desk. "Follow me."

"Not necessary. I know where it is." Jill turned to the right.

"There've been changes, Ms. Lewis." Armando turned left, going in the opposite direction of where the conference room was. In fact, he headed down the hall directly toward her office. What lovely surprise did Annabelle have cooked up for her this time? A newly redecorated office to woo her back to the *Gazette*, perhaps?

She noticed that the single door to her office was now a double door. Smiling, she stepped inside, imagining throwing open both doors every day if she came back. Not that she was coming back, of course.

She gasped when she entered the room. "What happened?" The four offices along that side of the building, including her office, had been combined, making it into one huge room with floor-to-ceiling windows. A mammoth-sized table sat in the center with nearly twenty chairs around it. Yes, it was a brand-new conference room. Her personal space had been obliterated. Perhaps Annabelle hadn't planned on her return after all.

Armando shut the door behind her as Annabelle and Rubric came over to greet her. They took turns saying how well she looked and how much they had missed her. Annabelle was the first to notice Jill's ring back on her finger. "Well, looks like Tommy struck out yesterday. But you have the better of the two. John is husband material, whereas Tommy is . . ."

"Food for the tabloids," Rubric supplied.

Annabelle, obviously done with small talk, put her hands on her hips and said, "Okay, let's get down to business. What will it take to get you back here?"

So they do want me back. "I'm not for sale," Jill said, thinking about the big story she carried right inside her briefcase. "I'm happy where I am."

"What are you doing here then?" Annabelle barked back.

"You invited me here, remember? When I told you I had an interview with Glenn Carlin."

"So?" Annabelle looked out the wall of glass as though she couldn't care less, but Jill knew she did. Turning back around, she asked matter-of-factly, "What did Carlin have to say?"

"Enough to make me think he's already distancing himself from Fleming."

"Interesting," Annabelle said tensely, folding her arms.

"It was interesting, all right. I ended up with an interview . . . with Fleming himself." Jill smirked at her former boss.

Annabelle sucked in air. "But word is Fleming isn't talking because of a gag order from his high-priced attorneys."

"Whatever his orders are, he isn't following them. At least not with me he didn't. I'm fresh from a long meeting with him."

Annabelle narrowed her eyes at Rubric, who quickly spoke up. "If I didn't know you so well, I'd call you a liar, Jillie. You see, I just came from Fleming's office this morning, and Carlin said Fleming was out of town. How do you figure that?"

"He lied to you," Jill answered simply.

"Looks like our girl still has the Midas touch. Want to share your information with us?" Annabelle's questions were always more like commands.

"My first loyalty is now with my own paper," Jill said, deliberately not revealing Fleming's desire to also have the story in the *Gazette*.

Annabelle walked over to Jill. "Can't you write for both papers, and we can print on the same day? Listen, agree to it and I'll give you and your little paper a byline in the *Gazette*. It's been done before, right, Rube?"

"Sure it has, but I can't remember when." He scratched his chin.

"Great, I think we can work something out then," Jill said. "Even though I'm not living in DC full time, I still have my apartment, contacts, and informants. It's taken me years to build this trust, and I'm not about to throw it all away just because I moved to Wisconsin."

"Good girl," Annabelle said.

"I'm a plane ride away, but with the Internet, teleconferencing, and phone calls, it's like I never left."

"What are you saying, Jillie?" Rubric asked, narrowing his eyes at her.

"Updates. Real-time connections. Here."

Annabelle shot her a puzzled look as Jill gave her file a good shove, making it whoosh down the table into Annabelle's hands.

Annabelle opened the folder and began reading. Her mouth twisted in disgust. "This is nothing more than a very expensive purchase order for high-end technical and video equipment."

"Exactly. Only the best, and it's all for the *Lakes News*."

"If you expect me to foot your renovations, the answer is no." Annabelle slammed the folder shut.

"Not so fast. Think about it. Regard my little hometown paper to be an offshoot of your paper."

Annabelle laughed so loudly she began to choke. Rubric ran to get a glass of water for her. Jill sat calmly and waited. When Annabelle had finished with her water, Jill continued. "Think about it. You and Rubric trained me well, and just as you love running this paper, I love running mine. But unlike you, I've pounded the streets in my high heels for years, developing contacts and paying informants. My dedication and long hours have paid off in big-time headlines for the *Gazette*. I can still make those headlines happen for you. Not only did I meet with Fleming today, but I also know the candidate who will take his place." Jill looked across the table at Annabelle.

Her former boss nearly salivated. "Who?"

Jill remained silent and smug as she crossed her arms.

"And your deal is?" Annabelle said.

"My deal is listed right on those forms." Jill pointed to the shut folder. "I want multiple TVs in my office so we can watch what's going on 24/7. I want updated cell phones with talkies so I can stay in touch with my crew and with you here in DC. I want all my employees to have laptops. There are various machines with different capabilities on the market. The one I chose is midrange in price."

"Anything else?" For the first time in her life, Annabelle looked caught.

"I'll let you know. Just because I am no longer working here doesn't mean I can't work here."

Rubric slapped his knee and looked at Annabelle. "Do it."

"Stop telling me what to do, Rubric." Annabelle contemplated for a few minutes. Then she pressed the speaker on the phone. "Armando, send Millie in here. I need her to draw up a new contract."

An hour later Jill walked down the street with a fresh contract in her purse, one that was beneficial to growing her paper.

Although anxious to get back to share the news with her employees, she would have to wait until Monday to do that. Right now it was time to meet John at the FBI headquarters.

When she arrived there, John was waiting for her in the lobby.

"We have our afternoon and evening cut out for us," John said. "I counted nearly fifty tapes."

"Good. We can order in." Jill pecked his cheek and then looped her arm through his.

"I had planned a romantic dinner at Milano's in Foggy Bottom," John complained good-naturedly as he held the elevator doors for her and explained the machine they'd put the tapes through. "The Frutoscopy machine we have here at the Bureau is a brand-new version. This is my first time to use it officially."

The bell chimed, and the doors slid open. "This is a patented algorithm, and it processes sequential video frames to produce detail. It also lessens noise, takes out artifacts, and sends a higher resolution. Just what we want."

Once they were settled in a room down the hall, John slid in the first tape. Jill took a seat by the control panel and leaned in to get a good look.

"If you see something, let me know, and I can stop it and show it frame by frame. I can slow it down to a millisecond and clear out the extra visual noise. If you want to get a good look at a far-off face, I can freeze it and clear the pixels, then enlarge. See? I can widen a large section of video output mode and I can zoom right in. See the mole on that lady's face?"

"Amazing. It's like a double frame, a picture within a picture. I want one of these machines."

He laughed. "This baby costs a few million. Even if Annabelle went for your proposal, I can promise you, she wouldn't get this machine for you."

"Well, she did go for my proposal." Jill beamed at him. "But I don't think she was too happy with the cost of the Pix-o-matic, so I won't push my luck any further than that."

John gave Jill a high five. "Congratulations! Now for the bad news . . ."

"Don't tell me. You're going to have to keep my tapes for the FBI investigation."

"How did you know?"

"I had my suspicions. Well, let's get to work." Jill took out paper and pen from her purse. She also opened her briefcase and removed her tape player, then inserted a new tape. "I want our conversation recorded. Since I won't have these videos to look at, I want to better recall what our conversation was about concerning them."

"I guess that'll be all right."

Jill tried to get comfortable in her chair. "This is like home movies."

"Home movies of people you don't know." John started the first tape. They watched someone clowning for the camera until the cameraman pointed it toward the sailboat race as it began. The entire tape was taken from the wrong angle. When the tape was over, John popped in the next tape. This time it was another race, and they spotted a dinghy in the distance.

"Hey, this might be our boy." John sat up tall, looking more interested. "Let's see if I can crop and clear the pixels on this." John worked for several minutes before they both plainly saw it was someone else swimming around their boat.

"It was really hot that day," Jill remembered.

John reached for tape number three and pushed it into the machine. After twenty tapes, they finally found a tape that showed a fairly good close-up of Fleming and Walker. Fleming was in the boat and Walker over the side holding on with one hand. The two men were talking.

"What I'd give for sound," Jill said. "Can you get closer?"

John adjusted the pixels before slowing the tape down and then cropped it frame by frame. When they were satisfied, he printed each image. Jill and John went back and forth from the printout to the tape. After the men talked, Walker appeared to push off from the boat, and Fleming began rowing again. Then they moved from the camera.

"I wonder if Fleming whacked him with an oar," Jill said, only half seriously.

"He was strangled, Jill. On the coroner's report there was no mention of whacking."

It was after midnight when Jill and John had finished with the tapes. They didn't see anything except what they already knew: Fleming rowing, Walker swimming. They didn't recognize anyone else in the tapes. No one else even came close to their rowboat.

"I'm turning these over to the investigative team, and they'll have another run through them," John told her.

"That's fine. You'll let me know if they find anything new?" Jill acted nonchalant.

"Of course I'll let you know."

The two of them walked out of the building arm in arm. Jill was exhausted, but she woke up quickly when a car slowly moved past them. The window rolled down a few inches, and there was the unmistakable face of Fleming.

19

The suspense is terrible. I hope it will last.

—Oscar Wilde

Once Jill's flight arrived in Chicago, Marge was waiting for her at the curb at O'Hare just as she'd promised.

"Ooh, nice ring," Marge said as she admired it and almost ran the truck off the road. "Your mom's bound to set off fireworks in the town square when she hears about this."

Jill wiped her brow. "Please, don't remind me. At least I'll have a reprieve. I have to stop by the office before I go home and tell her."

The radio was on Marge's favorite country station, but Jill reached over and pressed the knob for news.

"Just what do you think you're doing? That was Faith Hill and Tim McGraw. Are you crazy?"

"News, Marge. I've got to hear the news. That's our job, remember?" Jill reminded her just as a commentator's voice speculated on the short list of names of who might capture the Wisconsin seat. To her relief, John's name wasn't even on the list. What a coup for the *Lakes News* to be able to break the first story. The thought made Jill salivate. Fortunately, only a few

Washington insiders suspected John Lovell as the candidate, and they hadn't talked.

Having some time to kill in Washington until her flight, Jill had gotten her notes organized in the morning before leaving for the airport. A perfect day, except she couldn't shake the feeling that Fleming's eyes were on her, watching her at every turn. And she couldn't forget his cryptic words concerning John. *What did he mean, "Heads will roll"?*

Right in front of the *Lakes News*, Marge swung the company truck into a spot in front of the building. Parked next to the truck was Jill's Range Rover; Chad and Marge must have retrieved it from the impound lot as they'd promised. The car was now parked beside a sign that read "Thou Shalt Not Park Here. Jill Lewis, Publisher." In small letters at the bottom edge it read "Designed by Marge." Jill laughed. "You're the best, Marge. See you Monday."

As Jill walked into the dark office, she stepped into a puddle of water. She switched on the lights. "Oh please, the last thing I need is a leak." She groaned. No matter how skillful she was, she couldn't talk Annabelle into paying for that one.

Jill looked down and saw the puddle at her feet. Next to it was her purse, with water slowly leaking from its seams. At least it looked like the bag she'd lost in the lake. Marge had probably forgotten to tell her it had turned up. But why hadn't Marge cleaned up this mess?

The purse appeared to be jammed with something that had caused the seams to tear. Jill reached down into the bag. The object she touched was round with wild, fuzzy hair.

Jill screamed as she tossed the object up in the air and ran for the door and her Range Rover. Wildly she careened the car down side streets and through the center of town, pulling to a stop on the curb in front of the police station doors. She pushed through the front door and stopped at the front desk, demanding to see Detective Russ Jansen. Although Officer Connell offered to take her statement, she ran past him and barged into Russ's office. She didn't know why she expected him to be working on a Sunday night, but she was relieved to find him there.

"Russ, it's a head! There's a decapitated head in my office!"

Russ fell back in his chair with his mouth wide open. "Hold on a minute," he said. "What are you talking about?"

Jill couldn't answer him; she dove for a trash can and got sick. Her mind raced with wild thoughts. *Fleming had told me that heads would roll. Is this what he meant? He couldn't possibly have done something to hurt John, to make sure John didn't have a chance to publicly accept the nomination. No, it's not possible!*

Jill reached into her pocket and pulled out her cell phone. Slowly she punched in John's cell number, needing desperately to hear his voice. The cell phone rang. *Please, pick up, John!*

"Hi, sweetie!"

"John!"

"Yeah . . . it's John. Didn't you mean to call me? What's going on?"

"John! You're alive!" Jill screeched.

John spoke low and slowly. "Honey, were you having a bad dream or something? Are you all right?"

Jill assured him that she was okay and then told him good-bye and snapped her cell shut. She looked over at Russ, who was still looking completely mystified. "If it wasn't John's head in that bag, whose was it?"

A little while later at the *Lakes News* office, Russ held on to a white plastic bag. The thought of a head inside of it made Jill's stomach churn again. Now she wished she had gotten a good look at it before she had fled. Whose head could it be? Possible faces floated ghostlike in front of her eyes.

Jill waved to the detective, who walked over to where she stood at the office entrance.

"Do you know who the head belongs to?" she asked him.

"Let me know if this is someone you recognize." Russ reached into the bag, and to Jill's revulsion, he pulled out the head by the hair then dangled it in front of her face. At first Jill closed her eyes, but slowly she opened them, first the left eye and then the right eye.

"What?" Jill took a step closer to get a better look. "Hey, that's . . . that's a mannequin's head."

"That's right, but don't worry about it, it looked real to me too. Tricked you guys too, didn't it?" Russ laughed at the two officers who joined him. He then turned back to Jill. "Do you see anything missing?"

"Give me a sec to look around." Jill looked around the office and checked all the desks and computers. She then went to the safe in her office and worked the combination. When the tumblers clicked, she pushed on the handle and opened the door. It was all there, including the office's petty cash.

Relieved, Jill walked back to talk to Russ. As he placed the mannequin's head into an evidence bag, she gasped. "Wait! That's not just any mannequin. That belongs to the groom in my mother's bridal shop!"

Jill didn't wait for a response from Russ; she turned on her heels and ran out the door. She got in her car, turned the key in the ignition, and pressed the gas pedal until it hit the floor. The car jerked then lunged forward. Jill quickly arrived at String of Pearls, followed by police cars.

She ran inside the store. "Mother! Mother!" Jill's voice got higher and more desperate with each syllable as she ran throughout the shop. "Mother! Where are you?" She looked frantically around, even opening cupboard doors to look inside of them.

In the office, the bookcases were neatly arranged, and the top of the desk was clean with ordered piles of work. Material swatches lay across the gold brocade chair as if they had been lovingly placed there and not flung by an intruder. Not a single thing seemed out of place.

Russ came to Jill's side. "Maybe she's at home. Why don't you try calling her there?"

"No, she's not at home," Jill insisted. "Her car is out front, and the front door to her shop is unlocked. It's nearly ten, and I've never known my mother to work this late. Something is very wrong." Jill had a hard time catching her breath.

Russ directed his team of two officers. "Officer Connell, I want you at the front door. Officer Worford, go around to the rear and stand at the back door." Together Jill and Russ continued to search the premises, but very quickly they ran out of places to look. Jill began to pray just as she heard a racket above their heads.

"What's that?" Russ asked, looking up at the ceiling.

"It's coming from the second floor." Not familiar with the old building, Jill searched for a stairway, but Russ was the one who found it behind an old curtain inside of the storage room. On their way up the old metal steps, Jill started to call her mother's name over and over again.

"Jill? Jill, is that you? I'm in here." Her mother's shaky voice hovered above their heads. She began to knock from inside the room. "I'm right here. Let me out of here."

The door at the top of the stairs had an automatic locking device from the outside. "Well, look at this old lock, will you?" Russ said. "This used to be the town's bank vault. Locks only from the outside."

"Skip the history lesson, will you, and just get my mother out of there, please," Jill begged.

Russ broke through the old lock quickly, and just as quickly Pearl opened the door and fell into Jill's arms. "Thank goodness you found me!" she exclaimed. "I told the handyman I needed him here this morning to get this door switched out. I said, 'If you do not get here today, someone will get locked inside of that room.' But oh no, he had better things to do down at the site of the new jail, putting locks on those doors." Quickly recovering, Pearl turned to Russ. "Can you just go ahead and take the hinges off? That will settle the matter."

"I'll have one of my officers remove the door before we leave tonight."

"Mother, why did you go into the room to work when you knew you could be locked inside?"

"I was measuring the room for storage," Pearl said as though the answer were obvious. She started for the steps. "Well, let's go on home, it's late and I'm starving."

When Pearl walked into the shop area and saw all the cupboard doors open, she gasped and clutched at her chest. "Oh my! Someone broke in and ransacked the place while I was locked upstairs!" Frantically, she began folding material and setting perfume bottles straight on the shelves. "It'll take me days to get this place back in order and figure out what was taken."

"No one ransacked the place," Jill admitted sheepishly. "I did that, trying to find you."

"You made this mess? Then you can straighten it." Pearl went for the cash register. "Oh good, the townsfolk remain honest citizens. All my money is still right here."

"I'm glad you're all right, Mother."

Still angry at the condition of the store, Pearl began closing all the doors on the cupboards. "Yes, well it turns out the biggest disaster of the day was created by my own daughter. Tell me, why would I be inside a cupboard?"

"Your groom's head was stuffed inside of my old purse at the office tonight. It freaked me out, and I thought that maybe something horrible had happened to you . . ." Jill got choked up thinking about how blessed she was that the intruder only took a dummy's head and not the one on her mother's shoulders.

"So I was really robbed, after all, but just of my groom's head?

This person is definitely a sicko since he passed on all my designer gowns and money. Where is the head now?"

"Bagged for evidence," Russ replied.

"I need it back. I cannot have a headless groom in my front window. It's bad for business," Pearl said.

"Later. Right now it's evidence."

As they walked out of the shop, Pearl noticed Jill's ring. "I see Washington was productive."

"Oh, I didn't mean for you to see that for a few more days." The words were out of her mouth before she could stop them. Why was she always having to say whatever popped right into her mouth?

"And why not?"

"You'll find out soon, Mother," Jill said with more enthusiasm than she felt at the moment.

"I guess love had its way, and things worked out between you and John." Pearl opened the door on Jill's vehicle. "Give me a ride home, will you? With a wild man on the loose, we don't need to be riding alone at night."

"Of course. By the way, how about having lunch with me and John Tuesday at Millie's? I'll tell you in detail all about my weekend."

"All the details?" Pearl asked as she slid onto the passenger seat and smoothed out her Chanel dress.

"Down to the shoes. Does 11:30 work for you?"

"That will be lovely. I'll bring sketches of designer dresses for you to go over."

"No need. I already told you, I'll be wearing Muv's dress, the one you wore at your wedding."

"That's lovely, but we need an update, don't you agree?"

"Fine, but please don't bring the dress sketches. Not good for the groom to see them," Jill said as she put the car into gear. She had visions of John announcing his campaign while her mother held up placards of wedding dresses. A nightmare in the making.

"What's the date?" Pearl was anxious to know. "Please tell me we have at least until next summer to plan."

"Ah, that's something John wants to discuss with you," Jill said as they pulled onto the dark country lake road.

When Jill swung the car into the driveway, she panicked when she noticed an unmarked car pulled off on the side of the road up ahead. Obviously, someone was watching her mother's home, probably the same person who had stuffed the mannequin's head in her purse. Luckily, Pearl hadn't noticed the car, so Jill struggled to remain calm so as not to alarm her mother until she decided what to do.

20

There cannot be a crisis next week. My schedule is already full.

—Henry Kissinger

Jill hurried her mother into the house and grabbed her phone to call 911, but before she could dig it out of her purse, it rang. It was Detective Jansen.

"I've sent a patrol car to park outside your house this evening to keep an eye on things," he explained. "Officer Connell should be pulling up any moment now."

"This phone call's about five minutes too late," Jill complained. "I thought someone had followed us here. How much danger do you think we're in?"

"I think this perpetrator's nothing but a big bully trying to scare you off." Russ chuckled. "He obviously doesn't know you."

Jill hung up the phone and turned to Pearl, who was busily closing the shutters and the shades. "That was Russ, and he sent the car to watch over us. That's Officer Connell out there in our driveway."

"Where are my manners? Let's put a pot of coffee on for Officer Connell."

"Mom, it's midnight."

That didn't stop Pearl. Southern hospitality ran through her veins like iced tea.

"You can serve him coffee. I'm going to bed," Jill announced.

"Before you go, let me have another look at that ring," Pearl ordered.

The CSI dive team plopped backward from the sides of the dive boat like seals before disappearing into the pea soup waters. Minutes later, bubbles surfaced from their oxygen tanks. Jill timed it with her diver's watch. By now, she figured, they should be at the water's bottom, going after evidence in the ever-shifting murder scene. With Walker's death officially ruled as a murder, the police and FBI wanted to be sure nothing had been overlooked. A dropped diver's glove, a fin, anything left behind could mean the difference between solving the murder and a murderer going free. There were inches of lake bottom to sift through. By now a new team with fresh eyes were going down for their first look.

Russ stood restlessly at the pier's edge and looked back at Jill. His mind was on the present, not last night. He pointed out toward the boat. "They have a larger area to cover because of the fluctuation of the lake currents. I found it pretty interesting to watch as they calculated it out on their maps, charts, and weather information."

Jill nodded at Russ while she scanned the north shoreline behind her. No sign of John. It was silly for her to expect him on the scene this morning. There were last-minute details he needed to attend to, like officially requesting his Bureau leave of absence and meeting with the party. It was like leaping from one boat to the next, careful not to fall in the water between them. Jill wondered who wrote John's acceptance speech in such a tight time frame. She felt sure the party brought in a speechwriter for the occasion.

A horn blew, drawing Jill's attention back to the water. On the opposite side of the pier, she watched as Russ bent down so close to the water he nearly toppled in. Divers surfaced with more nets containing potential evidence. When the divers passed it off to the forensic team in the dive boat, they numbered the items and marked a grid map. Jill supposed most of what they'd found wouldn't be any good, just lake trash unrelated to the case.

"I wish they'd let me inside that boat. It's my jurisdiction," Russ complained.

Another flag buoyed up attached to a second bag. Russ hiked up on the tips of his shoes for a better look.

"Hey, beautiful!"

Jill heard him before she saw him. She turned around and saw John walking toward her in an easy stride. When she wrinkled her nose in a smile, it hurt. The bridge of her nose was sunburned.

This time John didn't hold back when Jill tossed her arms around him. He tethered her to him with his arms. Yes, this is what Jill had been waiting for.

"I love this new side to you." Jill nuzzled into his chest.

He whispered with a chuckle, "I've lost my head over you."

"Ah." Jill pulled back from him by a few inches. "Don't tease me about that."

"We'll discuss it later. Right now I need to get my head together for my speech."

Jill lightly slapped him on the arm. "That's not funny!"

John laughed and then turned around and called out to the detective, "Hey, Russ, any news from the dive boat yet?"

"Nothing." The detective never moved his gaze from the water, a true fisherman waiting for the first sign of a nibble. This time it wasn't a fish he was aiming to snag, but a suspect.

"I wish I could stay out here with you today, but I'm expected at Millie's," John explained, looking at his watch.

Jill looked around for her shoes. "Listen, I've got to get home right away to change. I can't wear this." She tugged at her tank top. "I have to get Mother to the restaurant, and then make sure Chad gets there in time with the paper's rickety old camera equipment. He's been trained on it, but this'll be his first time to handle it alone."

"Okay, we can drive together in my car. We can pick up your car later." John took hold of Jill's hand. "Detective, we'll talk very soon."

Russ flashed thumbs-up without taking his eyes off the dive boat.

—◆◆◆—

While Jill changed into blue cotton slacks and a blouse, John and Pearl sat in the kitchen, discussing wedding dates. Jill was relieved that John was the one to tell Pearl that they wanted to marry as soon as possible. She prayed her mother would take the news well. Once she was dressed, she took a deep breath and stepped back into the room.

Pearl turned toward her daughter and brightened. "We have our date!" She held up the wall calendar and pointed to a circle in red marker. Jill moved in for a closer look and saw June 28, almost a year away.

Shocked, Jill looked at John, who appeared to be chagrined. Plopping down in a chair, Jill said, "Don't feel bad. In all the years I've known her, no one's ever won against Mother."

"Then maybe she should run for Congress." John chuckled under his breath.

—◆◆◆—

At Millie's, Jill anxiously waited at a table with her mother while John sat with his dad and Max on the other side of the crowded dining room, along with the heads of the Wisconsin electoral party. Jill smiled, anticipating John's announcement. Her story for the *Lakes News* was written and printed, along with a close-up of John ready for the front page. Stacks of newspapers with the headlines about John Lovell's candidacy waited in crates back at the *Lakes News*.

"Oh, look, there's Big John Lovell right over there having lunch with Max and John," Pearl said. She frowned. "It's peculiar that Big John didn't tell me he was coming up this way today. I wonder why."

"You'll know in a moment, Mother. Patience." Jill looked around the room and saw her plan was nicely in position. Chad was there with the office camera equipment.

She got up from the table. "I'll be right back, Mother. I want to be sure Chad is ready to go . . ."

"Chad is ready to go where?" Pearl asked, but Jill was already halfway across the room.

Jill helped Chad take the camcorder out of the case, and she personally screwed it onto the stand. Frustrated when the back of the camcorder popped off for the third time, Jill said, "I can't believe the paper doesn't have a better camera than this." Chad pulled a knife from his pocket and cut a couple of five-inch pieces of duct tape to remedy that situation.

"Thanks. Hopefully, this is the last shoot for this old thing. Do you think these cables are still good for broadcasting?"

"I think they still should work okay."

"We'll find out soon enough. There's just a few more minutes until John makes his speech. Would you double-check everything for me?"

"Sure, I'll do that. What's his speech about, anyway?" Chad asked as he rechecked the plugs going into the outlets and camera.

"I'll never tell." Jill winked at Chad, then looked at her watch. "But you won't have to wait long, say, five minutes?"

"No problem."

Jill returned to the table, where Pearl impatiently waited for her. Their lunch had arrived in her absence, and Pearl was already eating her Reuben sandwich. "I suppose you're not going to tell me what that's all about, are you?"

"No, I'm not." Jill smiled as she spread smearcase on her bread, but her attention kept pinging between the clock and Chad. Obviously miffed at being left out of the loop, Pearl acted as though she didn't notice anything.

At the stroke of twelve, Max Clark rose to his feet. Jill looked at Chad standing across the room behind the camera. He gave Jill the A-OK sign, and a flood of relief washed over her. This was a tremendous coup for the paper, and for Jill personally.

"Folks, I won't take long, but John Lovell here needs your attention."

Customers looked from one to another quizzically.

"What was that name again?" a restaurant patron asked.

"Isn't that Craig Martin?" an elderly man said to his wife.

The usual lunch banter came to a halt. John looked uncomfortable and out of his element for a moment. But then he saw Jill's face, and he totally relaxed.

"I'm John Lovell, and I'd like to introduce myself as the new candidate on the ticket for your congressional district. I don't want to spoil Millie's good food with a lot of talk about politics. Kind of turns your stomach, doesn't it?" As the crowd's laughter bounced about the room, John continued, "I must confess, I'm as anxious as you are to finish my lunch, so you folks go ahead and enjoy Millie's cooking while I finish up here. I want to invite you and your families to a political rally tonight down at the Mill Pond at seven o'clock. There'll be lots of good food there too. Look, I need your support and your help. And I don't mind asking for it because I know you fine folks like helping your neighbors, so I know I can count on you. Come on out tonight, and I'll tell you all about my platform, which I know includes all the things you hold near and dear. Now if you don't mind, I'm going to sit down and enjoy my German apple pancakes. See you tonight, and bring your appetite."

"And your checkbook too," Max added.

A rousing sound of applause echoed through the room followed by a few female catcalls; then the room quickly returned to normal talk. Jill got busy on her BlackBerry and text-messaged Annabelle to double-check if she received the live feed. Just as she finished, her cell rang.

"Jill! You little sneak!" Annabelle shouted delightedly. "The live feed came through perfectly. You've pulled off quite the surprise this time. And to think you kept your secret from us while you were here this weekend. Even Rubric didn't have a clue."

"It was hard to keep it from you, believe me. I've got the story all written up too, and the *Gazette's* print room should receive my copy within minutes. You should also be receiving a picture of John."

"We can just take a clip from the streaming feed you sent us. You know with the murder and all, this is an exciting race!" Annabelle practically salivated into the receiver. "Fleming is removed from the race due to misappropriations of his funds, and now we find his friend, an aide, was murdered right beneath his nose. Now the special ops FBI agent has resigned his post to fill the vacancy. And my girl is engaged to the guy. Stories don't get much better than this. I can't wait to hear what happens on the campaign trail."

"Annabelle . . ."

"Oh, don't tell me you're putting someone else on it." Annabelle groaned.

"Of course I'll be on the campaign trail, but I also have a murder to look in to," Jill explained. "My time will be split."

"Every time you make a decision, remember it's my paper's money that's helping your paper."

"Thanks, Annabelle. I'll keep in touch." Jill flipped her phone closed.

Pearl slowly stirred her now lukewarm tea. "Didn't you hear

what John said about talking politics and business over a meal? Sours tummies." Pearl patted hers.

⌁⌁⌁

After the lunch was over, Jill called Russ on her cell. "Any news on this morning's lake digs?"

"Won't know for hours . . . but one piece of potential evidence was scooped from the bottom."

"What's that?"

"A piece of antique gold bullion in the form of a coin."

Interesting. Jill clicked her cell off shortly before arriving at the office. As she walked through the empty newsroom, she heard Olivia in the old broom closet, which was now her office. Jill leaned against its doorjamb. "Thanks, Olivia, for all your help writing about us and then pitching in when needed." Jill kept her voice casual.

"You're welcome." Olivia smiled that old girlfriend smile.

Jill turned to leave but then remembered she hadn't yet told Olivia of her engagement. She held out her hand for Olivia to see her ring.

"Congratulations," Olivia said. "But I noticed the ring before. In fact, everyone noticed it around here. Just because we were all running around making sure the announcement for the campaign would run smoothly doesn't mean we can't spot a huge emerald and diamond ring. We were all too polite to comment."

"Too polite to comment? What does that mean?"

"It's no secret you broke off the engagement when you met Senator Harrison," Olivia said casually. "We're just wondering how long the engagement will last this time."

Jill was so taken aback that she didn't know what to say for a moment. "What right do you have discussing my personal business with Tommy Harrison?"

"The poor man had a right to know where he stood with you. Someone had to tell him," Olivia shot back.

"And you decided it had to be you."

Just then the front door jangled. "Hi, Jill! Hi, Olivia!"

Jill turned around to see Marge waving papers in the air. "Jill, I have the papers here on all the Fundecks purchased in southern Wisconsin, northern Illinois, and eastern Iowa, along with their pictures and model numbers."

The words were enough to remove Jill from the spot. Taking a deep breath, she walked over to the reception nook. "Wow, this is great. You do good work," Jill said as she flipped through the papers.

"There's only Fleming's boat that resembles the craft that nearly killed us." Marge shook her head. "Open and shut case. Turn it over to the police so he can be arrested. My work here is done."

"Doesn't work quite that easily, Marge. There has to be proof . . . more than our eyewitness account. And we didn't see the driver. The boat may have been purchased by someone we don't even know about and hauled from another part of the state, or even outside the state, for that matter. We're not ready for the police, but still this is an important piece of the puzzle. Great job."

"We'll get our man, one way or the other," Marge said.

"And here he is," Chad said as he walked through the door.

"What?" Jill asked.

"Our man." Chad held up a dozen pictures of John. Olivia walked out of her office to see.

"And what a man," she said.

Jill bristled. Was Olivia really interested in John, or was she just trying to compete with her? Wanting to tear her apart for either one, Jill had to push it off until another time . . . one that would be more private. To her office crew, she had to be professional and diplomatic at all times.

Turning her back to Olivia, Jill asked Marge, "I have some personal business to attend to this afternoon before the rally tonight. Does the town's historian still live on Turtle Creek Road?"

"Gordon Yadon?" Marge asked.

Jill nodded.

"Is that where you're headed?"

"I sure am. Call me on my cell if I'm needed. I'm expecting a truckload of equipment from the *Gazette* this week. Let me know when it arrives, but don't open anything."

"Gotcha."

—⁓—

Gordon Yadon, a veritable icon in the town since his early days as the postmaster, didn't let retirement slow him down. He was still active in the community and a member of the Delavan Historical Society. He knew the town's past like a favorite storybook.

"Jill, this is an unexpected pleasure, especially since you've come to call the same day of the announcement of a local running for Congress." Gordon cupped his hands around the hand she offered in greeting.

"And it's always a pleasure to spend time with you, Gordon. I still remember those school assemblies you held with all those interesting artifacts." She smiled at him. "Today I'm here on folklore business."

"Oh?" Judging by the look on his face, she had piqued his curiosity.

"I was diving last week, and found some old bones at the bottom of the lake . . ."

"What kind of bones?"

"That I don't know. But they were large. Quite large."

"Have you considered the possibility of them being elephant bones?" Gordon asked.

"Elephant bones?"

"Yes, my dear. Barnum and Bailey wintered here for years, and what do you think they did when an elephant died?"

"Had a big bonfire?"

"No, no, no. The circus pulled the elephant on to the ice and waited for spring thaw to take the beast to the bottom. We have elephant bones in the lake's bottom."

"So this explains those bones I found." Jill felt deflated. "I must have looked pretty lame when I blogged on the greenhorn diver's site about mythical lake monster bones I found."

"Lake monsters are an interesting topic among the older generation. I believe in them myself." He seemed pleased with Jill's curiosity, and offered her a chair. Immediately she sat down as Gordon took the footstool a few feet away.

"Have you ever seen one of these monsters?" Jill asked him.

"No, but my grandmother told me about her experience with one when she was a girl. She was at times given to what was referred to back then as hysteria. Still, there are interesting accounts of others, perhaps dozens, of people who have had terrifying experiences with lake monsters. You may have found some bones."

"Possibly. I took pictures but lost my camera right afterward." Jill cocked her head to the side. "I do have another question for you."

"Ask me anything." He slapped his hands on his knees.

"Do you know how gold bullion might have wound up at the bottom of the lake?"

"Are you asking from curiosity, or has some been found?" Gordon's eyes shone with curiosity.

"Both."

"May I see the coin?" Gordon said, unable to hide the excitement in his voice.

"If I had the coin, you sure could, but Detective Russ Jansen has it."

"I must contact the detective right away. Meanwhile, let me tell you what I know about this mystery of the gold. At the turn of the twentieth century, there was one bank in town."

"Oh, like now?"

He laughed. "Just like we have now. Inside of the vault in the bank was half a million dollars in gold boullion in both bars and coins. In the late nineteenth century, the gold was stolen from the bank. Where was the gold found?"

"Would you mind if I checked with Russ? I have to make sure it's okay for me to pass along the information," Jill explained.

Gordon got up and went to his bookcase. He ran his fingers along the spines of the books, and once he found the one he wanted, he pulled it out. He sat back down on the armrest next to Jill and flipped through the pages, finally stopping at one. "Here's a picture of the coins and the boullion. These pictures were taken just days before the robbery."

Jill looked carefully at the pictures, but she had no way of knowing if what the CSI team divers had found matched what was in the pictures. "If I'm very careful with this book, may I borrow it for a while?"

"Of course. Just keep me posted on your findings."

"You can count on me." Jill rose to shake his hand before leaving.

21

There are no shortcuts to any place worth going.
—Beverly Sills

It seemed everyone at the Mill Pond arrived at the rally in high spirits, waving small American flags. Families came from every direction to greet the young politician. There was also no end to the homemade apple pies spread out on dozens of tables. Volunteers added scoops of ice cream on to plastic plates. Red, white, and blue balloons were handed to children, while the adults pinned on campaign buttons printed with John's name along with a slogan, "Leave It 2 Lovell." The high school band played their lopsided notes to patriotic songs. Baton twirlers caught some of their tosses.

Cars kept rolling in, and the latecomers had a hard time finding a place to park, so homeowners offered parking on their property for a small fee. This event showed the heart of the Midwest people, and in Jill's mind, it couldn't have been more perfect. Chad was taking pictures of anything that moved for the paper. Marge was working the crowd as Miss Cornelia took notes on what everyone wore for her write-up for the society page.

And there on the folding chairs sat her mother with Kathy and John's father. Gracie, John's dog, spread out nicely at their feet, swatting flies away with her tail while dripping a long stream of saliva from her jowls. Although Jill longed to join her family, she had to settle for smiles and waves since she was writing sound bites for two newspapers.

Jill was just turning back to her work when Gordon Yadon hurried up to her. "There you are!"

"Hi, Gordon."

"Do you remember when Delavan was named Circus Town USA?" Gordon asked her.

"Yeah, it happened when I was in high school. I recall that it was all your hard work that made it happen. Delavan was named Circus Town solely based on your research."

Gordon blushed as he looked around at the volunteers working to elect John for Congress. "As you know, it takes the effort of a team to make anything happen."

"I for one will never forget your hard work and commitment in making that happen. I still have the circus stamp I bought that day."

"That was a special time for our town," Gordon admitted. "Speaking with you today about the lake monster jarred my memory about something else. Twenty years ago this Wednesday, the day of the circus celebration, there was a man by the name of McGinnis Newman who came to talk to me. After buying Circus Town stamps, he handed me this envelope." Gordon passed a large brown business packet to Jill. She took it and looked up at Gordon questioningly, not sure if she should open it right now.

"Inside are articles dating back to the late 1800s. They're all about the lake monster," Gordon continued. "It was a busy day, and so I gave them a quick look and then slid them away in my bookcase. I thought you might get a kick out of them. Take good care of them, because I do want them back."

"Thank you, Gordon. I promise to take excellent care of them." Jill clutched the envelope to her.

"I know you will," Gordon told her, and then went to find a seat near the stage.

On the platform, the heads of the Wisconsin party began to take their seats on the folding metal chairs. Slowly, the crowd made their way to the grassy area. Some brought their own lawn chairs, while others spread blankets out on the sand; still others straddled fences or sat on the hoods of their cars. It was cozy and welcoming. Jill smiled. This was her town, and the man they had come to honor was her man, John.

When all were seated and the band stopped playing, Max walked to the podium. He picked up the microphone. After a few ear-piercing squeaks from the PA system, he greeted the happy crowd. "A great cry echoed from our political party a week ago. One man, a man of valor and of spirit, answered that cry. Ladies and gentlemen, here is the man of the hour, John Lovell."

Max stepped back and began clapping.

Applause was nearly deafening as John stood up from his front row seat and hopped up on the makeshift stage. Jill watched as his eyes searched the crowd for her. Once she caught his eye, she gave a wild wave. That charming smile took over his face when he finally saw her.

"Seeing you all here tonight, especially when you could be home enjoying your easy chair in the breeze of your window fans instead of being here swatting away mosquitoes in this heat, I know I can win this race. It's not me who campaigns, but you. It's not me who will win this November, but you. I am your surrogate . . ."

Jill marveled that John could connect with the lifestyle of small-town America so well. *The city folk will be a breeze.* Jill smiled again at her man for all seasons.

"Hey, Jill. There you are. I've been looking all over for you."

Olivia grabbed Jill's arm. "Listen, I'm sorry about our little falling-out this afternoon. Can you forgive me?"

Only hours earlier Jill had wanted to lock Olivia in the supply closet. Now it seemed Olivia was ready to put it all behind them. Although she suspected an ulterior motive, Jill was willing to forgive her.

"Of course I forgive you." After saying those words, she hoped the feeling would soon follow.

"Good." Olivia continued on, not recognizing Jill's inner struggle. "I know you're proud of John. I am too. My dad just goes on and on about him. You are so blessed to have him."

"I am blessed," Jill agreed, forcing a smile. "I hope you'll find someone just as special one day." Jill also hoped her old friend would find another seat, far away.

"Not like him." Olivia pointed to the stage and then clapped as another burst of applause rose up from the crowd. "From the first time I saw him in my daddy's office, I could tell great things were in store for him. I was right, wasn't I?"

"It's pretty amazing how you knew all that right away." Jill moved closer to the front to get away from Olivia. By now the sun had set, and the six stadium lights, used for night swimming, were snapped on to bathe the stage as John spoke.

"The great warmth of the welcome you've given me reinforces my decision to run for Congress," John was saying. "During this campaign, I won't tell you what I want to accomplish in this great state, because I will be too busy listening to you tell me what you think we need to do to keep Wisconsin the greatest state in the Union!"

The crowd erupted in ear-splitting cheers and clapping, so loud that John had to pause for several minutes. He began again. "I want to thank you for the generous support that has prompted my presence here tonight, because without you, I wouldn't be here. And without you, I won't be in Washington next year either. I'm counting on you, and you, and you." John pointed at the people throughout the crowd.

"Some of you may say that I didn't grow up in Wisconsin, but that's not true. Every summer of my childhood was spent in Wisconsin. The best times of my life! And I've had the good sense to get myself engaged to a Wisconsin woman. Jill, come on up here!"

Jill tried to hide her surprise as she walked up the steps to stand beside John. She smiled and waved at the cheering crowd. When John thrust the microphone under her nose, Jill took it and said, "The finest candidate in the land . . . John Lovell!"

With his arm around Jill, John continued.

"I don't want to talk to you. I want you to talk to me. So, I'm going to close now and walk among you and find out what you want to see changed in Washington. Together, we will make Wisconsin a better place to live, to work, to play, and to raise our families! And I am saying this loud enough to be heard in Washington. Watch out, here comes John Lovell!"

By midnight, the last of the cars had pulled away to return to their homes. John's voice was hoarse, and his shoulders began to slump with fatigue. Pearl and Big John had been among the first to leave for a late dinner at the Abbey in Fontana, and left Gracie for Jill to take care of until they returned. Jill kept the dog on a short leash at her side. While John had an impromptu meeting with the party members, Jill and Gracie waited. Olivia hung around as well.

Unexpectedly, Russ Jansen pulled up in his unmarked car, making Gracie prick up her ears. When the detective got out, Jill walked Gracie over to greet him. "It's nearly midnight, and that alone tells me you have news."

By then John had walked up to them.

Russ smiled at John. "I just got a copy of Walker's insurance faxed to me." Russ flicked it with his finger.

"I can tell by the look in your eyes that it's got to be interesting," Jill said.

"It's a policy with a two-person split." The detective held it up.

"Walker and his wife had children?" John asked as Russ handed it to him.

"Just read it," he said as he turned his car lights to high beam.

"A million-dollar split between his wife and . . . Fleming?" John shook his head.

"I'd say Fleming had a five-hundred-thousand-dollar reason to get rid of his best buddy," Jill said.

John nodded his head. "Jill, if I were you, I'd go see Anna again pretty quick. She might be mad enough about the insurance to open up more."

"No, I think I'll let Anna stew in it for a while before going back to see her. Right now, even half a million will seem like a huge amount. But let the cost of living sink into her head, and then divide what is left by about thirty or forty years. Once she sees what's left over, she may be more inclined to open up." Gracie gave a tug on her leash, anxious to walk around a bit. Jill headed toward the trees with her.

"Jill!" Russ called out. "Tomorrow I'm interviewing some people who were out on the lake near Fleming's boat on the day of the race. Could I persuade you to join me? Sometimes a pretty young woman has the advantage over an ugly lawman like me when it comes to opening up."

Jill knew he was kidding about his appearance. "I wish I could go along, but I can't right now. John leaves for Kenosha tomorrow, and then swings through the southeastern part of the state. I'm going with him."

"Okay, I understand that." Russ walked back to his car as John went after Jill.

"Jill, you need to be with Russ on this interview. Very seldom does a law officer call in support outside of his department. This could mean open doors for you on other cases in the future."

"I know that, John, but I'd much rather be with you. Politics is my forte."

"I know that, and I would definitely be disappointed if you didn't come with me." He took Gracie's leash from her. "But Jill, you need to stay put here at the paper and follow this investigation. It'll only be for a few days, and then you can catch up with me in Milwaukee, okay?" John opened his BlackBerry to show her his schedule. "Look, this would be perfect. In two days I'll be in Milwaukee speaking to the Daughters of the American Revolution."

"But who'll cover you in the meantime?" Jill wanted to know.

Suddenly Olivia was stepping up beside them. "What about me?"

22

The shoulders of the widow were hung in a long mourning dress, like the robes of exiled royalty.

—Franz Liszt

Jill studied the report she had written during the morning interviews with Russ. She compared them to Russ's earlier reports he had gotten within days of the murder. People saw things differently, and each interview seemed to cancel out what the next person observed. Russ just laughed about it, saying it happens that way a lot in homicide. But every witness spoke about the same kinds of things, how sad it was that a murder gummed up a perfectly good lake's reputation, how they suspected Fleming was the killer, or that the widow didn't act sufficiently bereaved.

Jill and Russ agreed to stop for the afternoon and were on their way back to the office when Marge rang Jill's cell. "Hey, what's up?" Jill asked.

"Anna Walker wants to talk to you right away. Says it's an emergency. Do you have her number?"

Jill looked over at Russ and smiled. "Anna Walker wants to talk to me."

"Hop on it before she changes her—"

Before Russ could finish, Jill had Anna Walker on the phone. "Anna, Jill Lewis here."

"Hello, Jill. Thanks for calling me back. I was wondering if you could come see me. I'd like to talk to you about something."

"Sure, I can come right now. Do you mind if Detective Russ Jansen from Walworth County tags along with me? We're investigating your husband's murder together. I'm with him right now."

"Yes, that's all right with me."

"Great. Give us an hour, and we'll be at your door. Thanks for calling." Jill smiled to herself in satisfaction.

"An hour, did you predict?" Russ said. "Nah, we'll be there in much less time than that." He smiled as he put his blue police light on top of the car. "This way we won't get busted for speeding." Chomping on a toothpick, he accelerated toward the interstate.

"I can't imagine what Anna wants to talk to me about."

"You can't?" Russ grinned as he tapped out a beat with his hands on the steering wheel. "Interesting that just as we learn of the life insurance policy split, you get a call from the widow."

"I don't want to walk into Anna's house filled with my own assumptions. It may be something entirely different. Feel free to step in to the conversation once we arrive."

"No doubt I will do just that." He smiled at her.

As they pulled up in front of the house, Jill saw Anna's slender form waiting on the front porch. The rocker was moving back and forth as if it were in a thunderstorm. From all appearances, this was not the meek and mild-mannered widow Jill had met only a week ago.

Russ took the blue light from the top of his car and put it into the trunk. He stepped back, allowing Jill to go first up the front porch steps.

"Anna, what's wrong?"

"Thank goodness you've come." She kept rocking, tears streaming down her face.

"What is it? What happened?" Jill knelt down in front of her.

Anna certainly wasn't as composed as she was the last time Jill had visited. Her face was raw from her tears, her clothes were rumpled, her hair uncombed. The box of Kleenex was empty.

"Joe is dead. He's really dead. I don't know what to do, how to live." The reality of it had finally sunk in. Anna covered her face with her hands. "I can't turn to Robert or Crystal anymore. I feel so alone and used."

Jill glanced up at Russ. "Anna, Detective Jansen has come with me. What can we do to help you?"

"Can you do anything about this?" From a pile of opened condolence cards she took a long white business envelope and handed it to Jill. Jill read the return address. "It's from an insurance company."

"Go ahead and look inside of it." Anna nodded stiffly.

Jill pulled out a five-page letter stating that as soon as the coroner closed the case she would be receiving a check for the amount of five hundred thousand dollars. Jill wasn't sure what to say to the woman. It was best to wait and let Anna have her say first, which she did, in the very next breath. "I've been robbed! Joe's insurance was for one million dollars. It was a financial strain for us to pay the premium on that policy. Robert sure didn't help us with that. But the other half was left to Robert just the same! I know Joe was fond of Robert, but I had no idea he had me, his wife, on the same level as a friend. It's not fair to me."

"I totally agree," Jill said a bit too quickly.

"Fair or not, it's all legal." Russ read over the rest of the papers.

"Maybe you should discuss this with Robert," Jill suggested. "He might give his share of the money to you."

"No chance of that with all his money troubles," she answered with disgust in her voice. She wiped away her tears. "One day my life was happy, secure, with no worries. Now I find myself not even wanting to get out of bed."

"Give it time. Look, may I get you some water to drink?" Jill put her hand on Anna's shoulder.

Anna nodded. Jill went through the front door and into the kitchen, shuddering as she remembered what had happened on her last visit here. Reaching for a glass in the cabinet by the sink, she noticed a bottle of peanut oil in the cupboard. She took it down and looked at it. Then Jill searched through the same cupboard trying to find a different oil product that could be used in baking, like canola or corn or vegetable oil. But there was none. Anna had only peanut oil. Was this the root of Jill's illness?

With the water glass in one hand and the peanut oil in the other, Jill went back out to the front porch. Russ was now seated on the porch swing. "Anna, did you make that banana bread you served me with peanut oil, by any chance?" Jill held up her find.

Anna turned around and looked at her blankly. "I believe so. I've been out of corn oil . . . Why do you ask? Oh, do I remember you telling me you're allergic to peanuts?" Her hand went to her mouth. "When you asked me about it I only thought about the raw peanuts. Oh dear. Did you get sick?" Anna rose to her feet and went over to Jill as if she were checking on her right then.

Jill nodded. "That's one mystery solved." She set the oil on a table. "At least now I know why I became ill."

"Don't you carry epinephrine with you?"

"I used to carry a few pen injections, but since I haven't had an allergic reaction since high school, I've become somewhat lax."

"Too bad you had to find out the hard way." Anna shook her head. "Now, how do you suggest I get my money back from Robert?"

Jill and Russ exchanged concerned glances. Up until this moment, Jill had regarded Anna Walker as a softhearted woman who just needed hand-holding during her time of grief. *No, Anna Walker isn't nearly as helpless as she would have you believe.*

23

History is not another name for the past, as many people imply. It is the name for stories of the past.

—A. J. P. Taylor

Jill arrived at the office just in time to see the huge delivery of boxes being unloaded from a DSL semitruck. Fortunately, Chad had already stepped up and was directing the delivery. "Looks like you ordered lots of office equipment," he said.

"I sure have. And, best of all, it's compliments of the *Gazette*. Looks like we have a busy afternoon ahead of us." Inside the office, Jill showed Chad where she wanted everything. "The TVs should be installed on that huge wall over there, the laptops should be stacked together there, and, oh look, here are the new cell phones with walkie-talkies. Wahoo!"

"Wow, this is top-of-the-line equipment! We've hit the big time. I can't wait to try some of it," Chad said.

"When I hired you, I sure hired the right person." Not being able to contain her happiness anymore, Jill hugged Chad. "I'm so glad you're here."

He blushed. "Thanks, I'm glad I'm here too. And where in your office should I put this very large machine?" His eyes widened as he watched the Pix-o-matic come through the door.

"You know what, Chad? I'm not sure where to put it. For now, we better leave it boxed up." Jill walked toward her office as her cell rang. It was Annabelle.

"Annabelle! Perfect timing. Your deliveries are all coming in through the front doors as we speak."

"Well, don't try to figure everything out for yourself. You're technologically savvy, but you don't have the expertise to install it. The *Gazette*'s tech genius will be arriving in a day or two to do all that for you. It may take him a week to get everything done, but he's the best and he'll do it right."

"Thanks. I owe you. Wait, you say he's arriving in just a day or two, for a week? That might be problematic. I'll be on the campaign trail with John by then."

"Our tech can handle it. Put what's-her-name in charge while you're away," Annabelle suggested.

"Her name is Marge, and she's very efficient. She can handle it."

"I'm sure she can, because my guy knows exactly what to do. The only thing that concerns me is the Pix-o-matic. He was going to hold a training session for everyone in your office."

Jill looked around the room. There was no way she'd postpone meeting up with John on the campaign trail again. Olivia was doing a great job emailing the coverage to Jill every morning and afternoon, but it was Jill who belonged by John's side, not Olivia. *How hard would it be to read a manual and figure it all out later?* "Marge will handle it."

"Great. Let me make a note of her name for the techie . . . Marge. Anyway, it's not you that I'm worried about. It's those other people who may not be familiar with how things work and tear up a machine in no time."

"How can I ever thank you?"

"Just keep writing those stories for us. I want up-to-the-minute information on John's campaign written as only his fiancée can write."

"You got it," Jill agreed and hung up. When she turned around, she bumped into Gordon Yadon.

"Oh, excuse me, Gordon!" She grabbed his arm. It was then Jill noticed another person standing alongside of him. They had obviously arrived together.

"I'm sorry if we've come at a bad time." Gordon looked at all the traffic in the office; he looked unsure whether they should stay.

"Nonsense. This is a great time for you to be here. In fact, any day is a great day to see you. Come on into my office." The men followed Jill. She closed the door as they settled into chairs.

Gordon held his arm out to the gentleman beside him. "Jill, I want you to meet—"

"McGinnis Newman? Hi, I'm Jill Lewis." She reached across her desk to shake his hand. "It's an honor."

"How did you do that? Know who I am, I mean?" McGinnis asked.

"It was just a guess." Jill smiled. "I haven't had a chance to go through your articles yet. But I'll get to them soon."

"No hurry about that," Gordon explained.

"We've come about another matter," McGinnis told her.

"Oh, the coin they found at the bottom of the lake?" Jill asked.

Both men nodded eagerly.

"I'll be seeing Detective Jansen later today, so I'll ask him if we can see it."

"Good. I tracked McGinnis down to tell him about the coin, but that's only one of the reasons we're here. He's really more interested in talking to you than seeing the coin."

"Me?" Jill wasn't really sure how to handle that. She had nothing to offer, other than some of Chad's coffee.

McGinnis leaned in to speak. "I wanted to meet the young woman who dared to believe in old men's tales."

"And here I am."

"Good." McGinnis cleared his throat. "I've got a story to tell you. In 1891, there was an infamous bank robbery in Delavan. All the gold boullion was stolen from the bank vault; bars and coin, all taken. Five years ago there was a robbery of gold coins from the Washington Mint. Both came from the same minting."

"I'm not sure what you're telling me." Jill began to scribble her notes onto a yellow legal pad.

"One hundred years separate the robberies, but the shipment was a one-issue minting in DC. It was purchased by the Delavan bank to sell off to private collectors. Until then, it remained together as one unit. Then the first robbery separated them," McGinnis said. "During the break-in, the robbers overlooked a bag. At the time, the authorities decided not to release that information to the public so that when the rest of the minting was recovered, the overlooked bag would be used for identification. But the stolen gold was never recovered, and this information I am telling you has never been made public. Government officials came into town right after the robbery and took the remaining boullion. They were able to deliver it without incident to the mint in Washington DC. Then five years ago, it disappeared."

"Stolen?"

"I'm afraid so." McGinnis sighed. "My great-grandfather was the president of the Delavan bank at the time of the first robbery. Darn near ruined our family. And it would've for sure if that one bag hadn't been overlooked."

"I've spent most of my adult life in Washington, and I know it's nearly impossible for anything to get out of the mint."

"Exactly." McGinnis nodded. "Had to be an inside job. Because of my family's history, and my interest in the boullion, my attention was drawn to the newspaper article."

"You say the coins are identical to the stolen ones?" Jill drew a large question mark on her pad and broke the pencil tip on the period. No matter, she chose another sharpened pencil from her desk. "Russ Jansen, our county detective, needs to hear about this," Jill said to McGinnis. "Just hang on, and let's see if we can't get him over here right now. I'll ask him to bring the coin so we can get a good look at it."

The two men looked at one another as if about to witness the eighth wonder of the world. It took Jill some doing, but finally she convinced Russ to bring the coin over to compare to the coin pictured in Gordon's book.

When Russ arrived and McGinnis shared his story, Russ became as excited as the three of them. Jill returned Gordon's book to him, allowing him the pleasure of finding the picture.

"Here it is!" Gordon's nimble fingers found the page, and he tapped his index finger on it. Everyone leaned in for a closer look. The gold coin was the size of a silver dollar. It was stamped with the American eagle and dated just a year before the robbery.

All eyes now turned to Russ. His hand reached into his right pocket. Between his fingers he pulled out the small plastic bag marked with evidence tape. Russ pulled on the tape carefully until it was off all the way. Then, he put an edge of the tape on the desk and unfolded the bag. From the bag he pulled out a coin partly encased in hardened mud and sand.

"May I?" McGinnis asked, as though he were asking for a small peek through the pearly gates.

McGinnis took a small pocketknife out, and with the dull edge began to scrape away at the sediment. When most of the mud and debris had been removed, he walked to the window and held it up to the natural light. "Once you're down in the water more than thirty feet, there is little sunlight. That explains why this has been so well preserved even after a hundred plus years."

"Okay, you lost me again," Jill said.

McGinnis smiled. "It's been in an oxygen-free environment where there's no decay. The sediment has served as a jacket for the coin, keeping it dry and well preserved." He tossed the coin back to Russ. "She'll shine up like a beauty. But now, let's go ahead and compare the coin to the picture in Gordon's book."

Russ placed the coin beside the picture. Everyone gasped, and the sound was followed by a hushed silence.

"It looks like a match to me," Gordon said.

"Aye," McGinnis agreed as everyone shook their heads affirmatively.

"If we let this out, then fortune hunters will be all over the lake," Russ said. "There'll be no stopping them. Boats loaded with sonar, not to mention tourists just jumping off rowboats. We'll have a three-ring circus here."

Jill laughed. Delavan was, after all, Circus Town USA.

"Can't we keep it a secret for now?" Jill suggested. "After all, we do need more time to have it checked out and confirmed . . . I mean, it has to be tested and examined, right?"

"Right. And to preserve the scene." Russ again pointed out the obvious. He placed the coin scrapings back into the evidence bag for safekeeping.

"It would take more than a court order to legally bring the gold up, if it's even down there like we think it is," McGinnis said.

"What do you mean?" Russ asked.

"The Great Lakes and most northern lakes, including Lake Delavan, are protected under the bottomland preservation laws. The gold cannot be removed because historical relics can't be disturbed," he explained. "Just like you can't destroy or disrupt national land reserves."

Jill felt disappointed. "Well, in that case, if it can't be removed, this secret will have to remain with us."

"Next question," Russ said. "How in the world did this gold coin from a bank robbery back in 1891 get in the lake?"

Everyone shrugged at once.

"Do we know who took the gold from the bank?" Jill asked, looking from Gordon to McGinnis. If anyone would know the answer to that question, they would.

Gordon took a deep breath. "Fingers have always pointed to the circus clown, Ralph Kolotka. About a month after the robbery, authorities found a gold bar and a handful of coins in his wagon. Although he maintained his innocence, no one believed him. When he was arrested, he had recently quit the circus, and they found him traveling in his wagon, heading out of state."

"It does sound reasonable for him to be convicted. If he were innocent, what was he doing with the bank's gold in his wagon?" Jill frowned.

"Ralph was in love with one of the animal trainers, but they had a quarrel, which led to their breakup." McGinnis picked up the story, taking the clown's side. "Very soon after that, she up and married the circus master. Ralph was devastated, and he quit the circus. Then when he got trapped in town because of closed roads from a blizzard, he waited out the winter by taking odd jobs. He planned to leave as soon as the spring thaw came. When the roads became passable, he left town. Ralph was two miles out when his wagon bumped over something hard in the road. According to historical accounts, he thought he had hit and killed a small farm animal. He climbed down from his wagon to have a look. Instead of a piglet or a chicken, he found a bag of gold! Thinking luck was finally on his side, he loaded the gold into his wagon and covered it over with blankets before continuing on his way."

"So they caught Kolotka with only some of the gold?" Russ said. "He must've had a partner in crime if he really committed the crime."

"Ralph Kolotka never admitted having a partner because he never admitted to robbing the bank. Even the young, local preacher, H. M. Clark, couldn't persuade him to confess his crime before he was hung," McGinnis explained.

"I know Rev. Clark," Jill said.

Both Gordon and McGinnis looked at her in surprise.

"Not literally, but I know who he was. I recently read his eyewitness account of the lake monster in the *Lakes News* archives."

The men smiled, seemingly pleased with Jill's interest in the town history, and Gordon prodded McGinnis to continue his tale. "After he was hung, people began to question if Ralph Kolotka was innocent of the crime."

"How very sad," Jill said.

"Yes," McGinnis agreed.

"And so we have the missing boullion due to a robbery in the 1890s, and another more recent robbery from the U.S. mint just five years ago," Jill said.

"Missing. Its legal term is missing," McGinnis corrected.

"Ralph Kolotka is buried out in Spring Grove," Gordon said. "In fact, 150 members of the old circus colony are buried there, or buried at St. Andrew's cemetery. My granddaddy once told me that Mabel, the animal trainer who broke Ralph's heart, used to leave a single rose on his grave every year until the day of her death."

"I bet it wasn't too popular with the ringmaster," Jill mused.

"Mind if I borrow this book from you for a while?" Russ picked up the old volume.

Gordon nodded his head. "Please, please take anything with you that might be of help."

Russ slipped the coin back into the evidence bag. "I guess I know where I'll be going with this: to the Federal Reserve. But for now, I won't say where it was found. When I find out more, I'll let you all know."

"But what about the forensic divers? Won't they want to keep it for possible evidence?" Jill asked.

"The head of the team is my buddy, and we do favors for one another. He knows how to keep his mouth shut. By the way, I'm only borrowing it until I know something for sure. Isn't it the truth we're all searching for?"

"And to preserve the scene," Jill said, as each one agreed.

After everyone had cleared her office, Jill shook herself into the present by walking out into the newsroom, where state-of-the-art technology awaited her. But she kept looking back into her office, where minutes ago three men and a piece of gold had transported her back into a very different time. She heard a story that was over a hundred years old, and seconds later she was checking her technology inventory: from wagon wheels to rocket science.

Before Chad left for the night, she had him tote back down one box of the old newspapers he had so carefully stored away for her only days before. Jill was determined to read every issue from 1890–1891 before she went home for the night. Jill sat on the old carpeted floor and opened the lid on the one box that contained two years' worth of the *Lakes News*. Lucky for her, back then her paper only went to press once a week, and most times it was just one page. Carefully, she picked through the brittle pages, laughing at the advertisements for elixirs and ladies' corsets.

Marge had left an hour before, and Chad was running an errand to pick up her new prescription at the doctor's office. She'd have the two auto injections of the epinephrine to take along when she met John on the campaign trail. Jill had to be prepared just in case a creative cook snuck some peanuts, in any form, into one of her dishes. What a pain. She wished she had outgrown this allergy.

Carefully, Jill laid aside each newspaper as she finished reading it. The next paper had a picture of the circus doing some of their stunts in the water during August of 1890. Evidently, they had returned to the area for a special show that summer. Jill looked closer, and there it was, that dinghy she saw hung up in that small cave. Of course, when you exchanged the order of the letters, *TC* stood for The Circus!

The papers for a few months later only discussed the early frigid weather and mounds of snow that never seemed to end. As usual, the circus was wintering in town and staying at the Delavan Hotel, while their animals were bedded down in what is now Spring Park. Moving on through the issues, Jill read how the beloved forty-year-old elephant, Sophie, had died from old age, and how she was dragged out on the ice and left there. There was even a picture. So much for her lake monster.

Finally she found what she was looking for: the headline "Robbers Take Gold Bullion from Mercantile Bank!" Jill kept reading through the issues.

When she started feeling sleepy, she decided to stop for the evening. But then something caught her eye: an article about how the weather suddenly turned warm a few days after the robbery and remained that way for a month. Jill grabbed a pen and paper and began a timeline.

1. The week of August 12, 1890, was the circus boat show. Maybe that was when the dinghy sunk. Jill felt it was irrelevant, but she didn't want to overlook that. She wrote it down with a question mark.

2. Early bad winter began sometime mid October of the same year. For several months the town was hunkered down with blowing snow, new snowfall, and frigid temps. *Sounds like a normal Wisconsin winter to me.*

3. Sophie died December 28 and was laid out on Lake Delavan by noon two days later. It took them that long to haul her just five miles in all that snow.

4. January 1, 1891, was the bank robbery. Within days of that incident, the weather turned unseasonably mild. Due to the fifty-degree weather, the winter wonderland began to melt quickly.

5. On February 2, the snow had melted enough for the roads to clear, and Kolotka rolled out of town.

Somehow all these events strung together meant something, but what? If the ground had warmed enough to melt the snow off the roads, then that meant Sophie was sinking down under the lake much earlier than expected too. Jill stretched her arms over her head. Her back ached from slumping over all the articles. She leaned against the old sofa to think.

Did Kolotka really tell the truth about just finding the gold? If his account was correct, then that meant the gold was on its way out of town long before Kolotka found some of it. With so much gold, it might have taken many trips to hide it.

Jill got up and paced her office floor. She started talking out loud to herself. "You can't keep all that boullion on you with the whole town looking for it. It must have been the tournament of the winter season to find that gold! Certainly you can't bury it when the ground is frozen. Where do you put it?" And then Jill screamed. She jumped up and down. "Of course, that's it!"

Jill rattled through the papers again. There it was: "Unexpectedly Sophie died within days of getting pneumonia. Up to that time she had been healthy. Her trainer, Ralph Kolotka, who also worked as the circus's most popular clown, was too upset to comment on his beloved animal's sudden death."

Jill doubted Ralph killed his beloved Sophie. Someone else did, someone who took the coins and used Sophie as the hiding place. Smart move, but spring came too quickly and thawed the ice and messed up their plans. Sophie went down with the treasure hidden inside of her. Jill sprang up in the air. "That's why the gold was found in the lake!"

Jill lunged for the phone to call Gordon. He answered on the second ring, and by the sound of his voice she guessed he was still excited over the coin. Jill picked up her pad and read her timeline to him, explaining what she thought it meant. While doing this, Jill felt rather presumptuous being the one to clear up what might have happened over a hundred years ago, to the town's historian. But when she finished speaking, Gordon said, "I think you've just exonerated Ralph Kolotka. His version of finding the gold on the road seems to be true. I would like to continue on with your research, with your permission of course, just to be sure."

"You don't need my permission. Just do it."

"I will . . . You know, Jill, all accounts say that at the twelfth hour, the minister prayed with Kolotka, who then accepted the Lord as his Savior. I think you've done our brother justice."

"If my assumptions are correct. On the way home, I think I'll drop by the graveyard to tell Kolotka our good news. I'll bring along my camera and take some pictures."

"Hurry along, now, while you've still got some daylight. Be sure to call me and let me know what he says." Gordon chuckled before saying good-bye.

24

We hang the petty thieves and appoint the great ones to public office.

—Aesop

Jill googled the Spring Grove Cemetery and located the spot where Ralph Kolotka lay. Next she dug through the closet until she found a working flashlight, just in case it got dark before she left the cemetery. On her way out, she turned out all the office lights before locking the door behind her.

Jill put her car into gear and turned toward Spring Grove Cemetery. She pulled into the graveyard and drove down the narrow lane until she came to a dead end where she parked under the shade of an oak tree. That's when she caught the first sign of evening fog rolling in over the property.

By the dashboard light, she read the map of the cemetery she had gotten off the Web and tried to figure out where Kolotka's grave site was from where she sat. Scrunching her nose, she looked out her car window and figured it'd be east of her car, right up the hillside. When she left the office, she hadn't realized how late it was getting. The light was fading so fast that she knew she'd have to quickly hike to find the grave.

Determined to get a shot of the tombstone for her article, Jill folded the map into her purse, next to the paper's digital camera and flashlight. She got out of the car and immediately sensed an atmosphere of decay in the damp air. Not only was the cornerstone of the mausoleum beginning to crumble, but also the bushes along the roadside struggled for life. Jill stepped off the main path and started up the hill. Layers of loose gravel made the incline difficult, almost causing her shoes to slip. Thankful for her good balance, she remained on her feet and turned onto the grassy knolls, walking in between the rows of headstones. Some of them had been knocked over either by weather or by prank; she couldn't tell.

Why was she given to such crazy notions like visiting a grave at night? Of course, she hadn't expected it to be so dark in the country, away from the small-town lights. The tip of her shoe caught the edge of a half-buried cement block, sending her down on all fours. Jill picked up her flashlight and sat looking around. The contents of her purse had fallen out across the grass. After she was sure she had gotten everything back inside of her purse, she turned in the direction of another much-narrower gravel walkway. The older part to the cemetery lay in the direction she was headed, and though it was dark now, she could see that this area hadn't been taken care of as well as the section near the road.

A noise from behind stopped Jill in her tracks. With her breath held tightly in her chest, she listened for the sound of footsteps again. Jill shone her flashlight in every direction. All she saw were ghostly white grave markers. Releasing her breath, she slowly and silently counted to fifty before proceeding.

As usual, the mosquitoes were fierce, so she took out her can of bug spray and used it liberally from head to toe. Now those little blood-sucking parasites could look elsewhere for their meal. She recapped the can and shoved it back down in her purse.

When she neared the crest of a hill, a strong breeze blew

through the cemetery. The moon was high in the sky, and the fog hunkered below in the valley. Now reading the tombstones was an easy task. Second row from the last, third plot from the left, and there it was: Ralph Kolotka's grave. His marker was a small white tombstone set deep into the ground. It had his name, the year of his birth, and the date of his death carved in the stone. Nothing more. It was plain and simple, although his demise had been anything but. A few weeds sprouted from between the cracks in the stone. Jill found it sad that no one was left to come and tend to his grave. But who even knew he existed except for perhaps the groundskeeper?

Looking around, Jill decided this would make a good eerie shot for her story in the newspaper. Jill worked her position until she found the perfect angle. After taking several shots in one direction, she repositioned herself so she could also get a shot of his grave along with the moon. The wind unexpectedly stopped, and as if set free, the fog began to roll up along the sides of the hill. Finished with her photo shoot, she reached down and pulled the weeds from the cracked places of the headstone and cleared away the stone of debris. She looked at her wristwatch. It was after ten, and she was anxious to leave the premises and get home.

Going down the hill was much easier than climbing up it. But now, she was locked in by thick fog. Her flashlight only made things worse, washing everything in the same color of nothingness. The visibility was only at about four feet. As she rounded a grove of trees, she realized she hadn't seen these scraggly old maples on her way up.

She suddenly felt fear squeezing in her chest. She felt like she was being followed. She began walking quickly until her walk became a run. She was sure she could hear the footsteps coming hard after her. Running as fast as she dared, Jill plowed into an unseen immovable object. The force of it made her fall to the ground, and for a moment, she was unable to catch her breath. Finally, she sat up. What she had hit was an old stone wall that had once separated one farmer's field from another. Hearing someone coming through the trees, she dove over the wall and crouched down to hide on the other side. From her purse she got ahold of the mosquito spray. She intended to use it as if it were mace. She crawled on her hands and knees to the end of the wall.

Suddenly something collided with her. Screaming wildly, she pressed the top of the bug repellent and sprayed not only her attacker but herself as well. A few expletives later, the person ran back into the woods. Jill hopped to her feet and ran in the opposite direction toward her car. When she reached it, she jerked open the door and dove into the interior. Like a crazed woman, she pounded down the main lock that made her Range Rover a fortress. She sat for a few minutes trying to catch her breath. Her hands shook as she tried to find her car keys in the black hole of her purse.

"Jill?" From the darkness a human form sat up in the backseat of her car. She screamed and attacked the door, doing her best to get back out. The voice kept calling her name. Breaking free of the car, Jill hit the trail as hard as she could. The person behind her bull-rushed her until his arms wrapped around her.

"Stop fighting me, Jill! It's me, Chad Stokes." His voice was high and shrill, almost like a girl's.

"Chad?" Jill struggled from his embrace.

"Yeah?" Chad smiled crookedly.

"Want to tell me why you were hiding in my car? And don't tell me you had a fight with your cousin, and he kicked you out." Jill tried desperately to catch her breath.

"No, things are fine between my cousin and me. I have your epinephrine that you sent me out for. I saw your car peeling out of the parking lot of the *Lakes News* and thought you'd want to have the medicine before you left tomorrow morning to meet John in Milwaukee. I followed you."

"Where's your truck?" Jill asked him suspiciously.

"I parked it under the oak trees over there. See?" He pointed. Jill thought she saw a glimmer of metal. If he hadn't said it was a truck, she'd never have been able to tell in this weather. "Then I waited for you in your car but fell asleep in the backseat."

"Where's my medicine?" Jill still wasn't convinced he was telling the truth.

"It's in the pharmacy bag in your car's backseat. Sorry I scared you." When they got back to the car, he opened the back door, took out the bag, and handed it to her.

"Let me see your face and eyes," Jill said.

"My eyes? What are you talking about?"

"Someone was following me through the cemetery. I sprayed him with bug spray, so I need to see your face."

"It wasn't me! I was waiting for you in your car," Chad insisted. "Sheesh, I was just trying to be helpful." Chad stomped over in front of Jill's headlights and obediently crouched down. Jill took his face in her hands and studied his eyes carefully. "Your eyes look normal. I guess you're not my attacker."

"I told you it wasn't me. I was sitting in your car, waiting for you. What are you doing in a cemetery at night anyway?"

"Working on a story for the paper."

He looked at her and shook his head. "Wait in your car while I run up the hill to see if there are any signs of anyone hanging out up there. And don't forget to lock your doors." Chad took off up the hill with the flashlight. Jill slid back in her car and locked it.

Fifteen minutes later, Chad was back and tapping on her window. Jill rolled her window down. Out of breath, Chad announced, "No, nobody's up there. At least not anymore."

"Thanks for checking. Look, I'm sorry, Chad. I've treated you unfairly. You deserve a raise."

He grinned. "But let me guess: you can't afford to give me one."

"I didn't say you were getting a raise, I just said you deserve one. To make it up to you, how about driving me to Milwaukee tomorrow to meet John? You can hang out with us for a couple of days and run the paper's new camera to video John's speeches. Consider it a vacation. How about it?"

Chad laughed. "Thanks. I could use a vacation after tonight."

25

I am not afraid to die. I just don't want to be there when it happens.

—Woody Allen

Chad arrived at the office the next morning within minutes of Jill. He stood in the reception area with his duffel bag. "You got a haircut," she said. "Where did you find someone to cut your hair so early in the morning?" She admired his clothes. "Nice suit too."

"My sister Lynn cut my hair. The suit belongs to my cousin. The only things I own are shorts and a half dozen swim trunks. You're sure I look okay and not dumb?" Chad fidgeted a bit, pulling at the sleeves of his shirt.

"Actually, you look quite professional." Jill scrutinized him, then straightened his tie. "And since you'll be down front getting the live feed, that's important." Jill thanked him and patted his lapel. "One of my goals is to upgrade the image of the *Lakes News*, so my well-dressed cameraman with his state-of-the-art equipment is a good start."

"Are you ready to go then?" Chad set down his duffel bag.

"I just need to sign out the paper's equipment—Marge's orders—and I'll be good to go."

"Before we go, I promised the staff I'd hand out their new cell-talkies. It won't take long." Jill called everyone into her office and began to assign the cells.

"Don't they come in pink?" Marge asked.

"No pink phones, Marge. They're all identical—red. I could've gone with silver, but then you might confuse them with any private cells you may have." Jill held one up in the air. "And I labeled each cell with a number. Each cell is programmed and automatically connected to the office. To reach the *Lakes News* just push *777."

"Wait, what's that number again?" Miss Cornelia asked. "I need to get that written down someplace."

Jill looked to Marge for assistance.

"I'll take care of it, boss." Marge gave her a wink.

Olivia, fresh from the campaign trail, seemed slightly agitated. She sat swinging her foot back and forth, smirking as the small group practiced talking to one another through the talkie feature. Turning her back on Marge and Miss Cornelia, she plugged one ear and said, "Jill, I must congratulate you doing this with your wits and not your wealth. I'm impressed."

"Thanks, it means a lot for me to hear you say that." Jill smiled at her.

"Have a good trip, and I'll see you when you get back. I'll take care of things around here while you're gone."

"Oh?" Suddenly Jill felt alarmed. She didn't want Olivia bossing her staff around.

"I wish I were going back on the campaign trail with you. That first night in Appleton was amazing. It was the best of all John's speeches, although he hasn't given that many yet. But it was great. John is great."

"Well, I'm glad you're back. Now it's my turn."

Olivia put her hand on Jill's shoulder and said sweetly, "And you don't need to worry about a thing while you're gone. I've grown up in this business, so I can take care of things."

Jill tried to keep the annoyance out of her voice. "Well, don't get too comfortable. I'll only be gone a short while. I've put Marge in charge, but I suppose an extra pair of eyes around here will be helpful. If there's a problem, Marge will call me right away."

Jill sighed as she looked at Miss Cornelia and Marge having an animated conversation with each other over their new cell phones. Leaving the paper was bittersweet; she wanted to see John and yet she and her staff had become such a tight-knit albeit dysfunctional family in the past few months that she hated to leave.

—⁓—

The trip into Milwaukee took less than two hours. They parked their car in the garage next to the convention center. After getting their suitcases and gear from the trunk, Chad and Jill hurried inside the modern building. Jill needed to freshen up in the bathroom. In front of the mirror, she smoothed out her dress and then plumped her hair before applying fresh blush and some lip gloss. A few old friends were waiting for her in the lobby, FBI agents Jimmy Allen and Sally Weinstein, and Jill wanted to look her best.

"It's great to see you again!" Jill hugged them. "Are you part of John's security detail today?"

"Yes, we've been assigned to the Milwaukee office, and we're here to help with security for this event," Sally told Jill.

"Where's Abe?" Jill asked, looking around. "Is he here too?"

"No, he's back in Washington, filling in for John until he comes back or his replacement is announced."

"Please say hello to him for me." Jill then introduced Chad.

"We'll have an aide take your bags over to the hotel," Sally said.

"And anything you carry inside of the auditorium will have to go through security," Jimmy told them.

Chad pointed to his camera luggage. "This is camera equipment from the *Lakes News*."

"Set it up on the conveyor belt so the guard can look through it," Jimmy instructed. He popped the lid on the metal case. There it was, RCA cables, the Sony camcorder, and the tripod. Jimmy was walking them backstage to where John waited when Jill spotted Glenn Carlin. "Glenn?" Jill approached him. "What are you doing here?"

"Hi, Jill. I was just hired the other day by the party to assist with John's campaign," Glenn said nonchalantly. "I packed up as fast as I could, and here I am in Milwaukee again."

"You certainly don't sound enthusiastic," Jill noticed.

"I was hoping to stay in Washington for a while. But since I helped with Fleming, Max Clark thought I could help John's campaign."

"I'm glad you're here. It's not everyone who can trick me into giving away information. You're good."

Glenn smiled and walked them backstage to John, who was now only minutes away from being introduced to the animated crowd.

When he saw Jill, John nearly tripped over his own feet on his way to hug her. He picked her up in his arms and kissed her. Breathless, Jill remarked, "You've never acted like this before. That's the best greeting you've ever given to me."

"Well, you'd better get used to it."

Jill framed John's face with her hands. "You're the best. No wonder I love you so much." She suddenly remembered that Chad was with them. She stepped to the side so the men could shake hands. "I brought Chad along with me."

"Looks like you're carrying a heavy load there," John said, pointing at the media case.

"This is our live feed equipment." Chad started taking it out of the case. "Jill wants me to record your speech and send the feed as it happens to the *Gazette* and the *Lakes News*, just like we did at Millie's. But this time, we have much better equipment."

"You seem to have a growing fan club," Jill said to John as she peeked out of the stage curtain. "Everyone is behind you. And I just heard the good news about Carlin joining your team."

"I just learned about it yesterday myself," John said. "I was a little concerned that he was coming straight from Fleming's office, but he hadn't worked there that long, and before that he was working for someone in the other party. It appears he doesn't let anything personal get in the way of his work."

Applause rose from the auditorium as someone turned to John to tell him he had been announced. John stepped forward with his backstage smile still in place. As soon as his feet hit the stage, the music started up followed by applause and hoots. Confetti floated down from the ceiling. Jill scooted Chad forward to start his feed, but she remained in the wings. Midway through his speech, John faltered, then stopped to look at Jill. She gave him an encouraging smile and a small wave. Then he held out his hand to her and asked her to join him on stage. Hurrying up to her fiancé, Jill grabbed ahold of John's hand as applause rose. Supporters waved their hats and chanted John's name.

When John was finally able to speak, he introduced Jill, and more applause followed. He kissed her cheek. John then continued with his speech. With a nod of her head to Chad, Jill motioned him to move closer. Just feet away from the podium, Chad stumbled over a cord and fell at the same time as an earsplitting shot rang out. The dropped camera slid across the stage as five men dove on top of John, and another three took Jill down to the floor.

Screams echoed throughout the auditorium as people fled in every direction. Agents and police scattered over the place. Agents Weinstein and Allen ushered the couple backstage into a secure room.

"John! John!" Jill cried. "Are you all right?"

"I'm fine. Are you all right?" They reached for one another.

"I think so . . . It just happened so fast." Jill hugged John tightly. A bevy of men and women in suits filled the room. They all wore earphones, and several had drawn their weapons. In the confusion there wasn't much information, but that didn't stop Jill from asking, "Does anyone know who shot at John?"

"Not yet, but you can rest assured that we'll find the person," someone answered.

Jill wasn't so sure.

"These special agents are professionals. We'll just sit here and wait until they tell us what we do next," John told Jill.

"Fine. Oh, where is Chad? I hope he got the action on camera," Jill said.

"Don't you ever quit being a newswoman?" Agent Weinstein asked her.

Jill didn't respond. "You know, Chad should really be here by now. Where is he? I need to find him!" Jill started toward the door as an agent blocked her path.

Just then, Jimmy Allen opened the door and walked inside with Glenn Carlin. "Jill, Chad Stokes has been taken to the Milwaukee Hospital. He's been shot."

Jill gasped. "Will he be all right?"

"We don't know how bad it is yet," Glenn said. "The EMTs took him away about five minutes ago in an ambulance."

Jill turned to John. "Chad saved your life. We have to go to the hospital."

Agent Allen shook his head. "As soon as the area has been cleared and it's secure to reach your car, we'll take you there ourselves. Orders say you are to be helicoptered back to your hotel. You'll have to stay there until the situation is assessed and a decision is made as to the safety of continuing with your campaign travels."

"Secret Service and FBI will make it safe; it's their job," Jill said. "And I'm going to the hospital to see Chad for myself."

"No can do. You of all people should know the danger of the situation," Jimmy Allen insisted.

Glenn stepped into the conversation. "Wait, I'm sure there can be a compromise. If we send John in a line of unmarked cars, and they all turn in different directions as they leave the convention center, each with its own police escort, it may work."

All eyes went to Jimmy for his final decision. "All right. Give me half an hour to set this up."

"Let me help you with that," Glenn said, stepping out of the room with Jimmy.

Jill felt thankful to have a take-charge, can-do person like Glenn Carlin as a member of John's staff.

Thirty minutes later, as she and John were on their way to the hospital under police escort, Jill dialed Mitch at the dive shop and told him all she knew. That an assassin's bullet meant for John had hit Chad instead. Mitch told Jill he was on his way.

At the hospital, Jill ran down the corridor and into the emergency room. Someone shouted that Chad was in room 12. What a relief to see he was sitting up on the gurney and flirting with a pretty nurse.

"Chad! Are you all right?" Jill cried. She pushed through the room until she got to his side, and John was right behind her.

"He's fine," an emergency room doctor answered. "We already got the bullet out." He pointed to it in the bottom of a sterile cup. "It just required a local anesthetic, and I'm stitching up his arm now."

"We'll need that bullet for evidence," John told him.

"*We'll* take it for evidence," Jimmy corrected John. "Your evidence days are over now, sir." With a pair of tweezers Jimmy lifted the bullet and carefully placed it in a plastic bag.

The doctor pointed to the X-rays hanging from a lighted board. "You can see how the bullet just entered the fleshy part and lodged right here." He pointed with a pen at a spot near the shoulder. "If it had been an inch higher, we'd be in surgery right now."

"And here I thought bringing you campaigning would be fun and memorable." Jill sighed, feeling guilty.

"You were right. It's very memorable," Chad said as the doctor carefully put his bandaged arm in a sling. "I'll have this scar to remind me."

Jill told Chad that she'd called Mitch. "He's on his way up here right now."

"My dad is actually coming to see me? He must be worried."

"How soon will he be released?" John asked the doctor.

"It could be as soon as this afternoon. We're running some tests as a precaution, and if they're clear, he'll be able to go home right away," the doctor answered before walking out of the room with the chart.

"Dad will take me home. No use in you guys hanging out here," Chad said.

"Chad, I owe you my life." John shook his hand. "I'll have all your medical bills sent to me. I'll take care of everything."

"I'm sure my dad still has insurance on me. But I'll let you know. Thanks for the offer."

Amid a myriad of reporters, Jill and John left the hospital. Reporters thrust microphones under John's chin in an effort to get a sound bite. The FBI driver turned on the radio, and every channel was filled with the news of the attempted assassination. Jill's phone rang.

"Hi, Annabelle. I'm with John right now." Jill glanced over at John for the fiftieth time since the shot rang out to make sure he was really all right.

"Did you get it all on tape?" Annabelle asked. Jill smiled at hearing Annabelle hyperventilate over the phone.

"I don't know yet."

"What? Weren't you with John at the time?" Annabelle snapped.

"Of course, I was right on stage next to John, but it was our cameraman who was hit," Jill explained.

"Oh, is he all right?"

"Yes, we all are. I'll have someone pick up the camera right away, but I imagine the FBI probably already has the video."

"Have John pull some strings and get that video back! I want a frame or two for my morning edition," Annabelle barked before hanging up.

Jill turned to John. "Is there any way we can get that footage—"

"No," John cut her off.

"Annabelle wants it . . ." Jill felt a bit trapped, knowing she would probably owe Annabelle for the rest of her life for all the equipment for her newspaper. It wasn't a good feeling. "If the FBI does have that tape, I want a copy. I have a machine that rivals the Bureau's Frutie machine."

"That's a Frutoscopy," John corrected. "How'd you swing that?"

"Annabelle footed the bill for a Pix-o-matic."

"Really? That's two steps under what the FBI uses and lots less expensive, but still, what a piece of equipment."

"Think Marge can learn how to operate it?" Jill asked.

"You're kidding me, right? It took me days of training to learn the Bureau's new machine." John laughed for the first time since the assassination attempt.

Jill changed the subject. "What I'd like to know is where Fleming was when that shot was fired."

"It's not very likely that he's the one who shot at me. He's too high profile right now with the murder and the funds."

"Maybe he didn't pull the trigger, but I have a feeling he was behind this shooting. He doesn't want you to run, and he intends to stop you. He told me as much when I met with him in Washington. Find Fleming, and I'm confident you'll find the shooter."

An agent in the front seat turned around. "Fleming was arrested yesterday."

26

Men are the cause of women not loving one another.
—J. C. Hare and A. W. Hare

John settled into one of the chairs at the conference table. At his insistence, Jill was allowed to sit in on the Secret Service debriefing in his hotel suite. The FBI, Secret Service, and the Milwaukee police met with the party leaders, strategizing on how security should be altered from this point forward in order to protect John and his entourage. Large pitchers of ice water and glasses were placed down the center of the table. Cutwork paper doilies lined the platters with sandwiches sliced on the diagonal situated on top of them. Silver trays piled with fruit were set at both ends of the table.

Up until this point, politics had meant laws, budgets, sparring with party opponents, and an assortment of other serious issues. The thought of an assassination attempt wasn't even in Jill's mind when she had pressed John to take the party's nomination. Since the attempt on his life, it was all she could think about. Maybe he needed to drop out of the race and join her at the paper. As if hearing her thoughts, John turned to Jill and whispered, "It's going to be all right."

Jill smiled back at him. As John listened to the discussion of the case, Jill studied his profile, knowing this had to be hard on him. Usually he was the one doing the protecting. Now he was listening to others as they formulated the plan to keep him safe from a sniper's bullet. Jill knew by the twitch of his eye that he wanted to give his input, but he behaved himself, listening intently to each person as they spoke.

"Has the shooter been caught yet?" Jill asked.

"Not yet," an agent answered.

"Do you have any leads?"

"We're working on it, ma'am," the same agent replied.

"Then no one has claimed responsibility for it yet?" John asked.

A few shook their heads no. Others shrugged their shoulders.

"Maybe you should all be out there interviewing people then," Jill said.

John put his hand over hers in an effort to calm her. "With the echo effect coupled with the panic of the moment, it'd be surprising if anyone did see something. Everyone was ducking for cover, or running out in terror. But it's still early, Jill. Someone is bound to come forward soon. I'm sure of it. It'll be fine."

"Which reminds me." Jill cleared her throat and sat taller in the chair.

"Jill, don't," John whispered.

"I want my camcorder back."

Someone rapped on the outside of the door and then opened it. A suit with an earplug leaned into the room so only his neck and head were visible. "Sorry for the interruption. Ms. Lewis, someone is here to see you."

Jill couldn't imagine who it could be, so she checked her cell phone for messages; there were numerous calls from both of the papers as well as her mother. If it were her mother out in the other room, she would keep on making a scene until she spoke to her daughter.

"Jill, you should go see who it is," John said.

"I'll be right back." Jill left the room and closed the door quietly behind her. When she walked into the living room, Jill saw the person she least wanted to see—Olivia. She looked like she'd been crying.

"I asked to see John. Where is he? I have to make sure he's all right." Olivia tried moving past Jill to get to the conference room.

Jill grabbed her shoulders. "Olivia, get a hold of yourself! He's in a meeting right now. Keep your voice down, will you? John's just fine. Chad is the one who was shot."

Not budging from her spot, Olivia blinked back tears. "You're sure John is fine?"

"Of course. If he weren't, he'd be hospitalized," Jill snapped.

Instead of moving toward the door, Olivia looked around the room and chose the couch to sit down on.

"You should've stayed at the newspaper." Jill didn't try to hide her annoyance. "I need you there, not here. The professionals are handling everything here."

"I just wanted to see for myself that he's all right," Olivia flatly stated.

Jill sighed. "Well, maybe it's fortuitous that you've come here." She pulled a chair to the couch and sat down on it. "We need to talk."

"About what?" Olivia asked suspiciously and flipped her long hair over her shoulder. She slid out of her loafers and tucked her feet up under her as she curled up in the corner of the large sofa.

Jill knew this situation with Olivia had to be improved before it reached explosive heights, so she said a prayer that what she had to say to Olivia wouldn't sound threatening. The words alone would put Olivia's hackles up even more than they already were, so it was important for her voice to soften them. "Are we really even friends anymore?"

Olivia looked shocked. "Of course we're friends. How can you even ask that?"

"At the moment, that's not how I view us. I see us in a tug-of-war after the same guy—my guy."

Olivia's answer was in her silence. She looked away.

Jill heaved a sigh. "What are we going to do about it?"

Olivia was quiet for a long moment, but then she spoke up. "Personally, I was waiting you out until you broke it off with John again."

Jill could feel her face getting warm, and she did her best to keep her words under control. "John and I have reached a new level of understanding and communication within our relationship. Situations that were once problematic no longer exist."

"You mean situations like your fling with Tommy?" Olivia answered quickly.

"Tommy was only a symptom of a problem. And as I said, the problem no longer exists." Jill paused, biting her tongue so as not to speak angry words. "Just so you know, I really resent the fact that you discussed my personal business with Tommy Harrison. It was unfair of you to interfere."

Olivia scooted to the edge of the couch and fished for her shoes. "You should know that Tommy and I clicked when we met, and we talk on a regular basis, but you flatter yourself to think we talk about you. Tommy's moved on, and so should you."

Jill was shocked at the animosity in Olivia's voice. "I never realized until now how much you resent me."

To Jill's surprise, Olivia started crying again. Jill waited for Olivia to calm down for a few minutes before saying, "I don't know what you want from me."

Olivia began wiping at her eyes, smudging the mascara that had run down her cheeks. "I guess I don't really know either. In some ways, I'm jealous of you and all that you have. But in other ways, I just want us to be best friends, like we were before." Olivia slid her back into the cushions of the couch.

"Best friends like when we were in high school?"

Olivia nodded.

"Best friends like when you stole my prom date . . . what was his name?"

"Scott Stewart."

"Yes, that's right. I don't remember us being best friends. I remember us competing—a lot."

"It's not fair to lay all the blame on me. You were no angel either. Shall I start making a list of all your little infractions against me? They'll outnumber your complaints by far. Truth be told, I'm not half as mean and cruel as you are."

Her accusation caught Jill off guard. It was true; she hadn't always been the nicest person either, fiercely competitive too. Jill just sat there for a few seconds unable to speak.

"Oh, come on, can't we just admit we were typical teenagers who most of the time loved each other?" Olivia pleaded. "I'm sorry. Can't we put all this behind us and start over?"

Jill didn't know quite what to say. In all the years she'd known Olivia, Olivia had never apologized to her, so Jill knew she had swallowed a lot of pride to say those words.

"Truce." Jill smiled, offering her hand as an olive branch. Olivia shook it. "Now, the best thing you can do for me right now is to go back to the newspaper and just be there in case anyone needs you, okay?" Jill used her Washington move and walked toward the suite's door, hoping to get Olivia going in that same direction. Jill wanted to get back to the meeting down the hall.

Jill signaled to the agent to open the door. He did, and Olivia walked through it and out into the corridor. With Olivia on her way back to Delavan, Jill went back down the hall to the meeting, hoping some of the sandwiches were still left. She was really hungry.

27

Having leveled my palace, don't erect a hovel and complacently admire your own charity in giving me that for a home.

—Emily Brontë

Marge stood in front of Jill's office door with her arms crossed one over the other. "I tried my best to keep them out, really I did." Marge slid a pair of sunglasses onto Jill's nose. "Here, put these on before you go in there."

"What are you talking about?" Jill knew better than to yank them off. It was best to just go along with Marge when she was in one of these moods. Jill gently moved Marge to the side, turned the knob, and pushed open the door to her office.

Jill gasped. "Who did this? Who painted this room bright yellow?"

"I was told it's called sunburst. You hadn't been gone for twenty minutes when your mother and sister showed up here with a truck loaded with furniture and their hands gripping paint cans." Marge shook her head in utter disgust.

"Why didn't you stop them, Marge?" Jill demanded. "And where was Olivia?"

"Olivia? Ha! She encouraged them. She told me that I had no

say around here, and sassed me from morning until night. She thinks she's Shirley Temple of the Good Ship Lollipop! I've called in sick the last few days just to get away from her. I wasn't actually sick, though, so those sick days don't count against me."

Jill hugged Marge. "Sorry you had a hard time. I'm hoping things will start getting better around here with her. Now let me have a closer look at what my mother and sister have done."

Her antique desk was gone, and in its place was a French provincial white desk with scrolled feet. Jill hated it. A very large overstuffed couch with a matching loveseat upholstered in English chintz bookended the room, making her feel hemmed in. Two striped armchairs, with hassocks, completed the cottage look. It was everything she didn't want in an office.

"Where's my old desk?"

"It's out by the dumpster." Marge pointed out the window just as Jill heard the rumble of the garbage truck.

"I have to get it back! It's been in this room for over a hundred years. Olivia!" Jill screamed toward the broom closet door. Olivia came out, and the three of them raced out to the dumpster and rescued the desk before it could be hauled away. Then they dragged the heavy old desk back inside. Olivia and Jill were on opposite ends as Marge helped with a corner. The uneven distribution made the desk dip, causing Olivia to step on Marge's foot.

"Ouch!"

"Sorry, Marge, but you were in the way," Olivia said.

Marge looked Olivia up and down. "Too bad such a pretty girl has such big feet."

Olivia gave Marge a nasty look, so Jill stepped in to the situation. "Okay, ladies, let's move this French desk out of the way so my old desk can be put back."

Soon the desk was back to where it had stood for the past one hundred years. The French provincial desk was relegated to the side under the windows.

"Much better," Jill said.

"Maybe if we get some pictures we'll be able to tone down the color in here," Marge suggested.

"Your entire turning-around space is gone," Olivia said as she tried to remove herself from between the wall and an armchair. "Some of this furniture needs to go."

"Like nearly all of it. I'll have to talk to Mother and Kathy."

After Olivia and Marge left her office, Jill sat at her desk and read her article about the attempt on John's life. It was nearly week-old news, but it still gave her chills to read it.

Jill overheard Marge and Olivia bickering with one another in the other room. She started to go in there and stop them, but then figured it was better if they learned to work it out for themselves. The door to the broom closet banged closed. Jill sighed. There had to be a way for the three of them to learn to get along. If not, it'd be a very long year for everyone.

Jill tried to concentrate on her work, but it was hard to think with the yellow glare in her eyes. With the lights out and the shades drawn, the bright color wasn't that bad, but then she couldn't see to do her work. She got up from her desk, grabbed her purse, and drove over to Wal-Mart. She looked through hundreds of paint chips and finally settled on one.

When she got back to her office, she shoved the furniture to the middle of the room, draped the furniture in drop cloths, and started painting. Since this was her first attempt at painting a wall, huge globs of paint splattered down her arms.

Olivia walked in and frowned at her.

"This isn't as easy as it looks," Jill said.

Olivia looked around at the office. "You do know that's going to take you all night."

"It won't take all night if you help me." Jill offered her a brush.

Olivia pushed aside the brush and went for the roller Jill was using. "You trim, I'll do the walls."

Within minutes, a curious Marge poked her head into Jill's

office. "Wow, look at that. It does look better. How can I help?"

"Want to help me trim out the room?" Jill asked.

"Sure." But the look on Marge's face sure didn't say sure. "Well, maybe I could just stand here and provide moral support."

After painting for a while, the girls decided to take a break and eat dinner. As they ate spicy Mexican food and sipped icy Diet Cokes, Jill took in their paint-splattered appearance and laughed. "Maybe I should just hire someone to do the painting for me."

Olivia laughed too. "Not a bad idea." She leaned over the table and said in a conspiratorial voice, "Okay, give us the real scoop, Jill. I have to know who you think murdered Joe Walker."

"I think Fleming did it," Jill told them as she snapped open another Diet Coke.

"Motive?" Olivia asked.

"Money. Robert Fleming was in deep financial trouble, and he must have had some kind of a hint from Joe Walker that he was named in the will for a big chunk of cash. Fleming saw it as part of his way out of debt. Maybe he counted on using that money to replace the money he stole and win the election on a sympathy vote from the public since it was his best friend who died. But it all backfired right in his face."

"No, that doesn't sound right at all to me," Olivia firmly disagreed.

"Then who do you think murdered Joe Walker? And you have to back up your opinion with facts." Jill reached for a tortilla chip and scooped salsa on it.

"I think he did himself in as a cruel joke," Olivia said, pointing at Jill with a soft taco.

"You mean you think he committed suicide?"

"It's a possibility. And how's this for a motive?" She smiled and waggled her eyebrows. "He wanted to frame Fleming because his best friend and his wife were having an affair."

Marge shook her head. "No way. Just look at Fleming. He's not affair material. I think it was none other than his very own wife, Anna Walker, who murdered him."

"Motive?" Olivia asked. "You have to give a reason."

"She was jealous over her husband's friendship with Robert."

"That doesn't make sense," Jill said. "If she were jealous of the friendship, it'd make more sense for her to kill Fleming than her husband."

"Well, whoever the murderer is, may he be found out very soon before he, or she, strikes again," Marge said.

Someone began banging on the front door to the office, making all three of the women jump. Stunned, they sat looking at one another. Jill was the first to speak. "Marge, aren't you going to answer that?"

Marge looked up at the wall clock. "No, I'm off the clock right now. This is considered overtime for me if I answer the door, and you know how you can't afford to pay me time and a half."

Jill looked at Olivia.

"Oh, okay. You both are such chickens." Olivia got up and went to the door.

Jill and Marge followed along right behind her as the knocking started up again. The bell over the door jangled when Olivia opened it.

"Is Jill still here? I'm Glenn Carlin, and I have something for her."

"Glenn!" Jill hurried up to him. "Come on in. We were just having some dinner. Care to join us?" Jill offered.

"No, thanks, I need to be getting over to the hotel to meet with the party tonight, but I have something for you." He handed her a DVD. "It's the footage from your camera on the day of the shooting. But the bad news is your camera is broken to pieces."

Jill clutched the DVD in her hand. "Cameras can be replaced. At least you were able to secure the video. How did you get it from the FBI?"

"Don't ask. I hope it's worth all the favors I had to call in." Glenn smiled at the women and then walked back out the door.

"Marge, can you run the Pix-o-matic machine so we can see this?" Jill handed the DVD to her.

"Can I run the Pix-o-matic machine? I sure can. Just follow me, ladies."

28

The truth is forced upon us, very quickly, by a foe.

—Aristophanes

"Two more videos from the boat race came today. These are from Chicago folks who own a cabin on the inlet." Marge held up two videos. "They missed the last few weeks and were catching up on the *Lakes News* when they read your ad. I put name and address on each video in case you wanted to interview them."

"Thanks." Jill set the videos on the Pix-o-matic and then sat down. "This machine is kinda fun."

"*Fun* is not the logical word to be using here. Let me help you. I know all about it." Marge put her glasses on and picked up the paper she had taken notes on when the *Gazette*'s tech was here teaching her. She looked back and forth from the two videos as if she were deciding which one to put in first until Jill picked up one and handed it to her.

"Just put this one in this little door like this, but make sure you slide it in like this," Marge said. "See how it takes it right in there? It just grabs it nice as can be."

"Just like my DVD player at home."

"Now press this red button, and it'll start. See? Oh, look at that picture. These knobs clear the pixels away, and this other knob will put a picture frame around what you want to see, and this computer mouse will enlarge it as you click on it, and this other knobbie—"

"Thanks, Marge, I'll take it from here," Jill told her, elbowing her away. "I'm just so disappointed that the video Carlin brought us had been erased. I better tell him his contacts pulled a fast one on him."

"If you run into any trouble, I'll be right over there listening to my new CD by the Dixie Cups."

"Dixie Chicks," Jill corrected.

"No, the Dixie Cups." Marge held up the CD for Jill to see.

"You're right!"

Marge slipped on her headphones, and Jill could tell a really good song was on because Marge began to shimmy and shake.

With her attention back on the screen, Jill worked the knobs and cleared the pixels. She tried out several buttons, experimenting with how they worked. One of her favorite features was the frame by frame. The lake almost looked better on the screen than it did in person. "Let me find Fleming in the water," she murmured as she searched carefully. She turned a few knobs, trying to locate the rowboat.

"Have you found what you're looking for?" a deep voice asked.

Jill spun around and was flabbergasted to see Fleming standing right beside her. She hadn't expected to see him until she covered his trial at the courthouse. "I . . . uh, I heard you had been arrested."

"My lawyer posted bond."

Jill suddenly realized she was sitting beside a blown-up picture of the crime scene, and he was looking right at both of them. She nonchalantly hit the off button on the Pix-o-matic, and Fleming chuckled hollowly. "There's no need here for pretense, Jill. I saw the tape you were working on just now. I hope you find something on it. I may have been charged with misappropriation of funds, but not murder. I hope you'll find a clue on it that will show you who killed Joe."

"You and me both," Jill said. She wondered if anyone on the street had seen Fleming come into the office. He was carrying a long satchel in the shape of a tube, and Jill worried it was just the right size and shape to contain a rifle.

"What's that?" Jill asked as she pointed at it.

"A little something I picked up for Anna."

Jill eyed it. She pushed back on her roller chair a little and looked around the room, trying to assess the situation if things should suddenly spin out of control.

Over in the corner, Miss Cornelia cheerfully hummed as she typed out her social column on her new laptop. Next she'd be working on the obituaries that had just come in to the paper. Jill looked across the room at Marge, who was sorting papers while listening to her CD player and dancing. Jill tried to get her attention by coughing, but Marge didn't look over at them once. She was too absorbed in her work.

The door to Olivia's closet was shut. She was on the other side of it writing. Chad was out on an errand and wouldn't be back until the following day.

"Should we step outside to talk?" Jill stood up, doing her best not to appear alarmed. She started to move toward the door.

"It's too hot out there today." Fleming seemed almost dazed, preoccupied with his own thoughts as he nervously pulled at his collar and continued to fiddle with the tube. Jill paid close attention. Suddenly she found the cylinder quite intriguing. It was a very old container, almost wood-like, and not cardboard as they were made nowadays.

"Your container looks old. What's in it, anyway?" She had to ask and get it over with.

Fleming shook his head. "I think they're diving maps. They're not mine. Joe . . ." His voice cracked a little, and he took a breath and started again. "Joe left them at the local dive shop." His tapping became louder. Jill saw Miss Cornelia glance up from her laptop to see who was making the irritating noise. Then she looked back down at her work.

"Anna asked me to pick them up for her the next time I was over in Delavan, and I ran into that fellow outside, the one whose father owns the dive shop."

"Chad? He works here now."

"So he said. Chad had the maps in his truck. Said he'd been meaning to bring them out to Anna but you kept him too busy. So I'll drop them off at Anna's house on my way home."

Jill looked back at Fleming. His forehead was shiny with perspiration. "Okay, so give me a direct answer. Why are you here?"

Fleming sat down on the couch in the reception area, then propped up the satchel against the couch. "I miss Joe. He was my best bud; Joe was the brother I never had."

He started to sniffle. Jill handed him a Kleenex and sat down at the far end of the couch.

"Thanks." He set down the long tube and dabbed at his eyes. Normally, she'd offer her sympathies, but she wasn't convinced that he didn't have something to do with Joe Walker's death. Once someone got into deep debt and became desperate, there was no telling what they might do. Especially if they were named as someone's beneficiary, like Fleming was on Walker's insurance policy.

Fleming seemed to read her mind. "So you must know about the insurance policy?"

Jill nodded. "Probate is a matter of public record," she said, not daring to tell him that Anna Walker had also confided in her.

Fleming pulled himself up off the couch and started toward the door. He stopped in the doorway and said, "It's no secret that you and I have no use for one another. But if you can find Joe's killer, I'll forever be obligated to you. I might even scrape up some kind of reward."

This man was always thinking about money. "That won't be necessary. And you can bet I'll find the killer." *Even if it's you.* "I do have a question for you before you leave. Remember when I was supposed to talk to Carlin in Washington but met with you instead?"

"What about it?"

"The last words out of your mouth were that heads were going to roll. What did you mean by that?"

"It's only an expression," he said.

"I know what it is, but why did you say that particular phrase to me?"

He gave a bit of a laugh. "I was mad and wanted to scare you, but I quickly found out that you don't scare easily."

"When I got back the next day, I found a mannequin's head inside my purse, here in this office. Did you put it there?"

Now he laughed harder. "Why would I do something like that?"

"You were mad and wanted to scare me, remember? You just said so yourself."

"I had nothing to do with whatever you found inside of your purse. I've made verbal threats, but I've never delivered on any of them. Kind of like my campaign promises," he mused.

After he pushed out through the front doors, Jill leaned up against them and closed her eyes for a moment, willing her heart to stop its frantic beating. After a few minutes, she opened her eyes and saw it. There, still propped up against the couch, was the mysterious satchel.

29

The wind and the waves are always on the side of the ablest navigators.

—Edward Gibbon

Torn between her integrity and her curiosity, Jill allowed her good side to win. She jumped up, grabbed Fleming's satchel, and ran out the front door after him. But Fleming had already driven away. There was no sign of him anywhere.

Too bad. Well, it wouldn't hurt to have a little peek at what's in here. Jill went to her office and closed the door behind her. She carefully pulled the maps out from the old tube and began to unroll them on top of her desk to see what she had. Rather quickly she found out just how fragile they really were, as the edges began to crumble from the touch of her hand. The top map was dated 1880.

She carried the map and placed it across the couch, and then she went back for the next one. Handling that one with even greater care, she set it down on the French provincial desk her mother had bought for her. Jill followed this same routine with each map until her desk and nearly every square inch of floor space in her small office was covered in maps. There were five in all.

The papers were delicate and stained with age. Since they'd spent so much time in the tube, they tended to curl back up. Jill gently placed small books on all the corners to make them stay. The maps needed an interpreter, but Jill wasn't about to wait for someone to explain them to her; she'd figure it all out for herself.

Jill discovered that the name of the body of water had been rubbed out, leaving the date untouched. The first map she looked at had almost an aerial view to it. The artist had only his imagination to use for a compass when he drew, since there were no airplanes at the time of its creation. Jill's eyes followed the lines of the amoeba-shaped lake. It sure resembled the shape of Lake Delavan. She wished she knew for sure if she was right. Jill moved to the next map that gave a slightly closer view. The third map gave seasonal water depths, and she read the water flow chart written in a careful hand. The fourth map had an enlarged view of one section of the lake. When she got to the fifth map, she pulled up her chair and sat down to get a closer look.

On the fifth and last map she noticed very small numbers stamped near the water. She almost missed them because at first she thought they were part of the vegetation. Jill tried to read them, but it was no use. They were just too small. That's when she noticed all the maps had these small numbers. Intrigued, Jill dug through her desk until she came up with a magnifying glass. She scanned the glass over the top of the maps and saw that those numbers read like coordinates and each map's coordinates were different. Were they the lake latitude and longitude coordinates, or did they locate something much smaller?

Her cell rang. It was her fiancé. "John, you'll never guess what!" she said as she leaned over one of the drawings and peered at land formations through the glass.

"Then I won't even try. Tell me."

Jill swiveled around in her chair and looked out through the window at the evening sky. "Fleming came into my office today."

"Fleming?" John echoed in reply. "That can't be good."

"The man is out on bail," Jill explained as she put one foot up over the other at the corner of her desk, reminding herself of her Washington mentor, Rubric.

"Maybe I should come back right now instead of tomorrow as planned." John sounded worried.

"Hold on. There's no need. I'm beginning to think he's innocent of the murder after all."

"How so?" John sounded interested now.

"I don't know, just a hunch. He stopped by to ask me to find Joe Walker's killer, and somehow I think he was sincere. But listen, he had some maps with him that he unintentionally left behind. They're Walker's maps of Delavan's lake bottom. I think I might find clues in them." With the cell cradled between her ear and shoulder Jill walked around her office, shutting windows before turning on the air conditioner.

"Don't be too trusting, Jill. There should be maps like those logged at shipyards and even at dive shops. Mitch might have those as well." Jill could tell John didn't understand the importance of what she had. Once he saw them in person he'd surely change his mind.

"No, John, these are all hand drawn from the 1800s. They're original and one of a kind. At least that's how they appear to me." Jill looked closely at the paper again. "I'm afraid Fleming might come back for them when he realizes that he left them. Give me a chance to look them over, and I'll call you back." Jill hung up the phone and worked quickly.

A moment later Chad walked in wearing cutoff jeans and a T-shirt. Jill was glad he wore sneakers and didn't come in barefooted. "Hey, there, Chad. I really didn't expect you to come back to the office today. How's your arm feeling? Still stiff?"

"Stiff and sore, but much better. I can lift it higher, see?" He raised his elbow up in the sling.

"Ouch, okay, just be careful." Jill tucked her hair behind her ears, picked up her magnifying glass, and returned to reading the small faded print.

"What do you have here . . ." Chad's voice trailed off as he began to have a look for himself. "What are you doing with these maps? Walker's widow has been calling my dad every day wanting these maps. He gave them to me to deliver, and I gave them to Fleming. How did you get them?" Chad had a look for himself. "They're old ones."

"Fleming stopped in to see me and inadvertently left them behind. I thought I'd have a look."

"Man, I still can't believe he's out on bail." Chad shook his head.

"He was arrested for misappropriation of funds, not murder."

"But he's still guilty, right?" Chad sounded unsure of himself, as if he were seeking her approval.

"Of the funds . . . but maybe not murder. These maps he left here are interesting. You know water. Maybe you can help." Jill stepped to the side so Chad had room to move in and have a closer look. "If you notice, the lake goes down in five-foot increments. It's hard for me to interpret everything else. Some of these formations look like amoebas to me."

Jill sat down and watched Chad as he carefully examined one map after the other. When he picked up a particular map, part of the edge crumbled. Jill nearly leaped out of her chair. "Ah, maybe you can just study them untouched?" She handed him her magnifying glass.

"Sorry." As he looked and compared the maps, Jill logged on to her laptop and typed the words *map keys* into the browser. She needed to be brought up to speed. Nothing that came up was remotely similar to what she had in her office.

"Supposedly, there's a legend about sunken boullion in the lake," Jill said over her shoulder to Chad.

"Really? Well, now, that just proves legends are wrong. A few years ago the lake was drained and cleaned. If there was gold down there it would've been found at that time."

"Not necessarily." Jill spun around on her rolling chair and looked at him. "There are different levels to the lake, see?" Jill pointed back to one of the charts that showed elevations. "Lake Delavan has hills and valleys in the bottomland, just like land formations above the water. The lake wasn't totally drained down to the mud in every place; it couldn't be. If I'm reading this map correctly, there are places that probably still had ten feet of water while another place may have had two or three, just depending on the lay of the land, so to speak. See this craterlike area? It would hold the water like a bowl. Why don't you know this? You're a diver."

Chad shrugged and looked embarrassed at Jill's question.

"The boullion was in canvas bags when it was stolen. From that point we aren't sure what happened, but I think it was accidentally dropped into the lake over one hundred years ago. And since the bags were canvas, and environmentally friendly, they are most likely totally dissolved by now, just leaving the gold to separate and dig even deeper into the bottomland. Simply draining the lake wouldn't reveal it. That gold could be as far down as five to ten feet under the bottomlands. But, of course, this is old folklore, and you don't believe in it, right?" Jill winked at him.

"Right." He chuckled. A particular map drew Chad's interest, and Jill wanted to get a look at it. To her delight, she suddenly understood what she saw. "Hey, look at the name on this small settlement. Over a hundred years ago, Lake Lawn Resort was known as Lake Lawn Lodge. Right here on the map, it's marked LLL. And that's the point it juts out on. I'm seeing the area of the lake that forms a cove just between North Shore and South

Shore Drive." Jill moved her finger just above the map, following the line. "My mother's house would come to be built about here sixty years after this map was drawn. And that means your dad's dive shop should be about here." Jill pointed to a spot on the shore. "It's even marked where Sophie was laid to rest on the ice in 1891. Strange. Why would she be marked on the map? Then over here is an X."

"X marks the spot," Chad said. "But who's Sophie?"

"Long story, never mind. Look Chad, that X is marked in newer ink." Jill placed her magnifying glass on the spot. "And this map feels slightly different than the others, as if it's been treated with some type of preservant." Wanting to see if she was correct, Jill put more pressure on the edge of the map. It didn't crumble. Now why was this map specially treated whereas the others weren't? This one must have been more valuable.

"Are you sure about the ink being newer? How can you tell?" Chad kept squinting his eyes.

"See how the ink of the map has faded with time? Well, this ink splotch of the X is newer. It's a bright blue, in fact. And it's also the exact route Walker swam every time he was in Delavan. Why? Why did he keep swimming this same route?" Jill asked herself.

Chad shrugged and then snickered. "You don't believe all that lost gold stuff, do you?"

"Laugh all you want, but it doesn't matter what I think. Only facts speak loudly, and right now I don't have any. John is a Navy Seal. When he gets back tomorrow, I may just ask him to go down to this spot and have a quick look. Maybe dig around a little." Jill straightened up. "Maybe you could drive the dive boat and go with him."

"John is coming tomorrow?" Chad turned around in surprise. "I didn't know."

"Yup. And Russ Jansen has a coin that was recently found in the water very close to this location." Jill knew then that she had said too much, so she tried to minimize the damage of her loose lips. "Of course, we're still trying to get its authenticity established."

"Well, I don't believe in any of that stuff."

"Then don't. But I think it's fun trying to believe it." With great care, Jill took the books off the edges of the map. "Truth or not, Walker believed the gold was there. He must have. Anna told me her husband always swam the same route each time they came to the resort. I had wondered why Walker was so intrigued with Delavan. Anna Walker said they liked the smaller lake, but that answer never set well with me. The lake here is so much smaller, and the water mucks up a lot, especially this time of the year. Other area lakes offer much better diving in clearer water. Maybe the legend of the boullion is what brought the men here."

"Aren't we getting a little carried away now, Jill?" Chad folded his arms and laughed at her again.

Jill whispered the answer. "He was testing the currents, trying to map out on his own where the treasure was. I bet Walker is the one who marked the blue X on this map." Jill tenderly picked up a map and held it up to the ceiling light for a closer look. "I bet Fleming didn't have a clue the entire time. Huh, maybe he is innocent after all."

Jill started to put the maps back into the tube, but she thought better of it. They were too fragile, and putting them back inside the tube might totally destroy them. Jill laid them one on top of the other.

"Okay, just to prove or disprove the folklore about the gold, I have an idea," Chad said. "Let's go right now and check it out. It'll be fun. Think of the boost it'll give the paper." Chad could obviously tell by the skeptical look on Jill's face that she needed convincing. "Let's go and see for ourselves, and then we'll know what the truth is once and for all."

"Oh, I don't think so. No way am I going down under the water again." Jill patted his arm. "Slow down."

"This wouldn't have anything to do with your fear of scuba diving, now, would it? If it is, I'll go down, and you can captain the dive boat. You can't tell me that reporter instinct of yours isn't dying to find out. Besides, I'm for preserving the bottomland relics too." Chad shrugged. "I won't tell."

"What about your arm?" Jill asked.

Gingerly Chad removed his arm from the sling and rotated his shoulder carefully. "I'm on the mend and am at about 80 percent now."

"You shouldn't dive unless you're at 100 percent, and even then it's still not really safe. And safety is the reason I'm not diving again. Too much can go wrong. Besides, finding out for sure opens up too many possibilities for fortune hunters, and it's just not worth doing that."

"Okay," Chad agreed as he watched Jill fixing the maps. She waved him off as he tried to help. "Hey, did I tell you that my dad found your camera?"

"No, you didn't tell me! Mitch found my camera? That's great. I've been anxious to see my pictures. But what's even better, it sounds as though you two have made up since your injury. Have you?"

"Things are getting a lot better. He even gave me the key back to the shop." Chad held it up. "Come on, let's go to the shop, and we'll get your camera right now."

"Okay." Jill picked up her purse.

"Hey, Dad loves old maps. Can we take those along and show him?"

"He's probably seen them. Fleming said Walker left them at the dive shop, but then you know that, because you had them in your truck."

"Yeah, they were in a locker Walker leased from us at the dive shop. Dad didn't really look at anything when we packed it up for Mrs. Walker."

"How did Mrs. Walker know the maps were there?"

"She didn't. She just asked for the contents of the locker, and Dad told her that Lynn would bring them to her the next time she went to Milwaukee. This morning he gave them to me and asked me to give them to Lynn."

Jill looked from Chad to the maps. "I guess we can bring these along with us. Besides, I'm really anxious to get my camera so I can send those photos to the zoo archaeologist at the university just to make sure it's not the lake monster."

Together they walked through the office to the front door. As Jill passed by the reception desk, Chad held the door open for her.

"Marge, you can lock up when you leave. I won't be back tonight."

"Not so fast. I'm your assistant investigative reporter, not Chad." Marge snatched her keys and her purse. "You check things out with me, not him."

"And as my assistant, I need you to stay here and close up the office. See you tomorrow."

"You guys get to have all the fun," Marge grumbled as she watched them walk out the door.

"Patience, my dear budding reporter," Jill said. "There's nothing to investigate. I'm just picking up my camera from the dive shop."

30

The idea of why a person would commit a murder still draws me to read every single article about murder in the newspaper.

—Judith Guest

Jill followed in her car behind Chad's truck. She was excited, knowing that the case was coming together so nicely and soon would be solved. Tomorrow, she'd lay it all out for John and Russ. Walker was after the gold boullion. With the bottomland maps to guide him, Walker swam the marked-out areas where the gold was buried. Being able to hold his breath for five to six minutes also gave him a strong advantage to hunt for the gold every time he swam. Later, when the time was right, he'd return in scuba gear and dive for a closer look.

The murderer obviously knew this. Wanting the gold for himself, he strangled Walker before he had the chance to excavate. Jill glanced in her rearview mirror at the lake drawings on the backseat. Rethinking her decision to show them to Mitch, she decided maybe it wasn't such a good idea. They were an important piece of evidence, and they needed to be locked up in the newspaper's vault.

For now, she had to get her camera and download the pictures. Then, she'd compare the rib cage to elephant bones, and if they didn't match, then she'd contact Dr. Holden again. Only this time, she'd have pictures to send to him. Jill pulled into the parking lot behind the dive shop and parked her car next to Chad's.

"I don't see your dad's truck here tonight," she said, looking around. "Let's leave the maps in my car for now."

"Good idea." Chad shrugged. "My dad must have gone home for the night, but I know where he put the camera. Just follow me."

Chad let Jill walk into the shop in front of him. "It's back there." He pointed the way. In the locker room, Chad went straight to his personal locker and opened it up. There on the top shelf was her camera. It was so good to see it again she couldn't help but grin. Chad handed the camera to Jill and then gently removed his arm from the sling. He grimaced as he stretched out his upper limb. Jill watched and asked him, "Should you be doing that?"

"Yup, the doctor said to exercise my arm throughout the day to keep my muscles from atrophying." Chad demonstrated and moved his arm around a bit more.

Jill turned her attention back to the camera and began pressing through the buttons to see her shots. She frowned.

"What's wrong?" Chad asked, looking over her shoulder.

"All my photos have been deleted. Wait a minute." Jill turned the camera over and studied it. "I don't think this is my camera." She flipped it back over. "Oh, it's not. See right here. It says 'Donna.'" Jill turned around to Chad, who by now had disappeared. "Chad?"

There was no answer. Shrugging her shoulders, Jill decided to look through the unlocked lockers in case her camera might be misplaced in one of them. Locker after locker, Jill opened then shut them. All she found was stinky socks and tennis shoes. The last locker seemed to stick at the bottom. She began to bang on it. Finally, she worked it loose. Her inner alarms began to chime with mounting intensity. Something, she wasn't sure what, made her afraid to peek inside.

Opening wide the metal door, Jill saw Mitch. His eyes were rolled to the top of the sockets, and his skin was ashen. It looked as though his neck had been broken, because his head was pulled to the side in an unnatural position. His right arm hung at his side. Rigor mortis had already set in; he looked like he had been dead for hours. Jill noticed all this detail in about two seconds before she clapped her hands over her mouth. On shaking legs she ran away from the body.

Back in the office, Jill searched for her purse to find her cell and call for help. Not able to find it, she grabbed the phone off the top of the desk and dialed 911. But the phone wasn't ringing out of the building. In fact, it wasn't ringing at all. Jill followed the cord down to the end and saw that the tip had been lopped off. Mitch's killer had cut the phone lines. She dropped the phone to look for her purse again just as Chad walked back into the room. "Jill? Jill, what's wrong?" he asked, seeing the look of terror on her face.

Jill put her arms around the young man. "Chad, I'm so sorry." She pointed toward the other room. "Chad, it's your father . . . your father's . . . he's dead." Her voice was wobbly, and she could hardly get the words out. "It looks as though he's been murdered. I don't think you should go in there. It's too awful. Not now. We need to find a phone and call the police. We need to get someone out here right away."

Chad walked toward the door to the locker room but stopped short of going in, as if he were trying to decide if he should have a look for himself or not. Then in a burst, he catapulted himself through the door. Jill heard a loud scream and then scraping of metal. Suddenly, it was silent. She stood watching the door, waiting for Chad to walk back out. Minutes passed. She couldn't keep quiet any longer. "Chad? Chad? Are you all right?" Jill walked toward the door, not wanting to have another look inside that room but at the same time worrying about her friend.

Jill pressed on the door with the tips of her fingers. The room was empty, and the locker Mitch was in had been closed back up. Feeling apprehensive, Jill forced herself to step into the room. The closed locker with its macabre contents mesmerized her. Slowly, she moved toward it. She didn't want to open it again, but for some reason she had to see if Mitch was still in there. She moved quietly with only the sounds of her breath for company.

As she reached out to the handle of the locker, she was grabbed from behind. An arm jammed around her neck, choking her.

"If you just relax, things will be much easier for both of us," her attacker whispered.

Jill tore at his arm with her fingernails, drawing blood. Quickly, he wrenched her right arm up behind her, dragged her to a chair, and forced her to sit. It was then that Jill got a good look at the attacker.

"Chad!" she screamed at her friend. "Stop! I wasn't the one who hurt your father. I found him like that . . . Chad?"

He grabbed four-inch silver duct tape and began wrapping it around her ankles and wrists. "I've waited too long to get that gold, to allow John and everyone else to know where it is. I've looked for that gold for over a year now, and it's mine." He moved toward the wall of cabinets. Rifling through one, he pulled out her purse. So that's why she couldn't find it to call the police. He had hidden her purse. Chad pawed through the contents and got ahold of her car keys. Then he left the room.

Chad had murdered his own father.

Jill sat there in shock for a moment as this realization washed over her. Then she began to struggle with the tape on her wrists. She moved her ankles around, trying to loosen the tape that bound them together. In a minute, she heard the sound of returning footsteps. They began at the back of the shop, went through the locker room, and now stopped right on the other side of the door. Jill kept her eyes on the entry, deciding she'd work the tape to the very last second. That's when an unexpected visitor walked into the room.

"Glenn!" Jill hollered out his name in desperation. "Thank goodness you're here."

"What's going on?" Glenn seemed perplexed at seeing her taped to a chair.

"Hurry, cut the tape and help me get out of this place," she pleaded. "Work fast; Chad will be back any second."

Glenn dropped to his knees and tried getting the tape off from around her ankles. "Chad is outside burning something," he told her as he looked up into her eyes.

"He's burning Walker's old maps! Listen, Glenn, you've got to stop him from doing that!"

"What are you talking about, Jill? You're not making any sense. What maps?" Glenn was rising to his feet when they heard Chad coming back through the front of the shop. Glenn grabbed a wrench from the workbench, dodged into the bathroom, and closed the door, leaving it slightly ajar.

Now Chad staggered into the room, looking wild in the eyes and choking from the smoke. Jill could smell it on him. "It was a bad move to burn those maps. How will you ever find the gold now?"

"I know exactly where the boullion is, thanks to the map. You found the coordinates, and I wrote them down. I just needed to get rid of them to keep anyone else from finding them."

"Chad, let me go," Jill pleaded. "You don't want to do this . . ." She kept looking out of the corner of her eye, trying to see Glenn without being obvious.

Finally, Chad turned his back on the bathroom. Glenn popped out of the bathroom and hit Chad over the head with the wrench, dropping him to the ground. "That should take care of him for a while," he announced as he dropped the wrench at his side.

With Chad knocked out, Jill could breathe much easier. "Please hurry, Glenn, and get me loose."

Glenn nodded his head, but he couldn't find the end of the tape. Exasperated, he ran his jittery fingers over the smooth surface in an effort to find the end. When he finally found it, he discovered that the glue on the tape was unyielding. As he struggled to remove the tape, Jill told him to just give up and call the police.

Glenn shook his head. "He knows it has to look like an accident, dumb kid," he mumbled, looking at Chad still unconscious on the ground.

"What are you saying?" Jill felt a slow, uneasy feeling flow over her.

"What I want to know is, where'd you get those maps? I just about tore apart Walker's office trying to find them." His head came up fast. He looked mad.

"You're in on this with Chad?" Chills rose from her toes to her scalp.

"Not really, but he thought so, which is all that mattered at the time. It's been weeks, and I still can't get rid of him. The kid has nine lives." Glenn bent over Chad to be sure he wouldn't be causing more problems. Seeing he was still out cold, he returned to Jill. "I needed him for one mission and one mission only," he explained to her. "To kill Joe and make his murder look like an accident. And we all sure know how that turned out, don't we? It was pretty easy to figure Walker was murdered. So now, it's up to me to get rid of the murderer. My job, always my job, is to tidy things up, smooth things over. I followed Chad that night you went to the cemetery. In the fog I followed the wrong person and ended up attacking you. I'm really sorry about that, Jill." He flashed a creepy grin. "By the way, that bug spray really stings."

Jill shut her eyes and cringed, suddenly realizing that Glenn was probably the one responsible for putting the mannequin's head in her bag. "Was Fleming in on killing Walker?"

Glenn chuckled. "Of course not. He'd never harm his good ol' buddy."

"How did Chad get involved in all this?"

Glenn glanced again at Chad sprawled out on the floor. "He was in it for the money in order to get his own shop on the West Coast. He wanted his old man off his back. Guess he finally got his wish when he killed him." Glenn nodded toward the locker room. "Anyway, it was easy to manipulate him." As he talked, Glenn kept rolling his shoulders and licking his lips. "I overheard Fleming tell you that heads will roll. Chad kept me up on what was going on in Delavan, so we came up with the devilish plan about the head in your purse." He leaned closer to Jill. "Scared ya, huh?"

"Chad dove down to get my purse?" Jill met his gaze and held it. "Then he had to be watching Marge and me out on the lake that day. He was in the Fundeck that smashed into us. It figures, since he knew the coves so well; he could haul it up out of the water really fast. And he had a good twenty-minute head start on us before we were rescued."

"Yes. Lynn was in the truck waiting for him. Oh, and by the way, I have something that'll make you feel lots better."

The man's words made her catch her breath at the back of her throat. She could hardly swallow. "What?"

"I hired someone to fire the gun that day in Milwaukee, but I never tried to assassinate John. That bullet wasn't meant for him, it was meant for the person it hit—Chad. It just didn't do the damage I had hoped for."

"So someone else is in on this. Who did the firing?" Jill looked over the top of Glenn's head. Chad suddenly stood over him, raising a hammer in the air. Eyes wide with terror she tried to scream, but the hammer slammed down on Glenn too fast. The sound of his skull splitting was sickening, but not as sickening as the blood that splattered across the ceiling and onto the floor. Glenn lay crumpled at her feet. Jill's heart pounded as bile rose in her throat.

Now Chad was rummaging through drawers, dumping them out one by one until he found a knife. He came at Jill with it. She turned her face to the side, trying to protect herself. But Chad kicked Glenn out of his way and dropped to his knees. He cut all the way through the tape and yanked it off in one pull.

"Thank goodness you've untied my feet. Now get my hands free and let's get out of here." Jill's voice quivered with tears. Chad was no better than Glenn, and her life remained in danger. However, Jill decided she needed to act as though Chad was her rescuer. He had saved her once; perhaps he'd do it again. "I knew you'd never hurt me."

Chad didn't comment. He went for her purse again and rummaged around a bit, tossing out her steno pad, writing instruments, billfold, cell phone, and more. When he found what he was looking for, a smile of victory crowned his face. Jill watched as he unfurled his right hand. Inside were her two pen shots of epinephrine. But he only uncapped one of them. "I hate to do this to you, Jill. You should know that I was honestly beginning to like you."

Jill tried to scoot the chair away from him, but it was no use. She couldn't get traction with all the blood on the floor, and her body weight held down the chair. "Chad, don't. I can't take that shot now. It could kill me."

"I know; that's the whole idea. I can't break your neck like I did to my dad." He gave her a big grin and with one fluid movement shoved the needle deep into her arm. She gasped in pain, then felt the liquid that was created to save her life suddenly increase her heart rate. Within seconds, she felt like she was on the last leg of a marathon. She squeezed her eyes shut, trying to breathe slowly, hoping to bring her heart rate back down. But it was no use; she felt her heart throbbing and her chest beginning to ache.

"Did you know that this medicine is one of the ingredients to a shot that vets use to kill old dogs?"

Jill looked up at him.

He stared her down. "Actually, I just made that up right now. Thought I would create a bit more drama and get your heart pumping a little bit faster." He rubbed his sore arm. "I did my best to get my dad mad enough at me to finally kick me out. I knew you'd feel guilty about it and offer me a job where I could keep a close eye on you."

"Then you knew my O-ring was defective when I went on my dive?" Jill asked weakly.

"No, that really was an accident. It was only when you mentioned the lake monster bones that I freaked." Chad pulled himself up on a workbench to talk. "Carlin told me the boullion was near to the rib cage of some circus elephant down at the bottom of the lake. He wasn't sure where it was. When you claimed to have possibly found the lake monster's bones, I knew it was only a matter of time until you had someone come to look at them. I couldn't take a chance on the gold being discovered before we could bring it to the surface." Chad jumped down and went around to the back of Jill.

"When you left the shop that day, I knew exactly where your camera was. It was under the front seat of my truck, and I destroyed it later. Saying that I found it was a ploy to get you here. It's too bad you had to find my dad like that." Through the windows, Chad saw the dark sky. "It's time," he told her and then dug through his dad's old oil barrels until he found just the right rag. He bunched it up and stuffed it so far into her mouth she thought she'd vomit. "That should keep you from calling out."

31

Life's enchanted cup sparkles near the brim.
—Lord Byron

Chad yanked Jill out the back door. He looked around, making sure no car headlights were coming around the curve to see them. Then he guided her across the deserted road down to the sandy shore. Her feet slipped on the slimy trails of beached pickerelweed deposited there by the evening waves.

Jill noticed Chad rubbing his sore arm a lot and holding it against his chest for support. Knowing exertion would cause further pain to his arm, Jill dropped to the ground and flattened herself as dead weight. Again, he was one step ahead of her in his planning, as he dug his fingers into pressure points. Yowling, she complied and got back on her feet.

Chad walked her out onto the pier, then led her onto the boat deck and laid her facedown on the floor between the bulkheads. The drug coupled with her terror careened Jill's heart to an alarming rate.

A twist of the boat in the water told her Chad was moving around. Jill kept track of where he was from how the boat stirred and by the sound of his bare feet. Now he went onto the bow of the craft to untie the rope from its mooring. Next he walked the narrow edge from the bow to the stern, where he cast off the last of the ropes. A second twist of the boat in the water meant he was back.

Chad took hold of an oar and with the fat end of it shoved away from the dock. He paddled the boat, walking between the starboard and the port sides. It was hard going, but he managed to paddle the boat far enough away from shore. It was obvious he didn't want any witnesses to say they saw him leave the dock in his boat. No, things had to remain quiet, unseen. Chad was clever, and she was sure he'd follow this same procedure when he returned.

He was next to her again, with the second vial of epinephrine. Jill whimpered as Chad poked it into her arm. Then he quickly tossed the two empty pen injections overboard and flitted to the front of the craft, where he finally turned on the boat's lights. The vessel rumbled and shimmied as it started up. Soon the engine was at full throttle, and they buzzed down the center of the lake. With only her wrists bound now, Jill found this to be the perfect time to continue working to free herself of the tape. She paid little attention to the chafing of her skin.

Soon the boat slowed, and the engine became silent. As in a cradle, they were rocked by waves. Jill tried again to relax, hoping to slow her heart rate, but it was no good. One way or another, time was running out.

At last Jill managed to free herself of the tape. She had both her feet and hands to use for self-defense, but she had to gauge her timing. Any exertion would surely push her off the blood pressure scales and send her into cardiac arrest. She prayed for an opportunity to escape.

Occasionally, she'd hear motorboats come close and then move away as Chad waited for potential eyewitnesses to go home for the night. Jill knew that no one would be able to hear her cries above the noise of any boat . . . only in the silence could she be heard.

Finally, Chad must have decided it was safe to finish what he'd started. He stood over her, and in a syrupy sweet voice he said, "It's time, Jill."

In an unexpected thrust, Jill used the force of both her legs to deliver a hard kick to Chad's groin. He stumbled backward. Breathing heavily, Jill struggled to her feet. She felt dizzy as she tried to figure out the boat's position in relationship to land. She scanned the shoreline, and there it was, the beacon she needed—the pink glow of her mother's boathouse.

She reached over the front seat and was just tall enough to get to the keys in the ignition. Trying to keep tabs on Chad's movements while turning the key was a difficult maneuver. As she curled her fingers around the key to turn it, Chad slammed her down against the wheel and desperately tried to wrestle the keys away from her. Just when he thought he had them, she thrashed her hand violently to the right and opened it. The keys jingled as they sailed across the dark waters and out of sight. Chad froze in place until they heard the keys plunk into the lake. He scrambled over the top of the front seat and switched on the searchlight. The light shimmered across the dark water. Jill immediately caught sight of the keys attached to a bobber floating yards away atop the water. Apparently, Chad saw them too. Frantically, he dove for a fishing rod and cast his line until he snagged them.

Now it was time. Jill opened her mouth and began screaming.

"Shut up!" Chad hollered at her while reaching for an oar. Jill waited until he raised it above his head. Then she lowered her body and charged him, thrusting her body into his stomach. The momentum threw Chad off balance, and he landed hard on his back, hitting his head as the oar dropped.

Chad appeared immobile for the moment. But light-headedness swept over her and her chest hurt so badly she doubled over. She felt like she was having a heart attack. She tried to call out again, but her voice wouldn't come. Staggering toward the front, she collapsed and tumbled over the side and out of the boat. From the water, she could see Chad was back on his feet. Weakly, she tried to grab the side of the boat. But the engine revved, and the boat began to move away.

Jill fought to stay conscious, but her rib cage felt like it was shattering to pieces. She could no longer catch her breath. And by now her arms were nearly paralyzed as her head slipped beneath the waters.

Numb with pain, she hardly noticed the arms that swept around her waist and moved her upward. She sputtered water out of her throat when her head crested the top of the waves. Someone grabbed her wrists and pulled her all the way out. A pair of arms carried her to the backseat and placed her on the cushions.

"Can you breathe?" someone shouted at her as a bright light shone in her face. "Jill! Jill! Can you hear me?"

Jill nodded and coughed up more water. Hands rolled her to her side to get rid of the rest before the IV line was slid into her vein. All she wanted to do was sleep. But then she heard his voice saying, "Jill, stay with me. Can you hear me? Stay with me, Jill. We're almost back to shore. Help is waiting for you there."

"Chad . . . ?" No, that name was wrong. It was someone else who called her from the darkness.

"Chad is in custody. Russ has him in the other police boat."

"He gave me a shot . . . epinephrine. My heart hurts . . . so badly."

"Stay with me, Jill. Your heart will always be safe with me." It was John's voice. It was John who had saved her. He was with her right now, keeping her safe.

※

When Jill opened her eyes again, she was greeted by the bright light of the emergency room.

"Welcome back," the emergency room doctor said. "How do you feel?"

"Awful," was all Jill managed to say.

"That was a close call, but you'll be just fine. Your heart rate and blood pressure are returning to normal," he told her while monitoring the medical machines. "We have a room for you tonight, and if all goes well, you can go home in the morning."

"Thanks." She smiled at him. "It felt like I was having a heart attack."

"You very nearly did," the doctor said. "Just relax and let us take care of you."

Just then John entered the room. "There you are," she said.

John sat down next to her and took her hand in his.

"How did you find me?" Jill asked. "How did you know where I was?"

"After we talked on the phone, I drove back to Delavan. I called your cell, and when you didn't answer, I decided to wait for you at the office. I turned on the tape you had been looking at. There it was: a clear shot of Chad and his sister Lynn in a Fundeck they 'borrowed' from a customer who was on vacation in Europe. With so much traffic on the lake, they blended right in, but with the *Lakes News* Pix-o-matic, I could see it. The tape clearly showed Chad suiting up and going over the side. Lynn acted as his lookout. As soon as I saw what had happened, I got hold of Marge, and she said you went to the dive shop with Chad. I called Russ, and he got the lake police out. At the dive shop we found both Mitch and Glenn dead. That's when we joined the lake search for you."

Jill squeezed John's hand. "It's over, it's just over now." She tried to sit up. "Take me home, John. I just want to go home."

John took her gently by her shoulders and laid her back down. "Oh no you don't. It's time to rest, Jill. This time, you're taking orders from me."

32

Those of you watching and listening, get a cup of coffee or a spot of tea and join us back here in just a few moments.

—Dan Rather

John and Jill sat together on Pearl's couch watching the November election returns, while Big John and Max sat across the room sprawled in armchairs. Jill's brother-in-law Jeff was in another room listening to radio reports. Olivia and Char walked between the living room and kitchen carrying trays of beverages and finger food. In the kitchen, Jill's sister Kathy and Marge helped Pearl with the food preparations. Gracie made herself at home as she lay stretched out on the floor, far away from the sizzling fire in the stone fireplace.

"May the best man win!" Miss Cornelia crowed as she tottered into the room. "I'm afraid my husband isn't feeling well, so we'll have to watch the rest of the returns from home. Don't worry," she called back to Jill. "I've already noted everybody who's anybody and what they're wearing for the society pages."

Pearl waved as they left and then asked John, "How can you see a thing the way you're channel surfing?" She set a tray filled with bowls of steaming hot chili, along with homemade corn bread, on the coffee table. "Come on, now, eat some more."

"Thanks, Mother," Jill said, looking away briefly from the TV.

"John," Pearl addressed the younger Lovell, "how can you be so calm at a time like this?"

"You're only seeing my exterior . . . inside's another matter," John admitted.

"You're going to win." Pearl's smile shone brighter as John reached for his third bowl of chili.

"Win or lose, I'm projecting your chili to be an early winner . . . it just won my vote for the best comfort food in town," John announced as he grabbed a linen napkin off the tray and spread it across his lap.

Pearl laughed and sat down next to Jill on the sofa.

"I wish Daddy were here so he could see this," Jill said, leaning into her mother's side.

Pearl patted her hand. "Me too, dear. He'd be very proud."

Jill reached over and took John's hand in hers. The TV reporter looked like he was ready to announce the winner.

"Quick, everybody!" Jill yelled. "They're about to announce the final results for the congressional winner for Wisconsin!"

Kathy, Jeff, and Marge ran into the room as the TV commentator announced, "And the winner of the congressional seat for the state of Wisconsin by a landslide of 75 percent of the votes is Republican candidate John Lovell from Delavan."

—⁂—

Anyone would have thought they were crazy had they seen the handful of people slip into the last remaining boat that wasn't in winter dry dock and drive down the center of the lake at midnight. Russ Jansen, Gordon Yadon, McGinnis Newman, John Lovell, and Jill Lewis stopped the motor in the region of the sunken gold. Above them the night bloomed with stars.

Below lay black waters and mysteries that would stay forever hidden.

"I'm glad the gold will stay down there," John said.

"Leaving it untouched is the right thing to do for everyone," Gordon agreed. "We're the only ones who know it's really there."

"What about Chad?" Jill asked. "He knows the gold is there."

John shook his head. "There's not much he can do from prison."

Russ stood tossing the gold coin up and down, up and down in the air, then suddenly he gave it a swift flick, and it flew into the water. Everyone looked over the side of the boat.

"Should you have tossed that coin back into the lake?" Jill asked, tugging her winter coat up around her ears.

"What coin?" Russ answered.

33

Reader, I married him.
—Charlotte Brontë, *Jane Eyre*

THE LAKES NEWS
DELAVAN, WISCONSIN
If You Don't Read about It Here—
It Never Happened!

Miss Jillian Winthrop Lewis Becomes the Bride of Congressman John Lovell III
The Social Event of the Delavan Christmas Season

WRITTEN BY CORNELIA SOUTHWORTH

December 26. What everyone assumed was the social event of the winter season in Delavan took a surprising turn as hundreds of guests in their holiday finery jammed the elegant lakeside mansion of the Lewis family for their annual Christmas Eve party. Halfway through the evening of traditional holiday cheer, Santa Claus appeared at the front door. As the children gathered around the Lewis's magnificent blue spruce beautifully decorated with the family's heirloom ornaments in the massive entry hall, Santa began distributing gaily wrapped packages.

His velvet bag almost empty, Jolly Old Saint Nicholas pulled out one last gift, an enormous family Bible belonging to John Lovell III. As candles flickered and Christmas carols floated softly through the halls of the Lewis mansion, the merry old gentleman opened the heirloom Bible to the book of Luke, reading the Christmas story with heartfelt feeling and expression.

Listening intently to the events of the first Christmas, many of the guests wiped away tears as they gazed upon the brightly shining star atop the Lewis tree and remembered that sacred night centuries ago.

"Who is this special Santa?" was the question on the mind of every guest. Mystery filled the air as music suddenly rang out of the antique pipe organ from up on the landing, which was covered in pink and white poinsettias.

To the surprise of everyone, the tune that the organ struck up was not a festive carol but the refrain of "Here Comes the Bride."

Suddenly a bevy of attractive bridesmaids descended the stairs, wearing gold silk blouses with skirts of emerald and gold velvet wrapped in gold and emerald silk sashes. They each carried a bouquet of ivory Princess Diana roses interspersed with green hydrangea and tuberoses and intertwined with gold ribbon. The bridesmaids also wore pearl earrings, a gift from the bride. Mrs. Katherine Lewis Kelley was matron of honor and Olivia Mays Clark the maid of honor. Bridesmaids were Ms. Annabelle Livingston Stone and Helen Morris Bell of Washington, DC, and Ms. Marjorie Kovitch of Delavan, who also happens to be the receptionist at the *Lakes News*. Flower girl, Miss Marion Pearl Kelley, was the last to appear on the landing leading the way for the bride. The flower girl wore an ivory velvet gown tied with an emerald green and gold sash. But who was the bride? No one knew, but this reporter guessed. It was none other than Jillian Winthrop Lewis, also publisher and managing editor of the *Lakes News*, beaming on the arm of her handsome brother-in-law, Mr. Jeffrey Maxwell Kelley, local Delavan attorney.

Resplendent in an ivory wedding gown of flowing silk satin and chiffon overlaid in French lace appliqués with thousands of hand-sewn seeded pearls, the bride wore a floor-length veil of Brussels lace that was attached by a pearl and diamond tiara that was also worn by her mother, Pearl Winthrop Lewis, and her grandmother Muv, Katherine Winthrop, on their respective wedding days. In her hands, the bride carried a white fur muff covered with a spray of ivory cabbage roses mingled with Casa Blanca lilies, blue spruce, orange blossoms, and anthuriums tied with gold French ribbons. The bride's only jewelry were the opera-length pearls given to her by the bridegroom and an heirloom pair of pearl-and-diamond earrings worn by all the brides in the family. In the bride's shoe was a silver sixpence belonging to the bridegroom's grandmother, Mrs. John Lovell Sr., of Chicago.

The surprised guests gasped as the lovely Miss Lewis began sweeping down the elegant curved mahogany staircase festooned with garlands of pine and white Casa Blanca lilies mixed with holly with berries, anthurium, and red roses.

The beautiful bridesmaids, the dainty little flower girl, and the blushing bride were eagerly met at the bottom of the steps by the handsome groom, Congressman John Thomas Lovell III, formerly known around Delavan as the popular and well-loved managing editor of the *Lakes News*. The famous FBI agent saved the lives of this writer and his beautiful bride on more than one occasion. Now, he is the newly elected Wisconsin congressman.

Words cannot properly describe the dazzling smile the young bridegroom wore as he glanced up at his beautiful bride, who was crying tears of joy that she dabbed with an heirloom linen and lace handkerchief that had belonged to her grandmother.

Santa, who was in truth the vicar at the Church of the Apostles, Reverend William Powis, married the young lovers surrounded by their friends and family.

And so . . . this writer would like to end this article by saying they lived happily ever after. But did they?

Sign up for a subscription to the *Lakes News* today, as this noted society editor continues to chronicle the lives of this dearly beloved couple, the new owners of the *Lakes News*.

New Arrivals

December 4. John Thomas Lovell IV and Katherine Winthrop Lovell were born December 4 at Elkhorn Lakeland Hospital to Congressman and Mrs. John Lovell III (Jillian Winthrop Lewis) of Delavan. J. T., the boy, weighed 5 lbs. 6 ounces and was 21 inches long, and the girl, little Katie, was 5 lbs. and 19 inches long. Both babies have blond hair and their father's big blue eyes. The little guy has big hands and feet like a linebacker, and the little girl has hands and feet as dainty as a princess. Proud grandparents are Mrs. Pearl Winthrop Lewis of Delavan and John Lovell Jr. of Chicago.

Acknowledgments

With deep gratitude to the exceptional Baker Publishing Group staff, especially our wonderful editors, Jennifer Leep and Kristin Kornoelje, for their efforts on our behalf, and our amazing and faithful agent, Beth Jusino, without whom these books could not have become a reality.

Our thanks for underwater exploration information from Thomas R. Holden at Maritime Center, U.S. Army Corps of Engineers.

Susan Wales is a writer and producer who has authored or co-authored more than twenty books. Executive producer of the annual Movieguide Awards, Susan has also co-written two books with Ted Baehr based on movies: *Faith in God and Generals* and *The Amazing Grace of Freedom*, also with her husband, producer Ken Wales. Originally from the South, Susan lives in Pacific Palisades, California, with her husband. They have a lovely daughter, Megan, an amazing son-in-law, JB, and an adorable granddaughter, Hailey Elizabeth.

A former missionary, **Robin Shope** is presently an eighth grade language arts teacher near Dallas, Texas. She has nearly two hundred articles in print and two dozen short stories in popular collections, such as the Chicken Soup for the Soul books. Married for thirty years, Robin has two grown children and a cocker spaniel dog.